A CLEAN CANVAS

A Lena Szarka Mystery

ELIZABETH MUNDY

Constable • London

CONSTABLE

First published in Great Britain in 2019 by Constable

ISBN: 978-1-47212-638-2

Typeset in Bembo by Photoprint, Torquay
Printed and bound in Great Britain by Clays Ltd, Elcograf S.p.A.

Papers used by Constable are from well-managed forests and other
responsible sources.

MIX
Paper from
responsible sources
FSC® C104740

Constable
An imprint of
Little, Brown Book Group
Carmelite House
50 Victoria Embankment
London EC4Y 0DZ

An Hachette UK Company
www.hachette.co.uk

www.littlebrown.co.uk

For Teddy

CHAPTER 1

The tiny dinosaur's head emerged, peering with its beady eyes at the modern world. At first glance its body seemed covered in translucent scales, but on closer inspection the scales revealed themselves to be tiny fragments of glass, each one rounded as if by the motions of the sea. The creature was entangled in string. A muscular tail poked out, adorned with a postage stamp. Wherever this dinosaur was going, it was getting there by first-class mail.

Lena Szarka gave the statue a quick dust, careful not to disturb the string or the stamp. Even if it looked messy by her high standards, everything had to be just as the artist had crafted it: Pietro Agnoletti insisted on it when he hired her to clean the Agnoletti Archer Gallery in Islington. It didn't matter how ridiculous Lena found the apparent works of genius. Her professional reputation depended on it.

Lena began to dust a hedgehog crafted from rusty nails. '"Tormented Illusions" is a victory!' declared Pietro, standing behind her. 'It is our best exhibition for years.'

It took a moment for Lena to realise Pietro wasn't speaking to her. Instead he was orating to an imaginary crowd, likely practising for the reception this evening.

'Today you will sell this animal, maybe?' she suggested, hopefully.

'Putting together an exhibition is like painting a masterpiece,' Pietro continued, full of rapture. 'Each painting is a brush stroke.

They must all be different, but each must work with its neighbour to create a beautiful whole, a "Tormented Illusion".'

Lena wished that she could clean the tetanus-trap hedgehog in peace. She had been delighted when she'd landed this client for her new agency, Lena's Cleaners, but the combination of the delicate and dangerous sculptures, the terrifying price tags and Pietro's constant orating was starting to make her wish she'd upped her rates.

'This will be the exhibition that will see *A Study in Purple* find its place in the heart of a discerning buyer,' said Pietro, gesturing to the fiercely priced painting that dominated the right-hand wall. 'And we are lucky enough to have the immensely talented artist, Trudy Weincamp, here this evening to tell you how she came to paint this delight. This whole exhibition has been built around her work of genius.' Pietro paused, and looked to the painting. 'Her larger pieces dominate a room in the MOMA,' he continued. 'But we have *A Study in Purple* right here in Islington. Her work is iconic. How often can you buy an icon for £84,000?'

Lena still couldn't believe something that didn't have three bedrooms and an acre of land could cost that kind of money.

Pietro's phone rang. He stopped practising and disappeared into the gallery's small office. Lena breathed a sigh of relief and got on with her cleaning. She ran her cotton duster over the top of an enormous clay eyeball, casting its judgemental gaze over *A Study in Purple* from its home in the middle of the gallery. Lena stood back for a moment, trying to appreciate what could cause this painting to be so valuable. It was about a metre square, and she knew from the small sign next to it that it was oils on canvas. But when she stared at it, all she saw was a mess of interlocking red circles and giant blue tadpoles battling it out to fill a purple triangle.

She shook her head and gently dusted the top of the frame. As she did so, she surprised a spider, which disappeared behind the painting. Although she had nothing against spiders, cobwebs were a definite no for Lena, certainly not on the night of the gallery reception. Carefully she levered the painting away from the wall and reached her duster around the back. She tutted at the rust that was on the tacks behind it – one had a pattern that reminded her of an elephant waving his trunk. The spider scuttled away from her. Lena carefully allowed the painting to rest back against the wall and went in pursuit of the spider. It was too fast for her and she let it escape to a tidy hiding place. She went to the store cupboard instead to fetch the mop.

She needed to find more clients, she thought to herself for the hundredth time that week. Since her mother had insisted on her hiring a cousin who'd left Hungary and found herself adrift in London, it had become hard for Lena to find enough work for the two of them to do. Her little cleaning agency was small and new, and was really only meant to be her for the moment.

Simon pushed open the door. His shoes squeaked on the exposed wooden floorboards.

'Why didn't you tell me Trudy Weincamp was coming?' he said. 'I'm supposed to be the manager of this gallery, yet I had to find out from a client! Oh, it's you,' he added, seeing that Lena was alone. 'Where's Pietro?'

'I tweeted it last week,' said Pietro, emerging from the office. 'How you think you can manage a gallery without even having a Twitter account, I've no idea.'

'I see you every day,' said Simon. 'You could have told me.'

'It's quite a coup, getting her here to our little gallery. I know you think I was mad for snapping up *In Purple* two years ago, and you're right it is taking a while to sell. But you'll be eating your words after tonight!'

'We're not ready for an artist like Trudy to see it here,' said Simon. Lena looked at him. He was pale and always looked a picture of misery. Even his voice sounded grey. 'It's not hung right.

It can't breathe in that horrible ebony frame you use for all the paintings.'

'Stop fussing,' said Pietro. 'I know these receptions aren't your thing, but this will be our best yet. Everyone's coming. I've prepared a killer of an introduction. Sebastian's is catering. My wife has a new dress. All will be well.'

'But the walls are the wrong shade of white,' continued Simon, 'like I keep telling you. They need to have more grey to offset the brightness of the colours. What will Trudy think of us?'

'Leave Trudy to me,' said Pietro with a wink. 'Remember when she visited our art school?'

Lena began to dust an enormous Perspex foot with a Campbell's Soup label stuck to its heel. The ground floor was her favourite part of the gallery. The basement had a few paintings displayed, but more in messy piles still covered in bubble wrap, and collections of frames and assortments of odds and ends yet to be fitted to their perfect pictures. She'd tried to rearrange it more neatly but Pietro insisted a little chaos was the sign of a good gallery. Upstairs, the first floor was dedicated to paintings, sculptures and handmade ornaments, all of butterflies. It was furnished with two sofas, a coffee table and a selection of art books. Pietro called it his chrysalis lounge. But this long room on the ground floor was definitely the smartest. She liked working at the back of the room best. When it rained, she could hear the pitter-patter of the drops on the glass roof, marking out time in irregular rhythms. And with the exception of the hedgehog, it was by far the easiest to clean.

Lena went to the kitchen and filled the bucket with water, squirting in her homemade wooden-floor cleaner: vinegar with a dash of ylang ylang for the scent. She didn't know whether they would succeed in selling that painting, but the floors would be as clean as hundred-year-old wood could hope to get.

Pietro gave *A Study in Purple* an approving look. 'I knew buying this masterpiece was the right thing to do,' he said, breaking Lena's reverie. 'It's genius. Just look at the vibrancy of the colours, the vivacious energy, the redolence of the symbolism. It's a celebration of creation, of life itself, yet at the same time death is present. I'm not sure I can bear to part with it. The sense of movement is divine.' He shut his eyes for a moment, swaying in time to a silent music. 'I can practically see the brush strokes dancing.'

Lena looked back at the painting. It just sat there. Perfectly still.

Pietro, however, was far from still. He twirled round, knocking the mop from Lena's hand. It flew towards *A Study in Purple*. Lena, heart in her mouth, leapt in an attempt to catch it but she was too late. It struck the frame with a sickening thump of wood on wood, sounding like an instrument Lena had briefly learned to play in nursery school. Water from the upturned bucket flooded the floor.

'Leaner!' shouted Pietro, rhyming her name, as he always did, with cleaner. 'The painting!' He rushed towards it.

'Keep still,' commanded Lena, having a vision of Pietro slipping in the water and breaking his neck. He obeyed. 'And my name is Lay-na.' She was starting to think that calling her agency Lena's Cleaners was a mistake. The British seemed much too fond of a rhyme.

Lena stepped carefully towards the painting. The mop had only struck the frame, leaving a tiny indent.

'I can't look,' said Pietro, his hands over his eyes. 'Is the painting ruined?'

'The painting is fine,' said Lena. 'There is only a mark on the frame,' she said. 'A tiny mark.'

Pietro breathed out heavily. 'You need to be more careful, Lena!' he exclaimed. 'That was almost a tragedy.'

Lena opened her mouth to object to being blamed for his ridiculous little dance but then shut it again. She needed this job. 'I am sorry,' she said, glaring at Pietro.

'No harm done,' said Pietro, looking a little guilty. 'All's well that ends well.'

Lena used the mop to wipe up the spilt water, wringing it out into the bucket.

The gallery phone rang. Simon disappeared into the back room, returning a few moments later looking concerned.

'That was Sebastian's,' he said to an expectant Pietro. 'They have cancelled the catering. Apparently there was an issue with their last invoice. You know how fastidious they can be.'

'A disaster!' exclaimed Pietro.

'Should we postpone?' ventured Simon. 'I don't see how we can have a champagne reception with no one to serve champagne.'

'I can do it,' said Lena, suddenly. 'And my assistant. We can serve the drinks.'

Both men looked at her. There was silence for a moment.

Then Pietro embraced her. She wriggled uncomfortably, his linen shirt crumpling in her face. 'The show must go on!' he declared.

'And the canapés?' asked Simon.

'Fromage d'Or!' said Pietro. 'I'll call in a favour with Jean-Marie. Ah, it will be exquisite. I'm sick of those overpriced, miserable so-and-sos from Sebastian's anyway. Leaner, sorry, Len-na, is our saviour.'

'It will be twenty pounds an hour,' said Lena, totting up sums in her head. 'Each. Four hours minimum. And I put flyers for Lena's Cleaners on the front desk.'

'That's what I like about you,' said Pietro with a laugh. 'Your continental directness reminds me of myself. None of this British reserve like poor Simon here. He wouldn't ask for a sausage in a butcher's shop!'

'You were born in Wiltshire and went to Eton,' objected Simon.

'My blood is Italian,' Pietro replied. 'I can trace my lineage back to Raphael.'

Simon scoffed. 'Really? You've never mentioned it.'

Pietro laughed. 'Perhaps I am a little too proud,' he said. 'But I'm sure if Lena here was a descendant of Franz Liszt, she would remind us of that regularly.'

'The only famous thing in my family,' said Lena with a smile, 'is my mama's chicken *paprikash*.'

CHAPTER 2

That evening, Lena looked around the gallery and smiled. She'd given the floor another mop, getting rid of the evidence of the day's visitors. There were freshly cut orchids in bowls dotted around the place, reminding her of the gift PC Cartwright had given to her when she was recovering in hospital after she'd been shot. To her these flowers were far more beautiful than anything else in the gallery, £84,000-worth of *A Study in Purple* included.

Fromage d'Or had done themselves proud on the catering. They had wisely declined Pietro's unappetising request to provide completely purple food, but there were burgundy shavings of beetroot adorning the wheels of sharp goat's curd, and some kind of purple sprouted vegetable that resembled a tiny tree on the puréed potato and chorizo towers. Lena had carefully put the platters in the large kitchen fridge and filled bucket upon bucket with ice for the champagne. She even had a small bag full of carefully washed violets from the florist next door, ready to pop a blossom into each champagne flute. Now all she needed was Sarika.

From experience, Lena had asked her cousin to come thirty minutes early. Evidently it was not enough. Lena wondered whether she could keep employing the girl. She didn't really have enough work yet for the two of them and Sarika was hardly reliable. But she couldn't bring herself to let Sarika go. She was a relative, as her mother kept reminding her, though on her disgraced father's side of the family. But there was another reason. When Sarika did show up, Lena liked the company. Although Lena enjoyed having time to herself, she found that she was alone much more than she wanted to be since Timea had died.

As if she could read Lena's thoughts, Sarika strolled in. She was ten years younger than Lena, and Lena found her a complete mystery.

'This is the fourth time this week you are late for a job,' Lena told her, sticking to English in her determination to practise. 'And it is only Wednesday.'

'Soz,' said Sarika, her attention still on her phone. Lena had picked up more English slang from her twenty-one-year-old cousin fresh from Hungary than she had in the three years she'd been living in London. But it didn't seem like Sarika had learnt a thing from her. Certainly not timekeeping.

'Where were you?' said Lena, taking the phone from Sarika's hand and putting an apron in its place.

'I said sorry,' said Sarika.

'Lena's Cleaners prides itself on being professional,' said Lena, breaking into Hungarian in frustration. 'It's hardly professional to arrive late.'

Lena watched as Sarika began to fiddle with the apron, for a moment unsure which way up it went.

'I wasn't meant to be working today,' said Sarika. 'So I'm a bit hungover. And besides, there was an emergency. Dragg needed help.'

'What is Dragg?' asked Lena, feeling bad now for her harsh tone.

'My flatmate.' Sarika paused. 'He had a fight with his girlfriend Kat and needed some comforting.' It hardly sounded like an emergency to Lena, but then again, she wasn't twenty-one any more.

'Do not let it happen again,' she said, taking the apron from Sarika and tying it deftly around her cousin's waist.

'I promise,' said Sarika.

'Do not stare at the guests,' whispered Lena in Hungarian.

'But his nails,' Sarika replied. 'They are longer than mine. And purple. Look, that one has a little animal painted on it. What do you think it is? A snake?'

'He is arty,' replied Lena. 'That's what they are like. We must get on with our work.'

'I'm going to ask him how he did it,' said Sarika. 'Perhaps he can do my nails too.'

Lena replied with a horrified look.

Sarika laughed. 'Sorry, only teasing. How stupid do you think I am?'

Lena didn't answer that. 'Take another tray of canapés round,' she said. 'I'll refill the champagne glasses.'

Lena had to stop herself from staring at a few of the guests too. There were some people who looked relatively normal. Two older ladies were busying themselves with the champagne and canapés and occasionally exclaiming on the lovely colours of the paintings. A few young people with the piercings and jeans of art students looked fashionably bored. An American man in a suit was glued to his mobile phone, and another man, wearing unflattering purple trousers with a neat crease down the front, was attempting to straighten the already straight picture frames. What really stood out to Lena, as she refilled glasses, was that no one was really paying any attention to the art on display.

Lena noticed Pietro and his wife Ophelia in a corner with empty glasses.

'It's a massive success,' Pietro told his wife, as Lena filled his glass. He was sporting a purple cashmere jumper for the occasion.

'I'm so glad I said to wear purple on the invitation. Everyone looks so festive. Trudy will adore it.'

'She is very late,' replied Ophelia. 'It is rude, but then I suppose she is American. Simon must have picked her up from the airport hours ago now.' Ophelia covered her glass with her hand just as Lena went to refill it. Lena's sharp reactions were all that stopped her from getting a champagne manicure. Ophelia's hands were adorned with a selection of amethyst rings that perfectly matched her mauve dress, floating like the evening mist over Lake Balaton. More drops of amethyst hung from her ears and gently jangled as she tilted her head in annoyance.

'Simon called,' said Pietro. 'Apparently Trudy insisted on a little tipple before the reception. He sounded a bit the worse for wear already, poor lad. He's not in her league when it comes to drinking. Still, who are we to judge the ways of the genius?'

Ophelia's earrings jangled angrily again. 'Ahh, Daisy,' continued Pietro, spotting a client. 'There you are. You look stunning. That lilac blouse exactly captures sunset in the Dordogne.'

Lena watched him wander off. Then she noticed that the two old ladies, empty glasses in hand, were edging closer to her. She smiled and poured. The fatter of the two gulped half of hers immediately and held her glass out for more. Lena smiled and poured again. 'Careful, Gertrude,' said her friend. 'Remember what happened at The Hasstrock Collection last month. My back won't take carrying you home again.'

'It's free champagne and I'm on a pension,' replied Gertrude, with a small hiccup. She turned to Lena. 'Don't you go too far away.'

'Of course not,' replied Lena. She turned her back and lingered nearby.

'So David is finally out of prison,' she heard the first woman say. 'Is he staying with you?'

'Of course not,' replied Gertrude. 'I'm not having that thief in my home, even if he is my nephew. He'd have his greedy mitts all over my grandma's emerald ring. I wouldn't even wear it to this reception. You never know what types will be about.'

Lena glanced at the ladies and noticed Gertrude was looking at her suspiciously. She moved away to get a fresh bottle of champagne. She'd make sure she refilled Gertrude's glass last this time.

Sarika looked up guiltily as she shoved the second half of a mini Gruyère and red cabbage tortilla in her mouth. 'I was just making sure it was okay,' she said, chewing furiously. 'Someone asked me which canapé was the best and I didn't know. I'm not stealing.'

'It is okay,' said Lena. 'No more, though. We do not want a client to see. People are so suspicious of the staff.' Sarika smiled at her.

'I will go take these round now,' said Sarika. 'That old fat lady has already had five of those purple sausage towers.'

Lena popped open a bottle of champagne, smoothed her hair and went back out. The American with the phone reached his glass towards her without even glancing up. Lena filled it and smiled at him nonetheless, noticing that although the golden buttons on his navy jacket shone, the shirt he wore underneath was wrinkled.

Serving drinks was much easier work than cleaning, she thought, and paid better too. She wondered whether she could expand her business to cover champagne receptions. Perhaps if she could make canapés? She looked at the platter Sarika was carrying. It seemed fiddly, and even if Lena could cook, which she couldn't, Hungarian food was probably too hearty. You couldn't put a goulash on a Ritz cracker. She'd need to find a business partner who could look after that side of things.

She refilled the glass of the man with the purple nails. He smiled at her graciously and said thank you before returning to intense conversation with his friend in the glittery jacket. The little man with the perfectly ironed purple trousers was picking invisible pieces of fluff from his white shirt while he chatted to an attractive woman in a well-tailored suit.

'We're in talks with a very exciting company in China, you know,' he was saying. 'Art dealers, some of the best. Looking to build a brand in the UK. They want to be seen as the Chinese Christie's. Of course, it throws up some interesting cultural challenges. People's perceptions are so skewed against the poor Chinese. It's not like they are all money-grabbing heathens, you know. What they need is a rebrand. Just the right shade of purple in their logo. Majestic, cultured, papal. That will change people's perceptions. Make them a real contender in the UK market.' Lena glanced at his companion, doing her best to stifle a yawn.

If she found a partner to provide canapés, or even full meals, they could offer a complete reception or dinner party service, she thought. She'd clean the house beforehand and do any decorations, then her partner would cook, Lena and Sarika could serve and wash up afterwards. Lena's Elite Evenings, she'd call it. Or did that sound like an escort agency?

Lena went back to the kitchen to open yet another bottle. These people were certainly enjoying the free booze. She almost fell over Pietro, standing in the kitchen with his head in his hands. 'It's a disaster,' he said, when he saw Lena. 'Simon and Trudy. They're both here and both blotto.'

Lena leaned out of the kitchen and glanced over at them, unsure what the word 'blotto' meant. It wasn't hard to figure out. Trudy, her short hair pink, was wearing a green silk kaftan that she'd hiked to her knees. Simon, as if Trudy's hair was reflected in his skin tone, looked much less grey than usual. He was laughing hysterically, his giggles interspersed by the odd hiccup. It was the first time she had seen him laugh, and she found it strangely unnerving.

'Do not worry,' she said to Pietro, handing him the champagne bottle, which he took with surprise. 'I will sort for you.' She put two Nespresso tabs in the machine and made two strong coffees. She piled a plate with the most carbohydrate-rich canapés, filled a large jug of water and grabbed two glasses. She put all of it on to a tray and carried it out, Pietro trailing behind her.

'Oh, I'd love a coffee,' said one of the guests, downing her champagne and reaching for one of the cups.

'Sorry,' said Lena, deftly sidestepping her. 'This is for the artist.'

It was easy to find them. Simon had taken his shoes off and was attempting to touch his own toes next to the soup label foot while Trudy shrieked encouragement and clapped.

'Hurry up,' whispered Pietro. 'I can't have a scene.'

Lena looked again at Simon. He wrestled the bottle of champagne from Pietro, took a slurp and then passed it to Trudy, who also took a gulp and then tried to balance the bottle on her head. 'Stop,' begged Pietro.

'You see to your guests,' Lena told Pietro. 'I will handle this.' Leaving an anxious Pietro behind her, Lena walked up to Trudy and Simon and waved the tray under their noses. 'There is a very comfortable sofa upstairs,' she said. 'And I have the best canapés here.'

'Is that coffee?' scoffed Trudy. 'Where is the vodka?'

'There is some in the kitchen,' lied Lena. 'Go upstairs and I will bring it to you.'

'Upstairs? Is that where the bedroom is?' said Trudy. 'Where's that Pietro? We could really have a party if he came up.'

'Pietro is busy,' said Lena, frowning at the woman. 'With his wife.'

'She can come too,' said Trudy, with a wink. 'So can you.'

'Come on, Trudy,' said Simon. 'I'll show you the butterfly room.' He took Trudy's hand and the two stumbled upstairs, Lena close behind them with her tray of sobriety tools. Once they were both sitting on the sofa, Lena snatched away the snacks.

'Drink your coffee,' commanded Lena. 'Then have snacks.'

'It's like being at school,' complained Trudy, obeying nonetheless. 'We're like the naughty teenagers smoking behind the bike shed. Do you have any cigarettes, Steve?'

'Simon,' said Simon. 'And no, sorry.'

'Drink your coffee too,' Lena told him. When he had, she lowered the plate of canapés and the two tucked in.

'Thank goodness,' said Pietro, as Lena came back down the stairs. 'How did you manage to contain them?'

'You better get on with your speech,' said Lena. 'Simon is coming down already.'

Simon wobbled over to them. 'She's asleep,' he said, in an exaggerated whisper. 'Shh.'

Pietro tapped his champagne glass with a spoon. The noise in the room faded to a gentle murmur, akin to the hum of a dishwasher. 'Art touches us deep within our souls,' said Pietro, launching into his speech. 'There is a quality to the colour, the dynamism, the emotion, that brings us to a synaesthetic state where we cannot just see the painting, but hear it. Hear its music, tingling inside our ears like a concerto by Mozart. We feel it, gently caressing our putty-like souls. Each piece of Trudy's work is individual and unique as a flake of snow at daybreak. But still, we see the *leitmotif* running throughout her work, her signature in colour.'

Lena's mind wandered. She watched Simon, who had settled down and was now staring at something. Lena followed his gaze. At first she thought he was looking at the sculpture of the hatching dinosaur, but then she realised he was looking beyond that. At Ophelia, Pietro's wife.

Ophelia did look stunning. Lena stared at her too, for a moment. Her auburn hair was long and wavy, and she had that otherworldly pallor that only adorns the translucent skin of a redhead. A whisper of sunshine would burn her. Totally impractical, Lena decided. Lena looked approvingly at her own arm, tanned like a nut already, even from the scarce sunshine of London in June. Still, she thought, it was not Ophelia's fault. We have as much power over the natural colour of our skin as we do over which country we are born in.

'In short, that is why this is a masterpiece,' continued Pietro, despite the fact his speech was not short at all. Lena noticed Trudy stumble down the stairs, blinking at the bright lights of the gallery and scratching at her short but vibrant pink hair. 'And why it deserves a place in history,' continued Pietro. 'A rare moment of solidity in the inevitable, ephemeral passing of time. We are fortunate indeed that the exquisite Trudy can join us, an artist who defines her generation, right here in Islington. I still remember the awe we all felt when she came to our humble art school as a visiting artist. It was a privilege to see her in action, to understand more about the inspiration and genius that underscores every piece she creates. And a stunning example of her work, that feeds the larger canvases displayed in the MOMA, is available here, at the Agnoletti Archer Gallery. Affordable culture, affordable history. I can hardly bear to part with it, but it is time for *A Study in Purple* to continue its journey into the *zeitgeist* of our time.'

Lena looked around to see if anyone was laughing at the painting being called affordable. Instead, they were nodding agreement. Even Gertrude, the old lady who claimed to be living off her pension. Some pension, thought Lena. Lena had no such luxury. She allowed herself a moment's concern for when she was too old to clean any more. Even more reason to make her new agency a success.

'So, let's raise our glasses to the inimitable genius of Trudy Weincamp!' Lena looked around. Everyone held up their glasses, though many had been emptied during Pietro's long speech. Trudy hiccupped and waved good-naturedly and looked as if she might say something. 'No no,' said Pietro hastily. 'You are jet-lagged and the work speaks for itself. So let's have some more champagne,' he said, looking meaningfully at Lena. 'And more of these delicious canapés. Enjoy!'

People dispersed, milling around. Lena and Sarika both grabbed bottles of champagne and began to circulate. 'They can drink, these art lovers,' said Sarika, casting a glance at the ever-growing shrine of empty bottles discreetly tucked in a corner. 'They put me to shame.'

'Rich people love free champagne,' said Lena.

'Everyone loves free champagne,' said Sarika, with a giggle. 'I'm starting to think I'd better hide a couple of bottles now or there'll be none left to swipe later.'

'Not funny,' said Lena, unsure if her cousin was joking. 'Go fetch the last tray of chorizo towers, then we'll start with the dessert canapés.'

Her bottle was empty by the time she walked past Trudy, Pietro and Simon, in the far corner from *A Study in Purple*. Trudy was looking at the painting from the distance.

'*In Purple* isn't as good as I remember it,' said Trudy, squinting at the painting.

'Gosh, don't say that,' said Pietro, looking around to see if anyone had heard. 'I need to get it sold.'

'Lena, Trudy has misplaced her glass. Could you fetch another?' Simon said. 'We have some very fine works downstairs too. Perhaps you'd like to take a look?'

'Underground art,' said Trudy with a laugh. 'Lead on.'

Simon smiled apologetically to Pietro, who had put his head in his hands again. Lena offered Pietro another glass of champagne. 'Thanks. I need it,' Pietro said. 'This is a disaster. I'll never be able to sell that painting with those two in that state.'

Lena looked around. The guests were thinning out now, but those who were still here were clearly enjoying themselves. The man with purple trousers came over to Pietro, the suited woman following behind him. 'Great piece,' he said, gesturing to *A Study in Purple.* 'It would work very well in the reception of my agency. The Chinese would love it. I wish there were two, so I could keep one in my home too. It's the triangle I love. Such a perfect shape. I really have to have it.'

Lena looked at him. What sort of agency, she wondered. Surely not cleaning?

Pietro beamed, then carefully moulded his face back to nonplussed.

'Ah, Malcolm, glad you could make it. Such fun trousers! I've never seen anything quite like them. And I agree, of course. It's just the thing to give an agency that little *je ne sais quoi*, don't you think, Leonora?' said Pietro, gesturing to the lady.

'You might want to win some new clients before you buy a painting of that price,' said Leonora, her voice concerned.

'Plenty on the horizon,' said Malcolm, with a tinkling laugh. 'Big prospects from overseas.'

'Exactly,' said Pietro. 'In fact, I was just chatting to Charles Saatchi about the natural affinity of advertising and art the other day. Lena, fetch Malcolm and Leonora some more champagne.' He turned his back on Lena and put his arms around his new favourite people.

Heading to the kitchen, Lena almost tripped over Gertrude, who was settled comfortably in a chair. Her friend had disappeared. 'Is purple trousers trying to buy that painting?' said the old lady. 'We'll see about that. Help me up.' She grabbed Lena's arm. Lena heaved her to her feet and pointed her in Pietro's direction. 'I'll get that painting by hook or by crook.' Gertrude wobbled towards him, her gait a picture of drunken determination.

Before Lena could reach the kitchen, she caught sight of Sarika, giggling away to the blond American, finally off his phone. To Lena's horror, she saw the girl sip from a champagne glass. Sarika saw her and smiled. 'I am telling Patrick that I love *A Study in Purple*,' she said, in her best English accent.

18

Lena forced a smile on to her face but she could see her dreams of Lena's Elite Evenings disappearing with every sip Sarika took of the guests' champagne. 'Excellent,' she said, grimacing. 'Could you open another bottle of champagne for Mr Agnoletti?'

'In a minute,' said Sarika.

Lena felt an angry heat creeping up her neck. She restrained herself.

'Now,' she said, as politely as she could manage. The smile faded from Sarika's face. Perhaps some of her fury had seeped into her voice.

'Yes,' the girl said, disappearing.

Lena looked at the blond man, noticing he was the person who had ignored her earlier, and went to follow Sarika into the kitchen. He reached out his hand to stop her. Lena glanced at it, large and muscular and adorned with a simple gold wedding ring. 'It's my fault,' he said. 'I wanted a woman's opinion on that paint-ing. I'm thinking of buying it for my wife.'

Somehow, Lena doubted that. She looked at the man again. He was old enough to be Sarika's father. 'Many people are interested in the painting,' she added. 'You will need to talk to Pietro right away.'

'It's not professional for the waiter to drink at the reception,' Lena explained to Sarika as soon as they were out of earshot of the guests. 'It's like stealing when we clean. Or trying on a client's clothes!'

'He offered,' said Sarika, her head in the fridge. 'I thought it would be rude to say no. And he is dishy, isn't he? I love that blond hair. Where is the champagne?'

'In the ice bucket,' said Lena. She looked at it, now just a bucket of cold water. The ice had melted and the champagne was gone. Pietro burst into the kitchen. 'Three people seriously interested!' he exclaimed. 'Three!' He began to do a little jig, waving three fingers in the air. 'All my problems are over. Champagne?'

'All out,' said Lena. 'I can go buy some more?'

'No need,' said Pietro. 'I'll open the special bottle of Châteauneuf-du-Pape I've been saving.' He reached into the cupboard and retrieved the bottle, then pulled his key chain out of his pocket and jangled it until he found the bottle opener on the Swiss Army knife attachment. 'Get rid of those other guests, will you, Lena?' he said, thrusting the spiralled opener into the cork with gusto. 'It's time we were wrapping this up. And the good stuff is just for the people who might buy. Decant it for me, will you? Good to keep the bidders together for now and create a bit of healthy competition. Maybe we can push up the price. I'll take them to the chrysalis lounge. Give it a few minutes then bring up the decanter and four large wine glasses.'

Lena carefully poured the red wine into the decanter and then went back out and began to collect people's champagne glasses. She turned up the lights. Most took this as a sign to leave. Sarika led Gertrude, Patrick and Malcolm upstairs.

As the gallery emptied, Trudy emerged from the basement, arm in arm with Simon. Her face was pale with a glistening sheen of sweat. She blinked like a mole in a sunbeam. 'I need to go back to my hotel,' she said, putting her hand to her flushed face. 'I haven't felt like this since I took MDMA at that festival in Texas last year.'

'I'll get you a taxi,' said Simon. 'Then one for myself. But first . . .' He embraced Pietro. 'Thank you for tonight,' he said. 'You are the best friend a man could have.'

'So Simon is an affectionate drunk,' said Pietro, as they went back inside. 'Must be middle age finally creeping up on him.'

'Maybe,' said Lena, closing the door behind them and looking around the room. It was time for some serious cleaning.

'That American artist. She drinks like a Romanian soldier,' said Sarika, phone in hand as always.

Lena debated with herself whether to change the conversation back to English for practice. She decided it was too late in the evening. 'You don't know any Romanian solders,' she said in Hungarian, picking up a champagne flute that was balanced precariously on the Campbell Soup label foot.

'I could do,' objected Sarika. 'I've been to the border, it's not so far from our old village. Mama told me to hide my gold bracelet up my sleeve. Hairy-footed Romanians.'

Lena laughed at the expression, impossible to explain in English. At moments Sarika reminded her of a younger version of her own mother, with her inbuilt distrust of anyone from countries that bordered her own. Inevitable, she supposed, considering the number of times those borders had been forcibly adjusted.

'Simon too. Did you see when he was trying to dance? It was like that castle spinning round on a cockerel's leg! Remember the stories Aunt Juliska used to tell!'

'Keep your voice down.' Lena laughed a little, despite herself, at the memory. 'Pietro and his clients are still upstairs.'

'They must be asleep. I haven't heard anything for ages.'

As she said that, Pietro came clattering down the stairs. 'The night has given us its joys,' he said, the others following behind him. 'But now it is time to retire to our beds. Can you lock up, Lena? I can't find my keys. I'll get taxis for everyone and then Ophelia and I will head home ourselves.'

'Of course,' said Lena, smiling at the guests, all three of whom looked at her bleary-eyed as they left the gallery.

'I am pleased they are gone,' said Lena, glancing at her watch. 'English people get as drunk as Albanian donkeys. And Simon too, I didn't think that he was like that. Usually so careful and considered.'

'He has the hots for Trudy,' said Sarika. 'Pietro too.'

'I do not think so,' replied Lena, picking up a napkin abandoned in the orchid bowl. 'I think they were just star struck. She is a famous artist.'

'Who do you think is fitter?' said Sarika suddenly, putting her phone down next to the hedgehog. She picked up one of the violets that had been decorating the champagne and that was now impaled on one of the hedgehog's spikes. 'Simon or Pietro?'

'Sarika!'

'They are both about a hundred,' continued Sarika, undaunted. 'Or at least forty. But I think Pietro is nice and strong and I like his tan. But he talks too much and he is getting fat. Simon is small and bad-tempered and pale, but more intense. I think that's sexy.'

'So you fancy both?' said Lena, with a laugh.

'If I was fifty like Trudy and had to choose, either would do,' said Sarika. 'Who would you choose?'

'That is not the kind of agency I run,' said Lena, thinking about her policeman. He was who she would really like to be with. 'Be careful with that sculpture,' she said suddenly, watching Sarika fiddling with the hedgehog's spikes. 'It hurts if it pricks you.'

'It is the ugliest cat I have ever seen,' said Sarika, continuing to fiddle. 'Ouch!'

It was not the ugliest cat Lena had seen. Lena felt her mind wander to Kaplan, the bald cat that PC Cartwright had rescued for her. He'd left it in the care of an accommodating neighbour when he went on attachment in Newcastle. He'd given her the address but she hadn't visited in the months he'd been gone. Too busy, she told herself guiltily. Maybe next week.

Lena gathered up a large bin bag of debris and hauled it outside. The night was cool now and she paused to take a deep breath of Upper Street's night air, which mingled with the scent of leftover canapés coming up from her rubbish bag. Lena heard an angry voice. She put the bag down and crept closer. Someone was lingering on a nearby side street.

'Of course I've made the transfer,' the man's voice snapped in an American accent Lena recognised from the gallery. It was Patrick, the man who'd offered Sarika champagne. Lena listened for a response but there was none. It must be a phone conversation. 'It's not my fault the exchange rate is where it is. We've agreed a price and that is what I am paying you.' Silence. 'No no, don't be ridiculous. If you need more, we can work something out. You can't stop. Maybe a non-cash alternative. An asset transfer? Ah, I thought you'd like the sound of that.' The voice grew nearer and Lena realised he was walking towards her. She ducked back inside the gallery just in time to see a flash of blond hair pass the window.

'Stop!' shouted Lena at Sarika, drawn back to the task at hand by what her cousin was doing. The girl turned to her in surprise, the offending cloth in hand. 'You must not touch the paint.' Lena hurried over to *A Study in Purple* and snatched the cloth from Sarika's hand.

'It had a smudge,' said Sarika. 'I was trying to wipe it off. Just with a bit of water.'

'The smudge is meant to be there,' said Lena, inspecting the circle of dried-up water droplets Sarika had left on the corner of the painting. They were very subtle. She turned back to Sarika. 'It is okay. No real harm done. Be more careful next time. Neither of us can afford £84,000!'

'Are we done now?' said Sarika. 'I've had enough and I'm tired.'

'Hungover you mean.'

'It is meant to be my day off,' said Sarika. 'I am allowed to have a hangover.'

Lena couldn't dispute the logic. She looked around. They had collected the glasses, rescued the abandoned egg and caper canapés no one seemed to enjoy, wiped up the spilt drinks. She was tired too. It was clean, she decided. There was to be another event the following afternoon; she could give it a final once-over at lunchtime. People would trail in more grime the next morning.

'Yes, it is done for now,' she said, feeling her own eyelids growing heavy. 'Let's head off.' They left, Lena taking one last look around the gallery, then she put on the alarm, closed the door and locked it carefully, popping the key into her pocket. She glanced at her watch. It was 1.15 a.m. She was more than ready for bed.

The two walked together in companionable silence. On a Wednesday, Upper Street was relatively quiet this time of night. The last trains gone, the tube stopped, the bars closed. Only a few stray people continued their journeys by the light of the moon and the pink of the streetlights.

'I'll just see what Lucia's up to,' said Sarika, reaching into her purse. 'She'll just be finishing work now and will still be out. We could go to a bar and then get the night bus home together.'

'I thought you were tired?' said Lena, stifling a yawn.

'Fresh air. Second wind. Shit.' Sarika fumbled in her bag. 'I left my phone by that prickly cat.'

'Hedgehog,' replied Lena.

'Whatever. Can I have the keys? I'll go back.'

'You can pick it up tomorrow,' said Lena. She saw Sarika's horrified face and laughed. 'I didn't have a mobile at all when I was your age.'

'Sorry, Grandma,' teased Sarika. 'But I need it.'

'You will not forget to lock up?'

'You think I am an idiot,' said Sarika. 'But I can lock a door. I am not stupid.'

'And the burglar alarm? I will come back with you.'

'You are tired. The code was on that Post-it note in the office. It is only four numbers. I remember.'

Lena looked into the girl's eyes. She could see the ghosts of tears. 'Of course you can,' she said, handing her the keys and yawning. Sarika disappeared into the darkness.

Lena continued on her way. Her bus stop was at the other end of Upper Street, and she walked through the empty streets, the screeches of an urban fox her only company. Tonight had definitely started her thinking. Yes, cleaning could just be one arm of her business. If she was to win new, profitable clients she'd need to diversify. She wondered if – amongst the assorted immigrants in Islington – she could find herself a talented chef, his skills wasted chopping carrots and peeling potatoes when he could be crafting canapés for Lena's Elite Evenings.

Lena heard a bang and froze. A fox ran past her, scurrying away from the alley as if its tail was on fire. She breathed a sigh of relief. It must have knocked over a dustbin lid and spooked itself. She paused for another moment, listening. She heard sounds from the alley. Human sounds. Pain.

Lena quickly crept around the corner, following her ears while her eyes adapted to the darkness. There were no streetlights in this alley. It was around the back of a restaurant and furnished mainly with bins. Her eyes adjusted to the dark. She saw two men playing football in the darkness by a couple of traffic cones. It stank of rubbish: rotten vegetables and used ashtrays. She squinted at the two men. No. Three men. No football. Two men kicking a third.

'Stop,' she shouted, hoping the authority she tried to infuse into her voice alone would make them obey. The men turned around. One had stubbly ginger hair, making his head resemble a scotch egg. The other had no hair on his head but a thick black beard concealing his chin. The light of the moon gleamed back at her from his scalp. Drunkenness and anger filled both their eyes. And now confusion. 'I call police,' she bluffed, wishing she had thought to do that before barging in. 'Police are coming.'

'You want some as well, do you, pikey?' threatened the ginger man. Lena pulled herself up to her full height like a threatened cat puffing out its tail. 'I don't normally hit girls, but I can make an exception for you.'

Lena looked around. There were two of them and one of her. But they were drunk. Unsteady on their feet. Out for the thrill

25

of a fight. She doubted they even had weapons. But it would be good if she did. Her eyes scanned the darkness, alighting on a stray brick. Keeping her eyes fixed on the men, she grabbed it. The bald man laughed, revealing a mouth crowded with crooked teeth.

'What you gonna do with that?' he asked. 'Build us a wall?'

Lena heard the wail of police sirens in the distance. She hadn't called the police, hadn't had a chance. But this time of night, round here. Perhaps the threat would be enough.

'See, police are here,' she said. 'Get out or I commit a crime too.' She held up the brick, making as if to hurl it at them.

The men looked at her in confusion for a minute. The ginger one stepped forwards. She saw the man they'd been attacking back further into the shadows of the garbage bins. A bottle crashed to the ground. Both men turned, startled.

'Not worth it,' said the bald one. 'Come on, Chris. Let's go.'

'I could murder a kebab,' said the ginger man, spitting on the floor. He walked past her, his broad shoulders deliberately bumping into Lena as he made his way back to the main road. His friend followed close behind.

Lena watched them leave, then bent down to the man, lying on a pile of garbage bags. He was still cowering, hiding his face. But she recognised the crease on his purple trousers. He was from the gallery reception.

'Are you okay?' she said. 'I will call police and ambulance.'

'No.' His voice was thick. He spat a red blob of blood on to the floor then recoiled from it in disgust.

'Let me help you,' she said. 'My name is Lena Szarka.' She looked at him, trying to recollect his conversation with Pietro. 'Your name is Malcolm,' she told him. He looked at her in surprise. 'I was at the gallery reception,' she explained. 'Serving champagne.'

Malcolm began to stare at his hands, grazed and dirty. 'I need to get cleaned up. I must get home,' he said.

'You might be concussed,' said Lena. 'I call ambulance.' She reached into her bag for her phone.

'No no,' he said, getting unsteadily to his feet. 'Dirty horrible places.'

'We should call the police at least,' said Lena. Those men were not the organised criminals she'd encountered before, like Yasemin Avci's gang. But they were dangerous.

'No, no police,' he said. Lena looked at him in surprise. Why wouldn't he want the police involved?

'I am fine, really,' he continued. 'I just want to get home. So dirty back here. Thank you for your help. Most brave.'

Lena watched him stumble off, pausing to straighten the traffic cones on his way. Hanging round this part of Upper Street at this time of night, not wanting the police called. She didn't know what he'd been up to, but it was clearly no good. Still, at least he was no longer being kicked to a pulp by drunken thugs. That was something, she supposed.

CHAPTER 3

It took Lena a moment to realise what the sound was, screeching in her ears. The phone. She'd fallen asleep on the sofa again, exhausted from her long day and late-night excitement. And a long way past her usual bedtime. The phone had slipped down behind the cushions so she reached in and fished it out, pressing the green answer button just in time. Pietro's voice bellowed gibberish at her.

Lena took a moment to let the words wash over her before she even tried to understand. Even now, feeling quite good about her English, she found phone conversations difficult. Without seeing people's faces and watching their expressions change, the words seemed much more foreign. PC Cartwright had tried to phone her several times after they had discovered together who had murdered her friend. Lena had ignored his calls, preferring to offer a text message response. It hadn't encouraged him and contact had all but dried up.

'So do you see?'

Lena snapped back to the present. See what?

'Umm,' she replied, noncommittally.

'You see how it looks? Good. Then you won't mind coming straight away. It's already eight a.m.'

'Of course,' said Lena. She needed more. 'Where shall I meet you?'

'The police station, of course. You were the last person who saw the painting.'

'You sold it?'

'Keep up, Lena. Haven't you been listening? *A Study in Purple* has been stolen.'

Lena breathed in sharply. Eighty-four thousand pounds' worth of painting gone. The police were involved. But, more importantly, her agency was involved too.

'Nothing to be worried about,' continued Pietro. 'They'll just want to ask you about locking up. I told them you were totally reliable. You'd never do anything like forget to lock up or put on the burglar alarm. Nothing that could jeopardise the insurance. Would you?'

'Of course not,' said Lena. There was no way Sarika would have forgotten to lock the door. Surely there was not? Still, she'd feel better when she'd spoken to her.

'Bring your colleague too,' said Pietro, as if he could read her mind.

'Who do they think—?' began Lena.

'Too early to say,' interrupted Pietro. 'Nasty business. I dread to think what Trudy will make of all this. It's a disaster.'

'It will be okay,' said Lena, trying to calm Pietro as well as the panic rising in her own chest. 'I go to station now.'

'Good, that's best. Tell them you locked up. At least I'm up to date on the insurance.'

Lena said her goodbyes and then a small prayer. Sarika must have locked up, she repeated to herself. Of course she had. It was the last words they'd said to each other. Still, she decided she wanted to look into the girl's eyes when she asked the question. Just to be sure.

When Lena had first seen Sarika's flat-share in Dalston she had offered Sarika a lifeline out of the squalor to come and live with her. Her offer was immediately refused. Sarika loved the

29

flat – apparently it was like a New York loft apartment. Lena supposed the girl was right. Perhaps she'd lost her ability to appreciate trendiness at the expense of comfort when she turned thirty.

Lena rang the doorbell then glanced at her watch. Almost nine a.m. None of the occupants would be up yet – apart from Sarika, she was pretty sure they all worked in bars and restaurants.

Eventually the door was opened by a pale boy Lena thought she might have once met, peering out at her through bleary eyes. Was he the flatmate Sarika had told her could cook? Lena doubted it, he had no fat on him at all. Never trust a skinny chef, her mother had always told her. 'I need to speak to Sarika,' she told him, pushing past and closing the door behind her. He just shrugged and disappeared into a room. Lena imagined that later he would think the lady at the door was just a particularly uninspiring dream.

Sarika was a lump on the bed. '*Kelj fel*. Wake up,' said Lena, giving the girl a gentle shake. Sarika blinked up as if Lena was shining a torch in her eyes. Lena pulled open the curtains. Sarika groaned.

'What time is it?' she said, wiping her eyes.

'It's almost nine a.m.,' replied Lena.

'Am I meant to be somewhere?' said Sarika. 'I have not forgotten again? I am so careful now.' She gestured to a scruffy piece of paper on the floor. Lena felt affection surge for the girl when she saw it was a carefully written-out timetable.

'No,' she replied, more gently. 'I just want to check something with you. It's very important.' Sarika pulled herself up to sitting and looked at Lena expectantly. 'Did you lock the door to the gallery last night? And set the alarm?'

Lena watched carefully for a reaction. She saw surprise, then hurt register in the girl's eyes.

'You think I am so stupid,' said Sarika.

'Are you sure?'

'Sure you think that? Yes. Sure of the gallery? Yes. I locked it. Of course I locked it. Here is the key.' Sarika reached to the floor by her bed, grabbed the keys and handed them to Lena. 'You keep them, check for yourself.' She lay back down and rolled over, her back to Lena.

'The gallery was robbed last night,' said Lena. She saw the girl's body tense under the duvet. 'The police want to talk to us.'

Sarika sat bolt upright. 'Why?'

'We were the last people in the gallery. But do not worry. They will be able to tell that the door was forced, or a window broken. I just wanted to make sure before we go there. Come on, get dressed.'

'Now?'

'Yes, now. We need to talk to the police as soon as we can. I do not want anyone suggesting that we are in any way to blame for what has happened.'

'I need to shower first,' said Sarika, her voice shaking. 'I'll meet you there.'

'I can wait for you,' said Lena. 'Be quick.' Her phone beeped as Sarika slowly rubbed her eyes. 'It's a message from Pietro,' she said. 'Get up, we need to go now.'

'I can hear Kat in the shower,' said Sarika. 'She will be ages.'

'Shower later,' said Lena, getting to her feet.

'I stink,' objected Sarika. 'What will the police think?'

This whole flat stinks, thought Lena, but the girl did have a point. They needed to make a good impression. Her phone beeped again with more hassle from an impatient Pietro. 'I need to go,' said Lena. 'You shower. I'll meet you there.

Lena sat in the police station waiting to be questioned. She wondered if Sarika felt the same sense of dread that she did. She thought it was probably a good thing for her to talk to the police first, to reassure them that they were a respectable agency before Sarika came in. It would dispose them more kindly to her. She wished PC Cartwright was here to help. He'd know just what to say.

Lena stopped herself. She was thinking like a guilty person. She had nothing to worry about. It wasn't like she was responsible. Still, mentally she added up in her head how long it would take her to save the £84,000 the painting cost. Forty-two years.

Lena felt her heart hit the floor when she saw the policeman. She closed her eyes for a moment, willing him to walk past her. Please, this couldn't be his case. She opened them. His bulky form was looming over her. 'You again,' he greeted her, his voice devoid of enthusiasm.

'Yes,' she said. 'Hello PC Gullins.'

'I thought I told you to stay out of trouble?' he said.

'No trouble,' said Lena, sweetly. 'I am a witness.'

'Come on then,' he said. 'Let's go to the interview room. 1B. I expect you know the way.' He stood back and allowed Lena to pass. She had no idea which room was 1B.

'Don't know everything, eh?' said Gullins with a chuckle. 'Maybe I'd better lead this time.' Lena stood back and Gullins squeezed past her. His heavy footsteps echoed on the linoleum as he led her to the room.

'Heard from lover boy?' he said, sitting down with a grunt.

'I do not know who you mean,' said Lena.

'Didn't work out? Never mind. I always thought you two were an odd couple.'

'We are no couple,' said Lena, feeling the volume of her voice rising. 'You want to ask me about the painting?'

'Calm down,' said Gullins. 'Just being friendly. Don't get your knickers in a twist.'

Lena shot him an intense look. Her knickers were none of his business.

'So,' he continued, opening a folder. 'This little picture of a triangle got stolen and you were the last person to see it. Correct?'

'Except for the thief,' said Lena.

Gullins chuckled. 'There's no catching you out,' he said. 'So tell me what happened.'

Lena began to recap the events of the previous evening. Gullins interrupted her.

'Pietro owned *A Study in Purple* himself, right? He wasn't selling it on Ms Weincamp's behalf?'

'That is correct,' said Lena, wondering where this was going. 'I have heard him talk about it with Simon. He bought it two years ago but could not sell it.'

'Why was that?'

'I do not know,' replied Lena. 'Perhaps it was not a good painting.'

'Perhaps,' said Gullins. 'Let's get down to business. What time did you arrive at the Agnoletti Archer Gallery yesterday evening?'

Lena filled him in on the details, at the same time staring at his cabbage-y ears. She paused for a minute after she described her and Sarika leaving the gallery. She didn't want to implicate her assistant.

'So you locked the door?'

'Of course,' replied Lena. She had done.

'And you have a witness, your assistant Sarika Tóth.'

'Correct,' replied Lena.

'You didn't go back, for any reason, and you haven't been back since?'

'No,' said Lena. She paused again. No good would come from lying, even with the best motives. 'But Sarika forgot her phone so she went back to get it. I gave her the key.'

'Interesting. And where is Sarika now?'

'She will be here soon,' said Lena. 'She is only twenty-one. Very innocent.'

'Good.' The two regarded each other for a moment.

'A man from the gallery reception was beaten up, just after,' Lena offered him. 'Nearby. I can give you descriptions. But he did not want me to call the police.'

'Not my case,' said Gullins. 'Unless one of them was clutching a painting of a triangle you can just fill in a form at the front desk. When did you say Sarika was coming to talk to me?'

'Any minute.' Lena shifted nervously in her chair.

'Let's wrap this up,' said Gullins. 'For now. This is an extremely valuable item that has gone missing. My colleagues in CID will want to talk to you as well, I expect, when they finally get here. So don't disappear off back to Poland.'

Lena didn't even bother correcting him. Gullins escorted her back through the police station to the waiting room. They both looked, but Sarika was not there. Lena left, feeling oddly guilty for telling the truth. Should she have lied to protect her cousin?

No, she thought to herself. Sarika had probably fallen asleep again, but would soon wake up, speak to the police, and even Gullins would be as convinced as Lena that the girl had done nothing. They could even search that filthy flat of hers, if they wanted. It wasn't a great advert for a cleaning agency, but at least it wouldn't contain £84,000-worth of *A Study in Purple*.

She should talk to Sarika about the state of her flat, though. She could make it much nicer than it was for her cousin. Lena smiled, thinking of the small flat she'd moved into. It was in a brand-new apartment and Lena kept it so spotless it looked as if it could still have the plastic wrap on. She felt alone without her best friend Timea and her ex, Tomek, at times, but she certainly didn't miss the untidiness he left in his wake. Perhaps she'd get a goldfish. It wouldn't be much of a substitute for a boyfriend, but it would be company. And it would be hard pressed to make a mess outside the confines of its tank.

Her phone rang in her bag and Lena struggled to pull it out in time to answer. Just before she did, she heard a voice behind her. A voice that made her stop in her tracks. It was a well-spoken voice, a little breathless. And it was calling her name.

Lena turned around. PC Cartwright stood behind her, panting a little. 'Lena!' he said. 'I saw your name on the board. So . . .' he paused to catch his breath. 'So I ran after you.'

Lena felt her own colour rise a little to meet his. She wanted to tell him how amazing it felt to see him, how much she had missed him while he was gone. She wanted to lean forwards and kiss those perfect lips of his. 'When did you get back?' she said instead, trying to sound casual.

'Just last week,' said Cartwright.

'Oh,' replied Lena. So he'd been back a week and hadn't been in contact.

'I tried to call,' he said, as if reading her thoughts.

'I have been busy,' said Lena, thinking of the missed calls that could verify his story.

'Of course,' replied Cartwright. 'Listen, I was thinking that maybe, if you'd like to, we could have dinner? You know, like we tried before I was called away? Just to catch up. It could be fun?'

Lena tried, unsuccessfully, to hide her pleasure. 'I love!' she said. 'I would love to,' she said, correcting her grammar.

'Sunday is my day off. Seven-ish? I'll text you. Your number is the same?'

'It is,' said Lena. Her phone rang again. She'd forgotten it was still in her hand.

'I'll let you take that,' he said. 'Oh, but first. Why were you at the police station? Is there any assistance I can offer?'

'Nothing I cannot handle,' said Lena. Cartwright walked back to the station, turning a couple of times to wave at awkward angles.

Lena cursed whoever the phone caller was as she picked it up. A female voice she didn't recognise began shouting at her. 'Sarika's gone, taken her stuff,' the voice snapped. 'Hasn't paid the bloody rent either. I'm going to call the police.'

CHAPTER 4

Lena tried to push her worry to the back of her mind as she walked to Penelope's house. She couldn't afford to let down a client. But memories of what happened to Timea flooded through her like the waters of a toilet flushing. This time was different, she told herself. She'd clean for Penelope, then focus on tracking down Sarika. She hoped for a little peace and quiet to think through what had happened as she scrubbed. Unfortunately, this didn't seem likely at Penelope's.

When Lena first set up her little agency, Lena's Cleaners, the agency she used to work for had given her a stern talk about how taking clients with her was akin to stealing. Lena hardly felt that was fair, but she obeyed for the most part. Both she and her best friend Timea had worked at the agency and she didn't want to take Timea's old clients. She still remembered her suspicions when Timea went missing. Even those clients who weren't involved had proved to have unsavoury secrets.

Lena had been touched when a few insisted on loyalty to her. Mrs Kingston, of course. Lena smiled, looking forward to her weekly trip to clean for her tomorrow. To Lena's surprise, Penelope Haslam insisted on keeping her too, although really she had been Timea's client. Before she even rang the bell she could hear the screams of an angry toddler, reminding her of a gaggle of baby otters shrieking for their mother. She'd heard them at the

Ludas Matyi Amusement Park Zoo back in Debrecen with Timea
and her son Laszlo. She didn't blame the mother otter for hiding,
attempting to catch a quick break from the gaggle of demanding
little waterproof furry bodies.

Sighing, she rang the doorbell. She'd been hoping to share this
client with Sarika. She was even prepared to provide Penelope
with two cleaners for the price of one, although what Penelope
really needed to do was hire a nanny. It would be a reward to
Penelope for her loyalty. And would save Lena's sanity. But
Penelope had switched her day to Thursday, one of Sarika's days
off. So far Lena hadn't been able to persuade either of them to
compromise. So she was stuck cleaning and managing the men-
agerie of two children by herself. She steeled herself and rang the
doorbell.

Penelope was still buttoning her shirt as she opened the door,
displaying a black lacy bra, partially concealed by the small child
she held awkwardly in one arm. She semi-passed, semi-threw the
child at Lena, who had her years on the school handball team to
thank for catching the boy cleanly.

'Thank god you're here,' exclaimed Penelope, as if Lena was late
instead of her customary ten minutes early. 'I'll go mad if I can't
have a proper macchiato before my conference call. It's my
keeping-in-touch day with the office but these little monkeys will
barely let me boil the kettle. I'll just finish getting dressed then
pop out to Le Péché Mignon.'

Crispin, the eight-month-old baby Lena was holding, began to
wriggle. Lena felt a wetness on her arm. Tears, snot or vomit, she
pondered, not really wanting to look. She began to make her way
to the kitchen.

'Can you grab my watch?' shouted Penelope from upstairs. 'It's
on the kitchen counter.'

Lena looked. There was nothing there but baby bottles and
squashed packets of healthy mush from Ella's Kitchen. Casper,

Penelope's three-year-old, was suddenly under her feet, scrambling to get on to the kitchen counter. He almost succeeded. She passed him the carton of orange juice he'd been reaching for. He instantly squeezed it on to his leg. From there it dripped on to the floor, leaving a sticky trail in its wake.

No watch in sight.

'It is not here,' she called up.

'Yes it is, by my keys in that lovely Iznik bowl I bought in Istanbul.'

'No,' replied Lena, wiping Casper's sticky orange leg roughly with kitchen roll. He grinned back at her.

'It's a Longines, with a rose-gold bezel. Little diamonds mark each quarter-hour.'

'There is no watch.'

'Yes there is.' Penelope came into the kitchen and rummaged through the bowl. 'I swear I left it here. Are you sure you haven't moved it? Cleaned it away?'

Penelope turned to face her. For a moment, Lena didn't like the look in her eye. She'd seen that look from clients before. Whenever they lost something.

'I have just arrived,' said Lena.

'Well, I'm sure it will turn up,' said Penelope, smiling again. 'But right now I need a coffee. I hope there's not a queue again at Le Péché. Perhaps I'll treat myself to a *pain au chocolat*. No, Lena, don't let me. I have to lose this baby fat. Just look at me.' She took a step back so Lena could appreciate her figure.

'I can get you coffee,' said Lena, hopefully, moving to pass Penelope back the baby.

'No!' Penelope practically screamed, before composing herself. 'That's hardly your job.' She smiled sweetly. 'I couldn't possibly take advantage of you.'

Lena looked at the child in her arms and heard another shriek from the next room. Then she thought about how much Timea had enjoyed working here. The children's yelps and giggles were like those of Laszlo, the son Timea had had to leave behind in Hungary when she came to London to earn money for his future.

'I will look after Crispin and Casper while I clean,' Lena relented. 'Enjoy your coffee.'

Penelope gave her a grateful wave, already halfway down the garden path. 'Thanks Lena,' she said. 'You're my hero.'

It wasn't like Lena to just lie in a park, but after finishing up at Penelope's house that's what she did. Prostrated on her front, she could feel the grass imprinting her face like iron wool. The sun was hot on her bare legs and she could feel an insect exploring her calf. An ant near her eye clambered to the top of a blade of grass for a better view of its surroundings, then scurried back down. It repeated this exercise several times, as if to reassure itself that its eyes could be trusted. Finally it reached the top and paused there. It waved its antennae in the air like the conductor of a tiny, silent orchestra.

So Sarika had gone. Lena found the fact that her belongings were gone too strangely comforting. Unlike when her friend Timea had disappeared. Timea's room remained eerily replete with her possessions.

It was a good sign, Lena told herself. She'd left on purpose. She must be okay. But did it mean she was guilty? Had she stolen *A Study in Purple*?

Lena turned her head so her opposite cheek rested on the grass. She looked at this new view, the grass forest-like from this height. Another ant, this one with a belly the colour of amber, scurried along in a confused-looking hurry, rampaging over the clover that dared to block its path.

No. She couldn't have. Sarika had been raised in a village on the other side of Hungary to her own, so they had not grown up together. But she was family. And in the months that Sarika had been working with Lena, she'd never known her to be dishonest. Late, perhaps, and even lazy. Silly sometimes. But not dishonest.

And it made no sense. What would Sarika do with a stolen painting? It wasn't like stealing a tenner from a client's wallet. It would take specialist knowledge and contacts to sell a painting. Neither of which Sarika possessed.

But then why had she left?

Lena got up, feeling a slight head-rush as she climbed to her feet. She glanced at her watch. Four p.m., and a Thursday. As good a time as any to talk to Sarika's flatmates and find out what was really going on with her young friend.

Lena stood awkwardly in the living room of Sarika's flat-share while the attractive but bleary-eyed boy who'd introduced himself as Dragg went back to his bedroom to put some trousers on. He'd opened the door in his purple boxers, displaying a pale but lean chest and an enormous tattoo of a fierce-looking creature crawling up his neck.

The room was filthy, with half-drunk cups of coffee serving as ashtrays and the stale smell of weed dancing on the air. Lena wondered if they would take offence if she tidied up a bit. A huge mural dominated the once-white wall, displaying a skull whose eyes were made of roses and whose teeth were composed of tiny beetles. It would fit well in the 'Tormented Illusions' exhibition at the Agnoletti Archer Gallery, thought Lena, admiring it despite herself. She looked more closely, trying to work out if it was on a giant canvas or painted on the wall itself, fearful for Sarika's deposit.

Dragg came back, wearing a ripped black T-shirt and tight black jeans. His bare feet were grubby, like a hobbit's. Lena tried not to look at them and politely refused the offer of a cup of coffee, imagining the state of the mug it would be served in. Dragg began to make the coffee, properly in a cafetiere. Lena breathed in its scent, regretting her choice.

'She did not tell you where she was going?' asked Lena, when Dragg finally sat down. 'What time did she leave?'

There was a long pause. Lena looked at the boy in front of her, who was in turn looking at the mural. She was trying to make out what the tattooed creature that seemed to be curled around his neck might be. Its head was right by his dark hairline, as if sniffing his skull. Perhaps it was some kind of snake, although its head looked more like a lion.

'I wasn't awake yet,' replied Dragg, rubbing his eyes. 'I was working last night. So it must have been before twelve.' Lena listened to his voice, trying to place his accent. He spoke well, but there was a foreign lilt. Greek perhaps?

'And what do you do?' said Lena.

'I'm a street artist,' he replied, with a touch of pride. Lena looked at him again. What did that mean?

'You paint pictures of the street?' she asked.

He looked amused. 'Something like that,' he replied. 'And some freelance graphic design.' Lena watched him as he reached into his back pocket and retrieved a tin of tobacco. He pinched some in his fingers and proceeded to roll it into a cigarette. Lena noticed that the tin also contained a small pouch of weed. That would explain the stale smell and reddened eyes.

'Graphic design?' said Lena, a little surprised this grubby boy could have such an impressive job. 'You are trained?'

'Yes,' said Dragg, 'I went to art school. That's why I came over from Greece. So do you know why Sarika has gone?' he asked, lighting his cigarette.

'I am not sure,' replied Lena. She decided not to mention the missing painting for now. 'I thought you could help. Was there anything going on with her? Was she upset?'

'I didn't know her well,' said Dragg, his voice careful. 'You'd have more luck with Lucia. They hung out together. Went to parties. Besties, I think the British say.'

'Yes, she has talked about Lucia,' said Lena. 'Is she here?"

'She's already left for her shift. She works five p.m. till one a.m. At the Black Zenith on Holloway Road.'

They heard the clink of a key in the lock. A blonde girl in a short leather skirt entered. She walked straight up to Dragg, gave Lena a hard stare and then kissed him on the lips. Lena averted her gaze. If she was marking her territory she was wasting her time. Lena couldn't think of anything worse than touching the none-too-clean Dragg. Finished with the kiss, the girl disappeared into the kitchen.

'That's Kat,' explained Dragg. 'My girlfriend.' Lena was pleased to hear a tinge of embarrassment in his voice. 'She'll say hello when she comes back.'

He was wrong. Kat re-entered the room, gulping from a can of Red Bull. 'What does she want?'

'This is Sarika's cousin. Lena, meet Kat.'

'I hope she's got the rent money,' said Kat, ignoring Lena's proffered hand. 'That bitch left without paying.'

'It was you who called me?' said Lena. 'Do not worry, she will be back.'

'In trouble with the police, is she?'

Lena looked at the girl more closely. She was wearing eyeliner that had smeared a little, making her look like a tired racoon. Lena thought she could detect a trace of glitter on her cheek as well. Dark roots divided the top of her head in two.

'Why do you say that?'

'That's why people leave, isn't it?' replied Kat. 'Money or police. Maybe both.'

'No,' replied Lena. 'That is not it.'

'You will pay her share,' said Kat. 'Of the rent. You are family, right? Takes me a lot of tips to make a month's rent. That's what she owes.'

'I will make sure you are not short of pocket,' said Lena. 'But we must give her a chance to come back first. I am sure it will not be long.'

Lena stood up to go. 'The Black Zenith?' she confirmed with Dragg.

'That's the one.' He was already skinning up again, and this time he picked up the little bag of weed and sprinkled it liberally into the roll-up. Kat had slipped herself on to his lap. Lena closed the door behind her.

'No, I have not heard from Sarika,' said Greta, Lena's mother, over the phone. 'Have you heard from that policeman?'

'That's not the point, Mama,' said Lena, enjoying the comfort that came from speaking in her native tongue. Without Timea and Sarika, she had no one in London she could speak to in Hungarian. It was exhausting, always translating in her head before she opened her mouth. 'I need to find Sarika.'

'You should never have left that lovely Tomek,' said her mother. 'He was a proper man. Ate every drop of his *goulash*.'

'He left me,' replied Lena. 'Not the other way around. You know that.'

'If only you had learnt to cook,' said Greta. 'This never would have happened. I tried to teach you. Over and over. But no, you always wanted to be climbing trees with that Istvan. And look what happened to him.'

'Can you call Sarika's mother? Just to see if Sarika has been in touch with her?'

'I'm not talking to that witch Boglarka,' replied Greta. 'She borrowed my best pot and burned her disgusting excuse for a chicken *paprikash* all over the bottom. It looked like the surface of Mars. I told her she needed to buy me a new one, and do you know what she said? "It was like this when I borrowed it." Can you imagine? I have never burned a chicken *paprikash* in my life! Have I? Have you ever known me to do such a thing? Well, that is it. She may have been the sister of my no-good runaway husband, but we are no longer family.'

Lena sighed. 'I'm worried about Sarika. Please?'

'That girl will be fine. She may not seem too bright but she's got peasant cunning. Just like her mother. And that good-for-nothing brother of hers that I had the misfortune to marry.'

'Just give me her phone number then. I will call Aunt Boglarka myself.'

'It will do no good. She's got her story about my poor pot and she is sticking to it. That's what happens when you live near the Romanian border. You catch their thieving hairy-footed ways.'

'I want to ask her about Sarika.'

'You won't get any honest answers out of her.' Lena heard her mother shuffling papers. 'But I'll give you the number. What's that daughter of hers done? Stolen a chicken?'

'There are no chickens running around London,' said Lena. 'Give me the number.' She scribbled down the digits her mother gave her and glanced at her watch. She needed to get to the gallery. She couldn't be late for work on top of everything else that had gone wrong.

'What do you mean "she's gone"?' shouted Pietro. He was standing outside the gallery with his wife Ophelia and the gallery manager Simon, peering in anxiously as the scene-of-crime officers intently dusted for fingerprints in their white boiler suits. A line of yellow and black tape prevented his entry.

For a second Lena wondered if she had pronounced the words

incorrectly. 'She is not here. Disappeared,' she clarified to the irate gallery owner.

'Where is she then?'

Lena considered for a moment. Perhaps honesty was best. 'I do not know,' she admitted. She looked at Pietro's face. It was reddening, but she guessed from anger rather than the sun. Honesty was clearly not best. 'But I am sure she will be back very soon.'

'How can she just disappear?' said Pietro, spitting out the words. 'Don't you get addresses, references? What do we pay you for?'

'I'm sure there's an explanation,' said Ophelia. She'd edged herself into a slender patch of shade against the building, but Lena could see inevitable freckles emerging on her pale skin.

'She's run off with our painting,' shouted Pietro. 'That's the explanation.'

'Do not jump to conclusions,' said Simon. 'Lena, how well did you know this girl?'

'She is family,' said Lena, miserably. 'She would not do anything wrong. I think that maybe she just got scared.'

'Scared?' shouted Pietro. 'I'm bloody petrified. I've had my most valuable painting stolen.'

'And my fingers have been inked by the police,' added Ophelia, holding up her delicate digits, each with an uncharacteristically dark tip. 'Pietro and Simon's too. I hope we're not suspects.'

'Of course not,' reassured Simon. 'It is so they know what our fingerprints are like as they will expect to find them here. So they can rule them out. Although with all the people at the reception last night, I don't know how that can help.'

'I cleaned after everyone left,' said Lena. 'There would be no fingerprints from the reception,' she said, with a touch of pride. 'I tell the police.' She tried to navigate the police tape to make her way inside.

'It's no good,' said Simon. 'They won't let you in. That's why we're standing in the street. They won't even let you near the door. They seem particularly interested in the lock, although we can all see it's been broken. We'll need to get the locks changed.'

'I'd take us all to Fromage d'Or,' said Pietro. 'Out of this heat. Except for the fact that I'm now destitute!'

'Don't be ridiculous,' said Simon. 'The insurance will pay.'

'That could take weeks to come through,' replied Pietro. He'd started to sweat in the heat. 'Months, if they're the stubborn sort.'

'We're not exactly poor,' interjected Ophelia. 'And I never liked that painting anyway. Ugly thing from an ugly artist.'

'Trudy is hardly ugly,' said Simon. Ophelia rewarded him with an angry stare.

Pietro grimaced. 'It's not just about the money,' he said. 'Trudy will bad-mouth me throughout the art world. My reputation is at stake.' Pietro buried his head in his hands. 'It is all your fault,' he said, pointing his finger dramatically at Lena. She stepped back, almost squashing a passing couple, their arms interlocked and their faces angry.

'Calm down, Pietro,' said Simon. 'There's no evidence that Lena had anything to do with it.'

'Not good enough,' said Pietro. 'Reputation is everything. She is fired.'

Lena gasped. 'This is not fair,' she said. 'Sarika is innocent. We both are.'

'Steady on, Pietro,' said Simon.

'And don't expect a reference either. I can't risk my clients or business connections losing things and blaming me.'

'But you do not think I took the painting? First you blame my cousin and now me?'

'I can't trust you,' replied Pietro. 'It's a good thing we're having the locks changed tomorrow. I'm afraid I simply don't feel safe with you having a key to my gallery any more.'

Lena looked to Ophelia for help, but the woman was busy inspecting her inky fingers. She looked to Simon. He was watching Ophelia. 'Ophelia, you're wilting in this heat,' he said, his voice full of concern. 'Let me take you to that vegan ice-cream place. A nice avocado coconut ice will cool you down.' The two left, leaving Lena to face Pietro alone.

'Fine,' Lena said, feeling her face heating up like a radiator. 'But you pay me one month's notice. I can work or if you do not trust me you pay me now. Then I go.'

'Don't be ridiculous. You're not getting a penny more out of me.'

'We have a contract,' replied Lena, keeping her eyes fixed on his. They were a deep brown, the colour of hot coffee. Or wet mud, she thought.

'It's like that, is it?' said Pietro. 'I'm pretty sure theft would void that. Gross misconduct. My lawyer will be in touch.'

Lena opened her mouth to speak, before realising that she had no words adequate to express her emotions. She turned on her heels and left.

Lena marched along Upper Street towards Highbury and Islington station. How dare Pietro fire her over this? She was innocent, she knew that much, and she was pretty sure Sarika was too. Innocent or otherwise, this painting had cost her one job and likely more. If the rumours spread, which is what rumours do, her nascent business would be ruined.

But if anything, surely Pietro was a suspect. She slowed her pace, thinking. Was he trying to use her agency to cast suspicion away from himself?

Lena stopped in her tracks. A dog tied up outside Budgens looked at her expectantly, willing her to be his owner. It was starting to make sense. The insurance had been Pietro's first thought when he called her. Did the gallery owner have secret financial troubles? 'I will investigate him,' said Lena, out loud. The dog barked at her as if he agreed. 'I will not let suspicion scare my cousin away,' she told him. The dog strained against his lead to lick her hand. 'Or ruin my business,' she said, giving his ear a quick scratch. 'No one can accuse Lena's Cleaners of dishonesty.'

Back home, Lena tried to relax in the cool bath she had run herself. She'd been clammy from the long walk in the hot sunshine, plus her own internal temperature always rose when she was angry. She added a few drops of cleansing lavender oil to the water and lay back, trying to force her muscles to let go of their tension. Finding Sarika had to be the priority, before things got further out of control.

She thought about that branch of her family. Aunt Boglarka, Sarika's mother, was her own father's sister. They'd lived in a distant village, but even so Boglarka had quickly become her mother's nemesis. Lena remembered her visiting only a few times, twice before her father left and once after, for a childhood friend's wedding. That final time Boglarka had seemed smug at her brother's disappearance, as if she had always felt Lena's mother Greta was not good enough for him. She had glossed over the fact that her brother had stolen money from the factory as well as his own family.

But Boglarka lived in a village hours away. Lena barely knew Sarika at all growing up. It was after Lena and Timea had already left for London that Aunt Boglarka had moved to the village just two along from her own. Either she'd then nagged Greta to help her daughter, struggling to find work in London, or more likely, Lena thought, Greta took the opportunity to show off and had offered Boglarka's daughter employment, working for her own daughter: 'the successful businesswoman'.

Lena heaved herself out of the bathtub and wrapped herself in a towel, enjoying the coolness of her shivers. Drying herself off, she went to the phone and dialled the number her mother had given her. After some awkward small talk with Boglarka, she filled her aunt in on the gallery robbery and Sarika's subsequent disappearance.

'But all her things are gone,' Lena added quickly. 'So I know she is okay. You are not to worry. Has she been in touch?'

'I don't know why you assume she has something to do with the painting going missing.' Her aunt's voice was abrupt, but she didn't sound too worried for Sarika.

'I do not think she took it,' said Lena. 'But she left at the same time. I want her to come back so that we can prove she is innocent.'

'Ha,' said Boglarka. 'You're just like your mother. Jumping to conclusions. Because I burned a *goulash* once, I will burn a chicken *paprikash* the next time.'

'What are you talking about?' Lena was baffled.

'People change, you know. They make one little mistake and are punished for it the rest of their lives.'

'What mistake are you talking about?' said Lena.

'Don't you play innocent with me. Sarika trusted you. She liked you. Even though you worked her like a slave.'

'But have you heard from her? Do you know where she is?'

'I would not tell you if I did,' said Boglarka.

Lena sighed. This conversation was not going anywhere. 'Tell her to get in touch with me,' said Lena. 'I want to help her.' She put the phone down.

Lena thought about what had just been said. What on earth was Boglarka talking about? She picked up the phone again. If any-one could find out the gossip back home it was her mother.

CHAPTER 5

'But you do know that she's okay? That she hasn't been abducted?'

Lena took a sip of her coffee and smiled at Mrs Kingston, her favourite client and her Friday treat. The old lady was staring at her with a concerned expression. She'd helped her through the drama when Timea went missing, and the trauma when she was found dead.

'Yes,' replied Lena. 'She took all her things. I think she chose to go. It was after I said to come to the police station. And her mother sounded okay. I think Sarika was in touch with her.' She accepted a garibaldi biscuit from the plate Mrs Kingston offered her and took a crumbly bite. She knew that Jasper, Mrs Kingston's pet rabbit, would hoover up any crumbs before she could get round to it. She could hear him scratching around under the floral sofa, his keen nose picking up the scent already. 'But I am worried. I do not know how she will manage on her own.'

'At least the police will be interested in finding her this time,' said Mrs Kingston. 'What with them thinking she's got the painting.'

'I wish her to come back,' said Lena. 'She is new to this country and . . .' Lena struggled for the expression. '. . . is not wise about the streets.'

'Streetwise,' offered Mrs Kingston. 'Does she have any friends? Someone she could be staying with?'

51

'She has not been in London for long. The only people she knows well are her flatmates,' said Lena. 'And I have spoken to them.' She thought for a moment. She hadn't yet met with Lucia. That would need to be added to her to-do list. 'I am worried about where she could have gone. What she could be doing.' Against her reasoning, Lena's imagination began to rebel, placing Sarika in all sorts of unpleasant situations. A pretty, innocent girl, on the run from the police in a strange country. Suddenly twenty-one seemed so young. Too young.

Lena shivered and bent down. Jasper bounded up to her hand and gave her a comforting sniff. She ruffled his fur, marvelling at its softness against her coarse fingers. She passed him down a small piece of garibaldi in gratitude, making sure it contained a fat piece of raisin. He sat on the carpet and munched away merrily.

'If you don't have any leads about where she could be,' said Mrs Kingston, breaking her reverie, 'then the best thing you can do is make it so that she wants to come home. When I was a journalist we used to say it was making them come to you.'

Lena looked to the older lady. 'How do I do that?'

'Find the painting of course. Prove her innocent.'

Lena sat back. That was a tall order. 'I do not know where to start,' she said. 'The police are working on it. Perhaps they will find it.'

'We both know how slow they can be,' said Mrs Kingston. 'And what if they find Sarika first? After running away like this they'll keep her in custody.'

'I did not think of that,' said Lena. 'I do not think that Sarika would cope locked up.' She took another biscuit and chewed on it as she thought. Jasper peered up at her, standing on his hind legs and scratching at her leg. Absent-mindedly she picked a raisin from the biscuit and passed it down to him.

'Even if I do find the painting, how will Sarika know? She does not answer her phone. No reply to my texts.'

'Come on Lena,' said Mrs Kingston. 'You're less than half my age. Surely you know young people are never without social media. Tweet it.'

Lena thought of Sarika, her hands constantly wrapped around her phone, her attention fully absorbed. She smiled. 'You are right,' she said. 'Wherever she is, Instagram will not be far behind.'

Lena looked down at Jasper, who looked back at her hopefully. She took yet another biscuit and broke a small piece off. He almost jumped to her hand in his eagerness to get it between his protruding teeth.

Lena thought for a moment. 'Pietro was very quick to blame Sarika for what happened and fire me. There is something not right. I know that.'

'Then you have your first port of call. But you will need more sources than that. More options.'

Mrs Kingston was right. She'd jumped to conclusions the last time she had investigated and it had clouded her judgement.

'The guests at the gallery reception,' said Lena. 'They all knew the value of the painting.'

'Were any of them acting suspiciously?'

Lena cast her mind back. Gertrude, the old lady with her nephew fresh out of prison for theft. Patrick, the American with his phone call about money troubles. Malcolm, attacked after the reception and not wanting the police called. 'Yes,' she replied. 'But I do not even know their full names.'

'Then you must find out,' Mrs Kingston told her.

Lena got up, taking the now empty plate of biscuits and her coffee mug into the kitchen and running the hot tap.

'You don't need to clean the house today,' said Mrs Kingston, her voice barely audible above the waterfall of the tap. 'You have investigations to make.'

'I will plan while I clean,' said Lena, clattering more dishes into the sink, determined not to leave Mrs Kingston with a messy house. Especially with all the detritus the rabbit left behind. She couldn't have her favourite client falling over a carrot stub. 'Cleaning is when I think my best.'

After leaving Mrs Kingston, Lena wanted to capture her thoughts there and then. She looked around. There was an American-style diner a short walk up the road. She'd suffer a cup of their coffee and get started on her suspect list.

Being neither breakfast nor lunchtime, the diner was quiet, but it still had the appetising aroma of fried potatoes and onions. She ordered a filter coffee and an espresso which she combined into one cup as soon as she could, and treated herself to a greasy chocolate-glazed doughnut. This kind of thinking required plenty of sugar, even after all those biscuits. She grabbed a couple of napkins and took a bright green seat in the window. She sipped her coffee. With the extra shot it was almost strong enough.

Lena bit into the doughnut, retrieved a pen from her bag and smoothed out a napkin. She paused to think, to organise her thoughts. What she needed was a list of suspects. She took another bite, feeling the sugar carried by the coffee straight to her brain.

She thought of the insurance and wrote down Pietro's name, pressing hard with the pen and damaging the napkin in the process. Remembering her last case, she added his wife Ophelia for good measure. And Simon. Then she put a heading for people at the drinks reception. Gertrude, the old lady with the nephew released from prison. Malcolm of the purple trousers and disinclination for the police. Patrick, the American with the blond hair, who'd flirted with Sarika and had the angry phone call. She added the nameless others she could recall. Another flamboyantly dressed man and some other hazy faces of bored-looking art students. Gertrude's elderly friend. She'd get their names from the gallery later, once Pietro had cooled down. One of them could have sneaked back in at some point and taken the picture. There were so many. She guessed at least fifty people had been to the gallery that night. She'd need to find some way to prioritise.

Lena wasn't sure why she felt suspicious of the artist, but she added Trudy Weincamp's name to the list. Had anyone else seemed interested in the picture, someone who had the contacts to sell it? Lena sighed. She'd have to make up with Pietro or Simon if she was going to find out more, but they couldn't know they were top of the suspect list. Then reluctantly she added Sarika's name. Was there anyone else? Could those two men in the alley have something to do with it? It was a long shot and she wouldn't be able to find them, but she put them down anyway. First, she'd start with her napkin list, then tomorrow she'd build up a proper suspect board, like she had with PC Cartwright when they were trying to work out who was responsible for her friend Timea's death. Then she'd work out how on earth to begin investigations.

Later that evening, Lena sank down into her sofa with a sigh, resting her head back on to the cushion so even her neck could be off duty. She missed her best friend and flatmate Timea every day. Sometimes she even missed seeing her ex-boyfriend Tomek, sprawled on the sofa or munching a sausage roll. The spark had gone a long time ago, but it had been nice to have a warm body snuggled beside her.

She liked living on her own, she told herself. She went out in the morning and her loyal flat would wait for her, everything exactly how she left it, until she returned home in the evening. And so quiet. No drama, no panics, no gossip. Lena looked around the room, drinking it in. Although the flat was rented, of course, it felt so thoroughly hers. Everything in the flat, modest though it was, she had purchased. A soft fleecy blanket adorned the clean leather sofa. A framed photo of herself with Timea, taken on a sunny afternoon in Clissold Park, smiled down at her from the mantle.

The only other living thing in the flat was the orchid from Cartwright. It had long since stopped flowering and lay dormant, its waxy leaves shining. Lena swallowed the impulse to water it again. Too much water would drown it. She still hoped that if she gave it just the right amount of attention it would flower again. She closed her eyes and felt herself drifting towards sleep.

The phone rang. Lena cursed whoever was calling and rooted around in her bag. It was a WhatsApp call. Lena saw who it was from and swiped to answer as quickly as she could.

'Sarika,' she gasped into the phone. 'Where are you?'

'I'm so sorry, Lena,' the girl replied. Lena could tell she was not far from tears.

'At least you are okay,' said Lena. 'Come home.'

'I can't,' said Sarika. 'I'm scared.'

'But why?'

'The police will think I took the painting.'

'Not if you come back,' said Lena. 'They will not suspect you if you turn yourself in.'

'I'm not coming back,' insisted Sarika. 'I can't go to prison.'

'There is no way you will go to prison,' said Lena. 'You do not have the painting. You didn't steal it. You are no thief. Someone broke into the gallery after you left. The lock was smashed. We will prove that you are innocent together. Now, tell me where you are and I will come and fetch you.'

Silence.

Lena held the phone away from her face. Sarika had hung up. She redialled but got no answer. Lena tossed the phone to the other end of the sofa. She closed her eyes again, resting her head back on the cushion. Lena couldn't believe how foolish Sarika was being.

Still, at least the girl was alive. Although everything had indicated Sarika had gone of her own free will, until Lena spoke to her she'd felt the fear that had become seated deep inside her since her dear friend Timea's murder. A fear that had been eating away at her guts like an ulcer.

Lena picked up the phone again and fiddled with it. Sarika was offline again now. Lena had seen in movies the police tracking where people are from phone calls. She wondered if they could do the same thing from her mobile. It seemed highly unlikely. But if anyone could do it, she knew who it would be.

A snooze wasn't to be had that evening. Lena had just drifted off again when the doorbell rang. Lena jumped up, upsetting the cup of milky coffee she'd been cradling as she nodded off on the sofa. It splashed a hazelnut pattern of liquid that resembled a misshapen violin on the floor. The cup took a circuitous route, travelling in fast concentric circles until it petered out, finally taking its rest under the coffee table. Lena bent to pick it up and then headed to the kitchen to grab a cloth, grateful for the umpteenth time that the floor was laminate. The world was an easier place to inhabit when your floor could be wiped clean.

It took a second, impatient ring of the doorbell to remind Lena what had awoken her. Sarika. It must be. The girl had listened to her after all. She ran to the door, still clutching the cloth, ready to give Sarika an enormous hug before she sat her down and chastised her for her foolishness in running away in the first place. Then she'd take her down to the police station and get this whole mess sorted out. But not before she'd wiped up the liquid violin spillage on her own floor.

With all these thoughts running through her mind, it took Lena a moment to place the woman who stood in her doorway.

Angry eyes, framed with thick black eyeliner, glared at her through her poker-straight blonde hair.

'You owe me a fucking laptop,' shouted the woman, pushing past Lena into the flat.

'Kat!' said Lena, finally remembering the name of Sarika's flat-mate. She slammed the door five seconds too late and turned around to see Kat already causing destruction in her beautiful flat.

Kat did a quick sweep of the place with her eyes before she started opening drawers and throwing their contents on the floor. Lena watched aghast as her neatly folded life crumpled on the floor.

'You must have one,' said Kat, giving up her search for a moment to turn to Lena. 'Where is it?'

'How do you know where I live?' said Lena, feeling like the victim of a tornado.

'You left your details with Dragg, remember? In case that little tart came back.'

'Has she?' asked Lena. 'Sarika, I mean?'

'No,' said Kat. She made to grab Lena's television, ignoring the cables connecting it to the wall. 'I'm taking this,' she told Lena.

'You are not,' said Lena. Kat was still yanking at the television. Lena grabbed her by the shoulders and pushed her round so that the women were forced to stare into each other's eyes. 'Now,' she continued. 'We will sit down and you will tell me what happened. Then you help me clear up the mess you make in my apartment.'

Kat's hostile face turned redder before resignation filled it. 'I will tell you,' she said. 'But then I will take the TV.'

'Sit,' commanded Lena. Kat obeyed.

For a moment Lena hesitated. The coffee spill was still weighing heavy on her mind. Laminate or not, she only had so long before it would stain permanently. But she didn't really want to take a position kneeling by Kat's feet. It wasn't exactly ideal for negotiations. 'To hell with it,' she muttered to herself. 'Move your feet,' she said to a surprised-looking Kat. Lena grabbed the cloth and wiped up the spill, retrieving the coffee cup and taking both into the kitchen. She breathed out, feeling relieved. The rest of the mess was just the contents of drawers on the floor. Not time-sensitive, though she'd feel better when things were back in their place. But first Kat.

She filled two glasses with water, deciding the woman didn't deserve coffee, and went back to the living room. Kat was sitting on the sofa, looking a bit calmer.

'Tell me about the laptop,' said Lena.

'The police took it,' said Kat, giving the water a tentative sniff, as if she suspected it might be poisoned. It passed the test and she took a long gulp, wiping the dregs off her lips. 'They think there might be evidence on it, about the painting that bitch ran off with. You didn't mention that when you came looking for her.'

'You shared your laptop with Sarika?' said Lena, trying to focus on the information that might help.

'Yes,' said Kat, quickly. 'I'm not a monster. We all used it. But I don't know when I will get it back. The police say it could be months. And I need it for work.'

'But you work in a bar,' said Lena.

'I need it back, all right!' said Kat, slamming the glass on the table with a bang that Lena felt reverberate around her skull.

'And you will get it back,' said Lena, her voice rising. 'Sarika has done nothing wrong. She is innocent.' Lena looked at Kat. 'If you have done nothing illegal on your computer, the police will return it,' she said.

Kat stood up. 'If the fucking police steal my laptop you owe me a new one,' she said.

'I am sure you will get it back,' said Lena, wondering how Kat had decided Lena was responsible for everything that went wrong in her life. 'The police are very honest,' she added, thinking of PC Cartwright with a smile.

Kat replied with a derogatory grunt as she left the apartment, slamming the door behind her.

Lena felt exhausted by the evening's events, but she hauled herself to her feet and began to tidy up the miscellany of her belongings that Kat had emptied on to the floor. She would sleep better knowing everything was in its place.

CHAPTER 6

On Saturday afternoon, Lena decided to track down Lucia, the only flatmate Sarika seemed to be on friendly terms with. She phoned the flat and was pleased to hear Dragg's sleepy voice, not Kat's angry hiss. He confirmed that Lucia would be at work, but her busy time in the kitchen would not begin for another hour. Perfect.

The Black Zenith was a cavernous bar on Holloway Road. The sun was fierce outside. When Lena stepped into the darkness of the bar she found herself blind for a moment. She blinked and waited for her eyes to adjust.

When they did, she took in an enormous room with a huge bar, empty stage and rigged lights, and a bearded man in a cowboy hat looking at her in amusement. He was leaning on the bar.

'Bright out there?' he said, in an exaggerated American drawl. Lena walked to the bar to see him better. His beard was greying and his tummy overspilled his jeans, designed for a younger, thinner version of himself. 'You here for the band? Because they're not on till ten p.m. You're five hours early. Get you a drink?'

'I am looking for Lucia,' she said. She rested her hand on the bar for a moment, found it sticking and hurriedly wrenched her fingers away. 'She works in the kitchen?'

'She sure does,' said the man. He stroked his moustache.

'Is she there now?' asked Lena, feeling impatient.

'You sure you don't want a drink? Most folks who come here want a drink.'

'No thank you,' said Lena. 'Can I go into the kitchen?'

'That won't help you,' said the man. 'She's having a smoke out back.'

Lena thanked him and walked through to the back. A girl with proportions her mother would have approved of was sucking on a cigarette in the sunshine by the bins.

'Lucia?' said Lena. The girl nodded, looking at her curiously. 'I am Lena, Sarika's cousin.'

'*Sì certo!* That's why I recognise you!' said Lucia, throwing her cigarette on the floor, stamping it out and hugging a surprised Lena. 'You look very like her.'

'I do not think so,' said Lena. 'But thank you. I take that as a compliment.'

'Sarika is *bellissima*,' said Lucia. 'You are too.'

'Thank you,' said Lena, again. She looked at the girl. She carried a shy voluptuousness about her and had an olive complexion; her curly black hair was tucked behind her ears. Lucia smiled back at her gaze. 'You and Sarika were close?' queried Lena.

'Yes,' said Lucia. 'I miss her. Come inside. Are you hungry? I'll make us a snack. I need to eat something before the rush comes because I won't have dinner till one a.m.'

After the stickiness of the bar, Lena found herself pleasantly surprised at the kitchen. Immaculate stainless-steel surfaces, a couple of giant cookers and an enormous barrel freezer greeted her. She perched on the edge of one of the worktops while Lucia removed a large tub of olives and an egg from the fridge. She switched on the gas under a saucepan on the hob and began pitting olives, dextrously removing the pips with surgical precision.

Lena watched her, fascinated. Lucia took a baking tray covered in breadcrumbs from the oven and left it to cool. She stirred the contents of the saucepan and Lena breathed in deeply. It was a meaty stew that smelled of home. 'Sarika and I are good friends,' Lucia continued. 'We needed to stick together with that Kat girl around.'

'Have you heard from her, from Sarika?'

'One WhatsApp to say she is okay.'

'Same,' replied Lena. 'Do you know where she went?'

'No. And it's awful with her gone. Kat seems to hate everyone. But me especially. And Sarika.'

'She is not pleased about her computer,' said Lena.

'She is not pleased about anything,' said Lucia. 'It's no wonder Dragg gets on so well with Sarika.'

'They are friends too?' said Lena.

'A little,' said Lucia quickly, taking the saucepan off the heat and breaking the egg into the bowl. 'But not close friends. Kat is such a nightmare to live with. Always angry. And selfish. Dragg told me it is because she has seven little brothers and sisters back in Russia that she needs to support. They Skype them all the time – apparently they all love Dragg. He draws little caricatures of them all and sends them by email. Her father is a strict Orthodox with little money and her mother is dead.'

Lena watched Lucia deftly use a teaspoon to scoop minuscule amounts of the meaty mixture into each olive. She poured the stuffed olives into the beaten egg, shook it around and then spread the olives over the breadcrumbs on the oven tray, coating them in crispiness.

'But Kat let Sarika use her laptop?' Lena asked.

'Never,' said Lucia, lowering the olives into the deep-fat fryer. A greasy but delicious smell wafted up as the olives fizzed and hissed as they fried. 'She'd have a fit if she thought we were on it. Kept it locked in her room. Only she could touch it. She might have let Dragg, I suppose. She thought it was bad enough having to share a kitchen and loo with us two. Let alone anything that actually belonged to her.'

Lena was thinking. This changed things. 'The police took the laptop as evidence against Sarika,' she said. 'But Sarika never used the laptop. Why did Kat not say that to them?'

'She did at first, when she didn't want them to take it,' said Lucia, removing the hot olives from the fryer. 'But she changed her story when they were so interested in it. Probably covering her own back.' Lucia shrugged, then put the olives on to a plate, garnishing them with a sprig of basil. '*Olive Ascolane*,' she said, with a flourish. 'A traditional snack from my region. Help yourself.'

'This is delicious,' Lena exclaimed. It was. She wasn't usually a fan of olives, but these ones, pimped up with meat and batter and served piping hot . . . well, they were something else. Lucia grinned with pleasure, her own mouth full.

She swallowed. 'Thanks,' she said. 'Sorry I couldn't be more helpful.'

'You have been most helpful,' replied Lena, wondering what the police had found on that computer. And who had put it there.

Lena sat in the police waiting room the next day, fiddling with her phone. It emitted an angry beeping sound and she almost dropped it in alarm. Then she realised she had caused the sound herself with her random button pressing. She put it back in her pocket and looked for something else to distract herself. Her hands found a tissue in her pocket. She proceeded to rip it into shreds with her fingers.

Gullins had called her an hour ago, insisting that she come to the station. Lena had spoken to Sarika on Friday, just two days before. She'd been alive then. Could something have happened to her so quickly? Something terrible? Lena didn't think she could go through this again.

She took her hands from her pockets. A few errant shreds of tissue escaped to the floor. She leaned down to collect them. She must stop thinking the worst. It wasn't healthy. Just because something terrible had happened to Timea, it did not mean that Sarika would not be safe. Still her mind rebelled, full to the brim with horrible scenarios. When she lifted her head Gullins was standing in front of her, a scowl on his face.

'There's been some developments,' he told her. 'We've got a special guest, rare for a Sunday. Come with me.'

Lena followed him to the interview room. A well-heeled lady in a bottle-green suit stood up as she entered and reached out her hand. 'DI Amy Blake,' she said, as Lena shook her hand. It was soft and cool. 'Due to the value of the stolen item, I am joining this investigation. I am from CID and my expertise is art crime. I will be heading things up now. PC Gullins is here to assist.'

Lena returned the woman's smile, feeling herself almost drown in the torrent of relief that filled her body. Art crime. That is not who she would be meeting with if they had bad news about Sarika.

'It is good to meet you,' said Lena. 'I hope that you find the truth.'

'That is certainly my intention,' replied the woman. 'And I intend to recover the painting in the process. That will be my priority. I hope not too much time has elapsed already. Timing is of the utmost importance in recovery operations.' She shot a look at Gullins, who was busy digging around with his finger in his ear. 'Let's get started, shall we?' she said. All three took a seat, Gullins and DI Blake on one side of the table, Lena on the other.

'Sarika did not take the painting,' began Lena, keen to get her case across first. 'She knows nothing about art and would not be able to sell it even if she had taken it. Sarika is innocent.'

'If it were not for her disappearance I would be inclined to agree with you,' said Blake, taking notes. Lena looked at the detective's hands. She had elegant fingers with deep-red nails. No wedding ring. 'However, Sarika was the last person to leave the gallery, she had the keys and the code to the burglar alarm and now she has disappeared. You must agree it is incriminating?'

Lena found herself liking Blake, even as she accused her friend. She'd pretty much said the same to Sarika herself. This woman was logical, she'd give her that. And it wasn't her fault that she didn't know Sarika.

'I know it does look like that,' she told her. 'But she did not do it. I would not trust her to get to work on time,' she admitted. 'But she has never stolen anything.'

Blake glanced up at her and made a note.

'And she would not know what to do with a stolen painting,' continued Lena. 'How could she sell it? She does not know the kind of people who might buy an £84,000 painting.'

'She would need connections in the art world,' agreed Blake. 'Does she have any?'

Lena thought for a moment. Dragg had gone to art school. But that didn't mean anything.

'Pietro, Simon and Ophelia. They are the ones with the art connections,' she said.

'Don't worry,' said Blake. 'We are investigating all options.'

'And Sarika has only been in London a few months. What would she do with a painting?'

'That is what we are trying to find out,' said Blake. 'It would be a lot easier if we could ask her.' Lena conceded the point with a small nod.

'However, you are also a witness and I hope that you can assist us. I have some questions. We have some other avenues of investigation that have not yet been explored.'

Lena readily agreed. Gullins grunted his disapproval in the background. Both women ignored him.

'Are you aware of whether Pietro had his gallery keys at the reception on Wednesday evening?' she asked.

Lena looked at her, thoughtful. Why would she ask that? She scoured her mind, trying to remember. 'Yes,' she said. 'I saw him use the corkscrew on his key ring at around ten p.m. We had no more champagne so he opened a bottle of red wine.'

'Was it definitely the gallery key? Couldn't have been his house keys or car keys?'

'I am sure,' replied Lena. 'I have seen him open the gallery with those keys.'

'Excellent,' said Blake, making a note. 'He had not lost his keys.'

'Wait a minute,' said Lena. She shut her eyes, visualising the gallery at the end of the night, champagne flutes and canapés lying around like casualties of battle. 'He lost them before we left.'

Blake looked disappointed. Gullins looked smug.

'You are sure?' said Blake.

'That is what he told me,' said Lena. 'He asked me to lock up.' She looked at Blake, who was busy making more notes. Gullins was scratching his ear again. 'Someone could have taken the keys from him, someone at the gallery reception?' said Lena. 'Perhaps that is the person who stole the painting? I saw Malcolm later that night. In the purple trousers. He refused to let me call the police when he had been beaten up. And Gertrude, the old lady. She wanted that painting very much but she is on a pension.'

Blake looked unconvinced. 'Now, let's move on to your own movements. When you left the gallery you locked the door?'

Lena thought for a moment before replying. 'Wait,' she said. 'The gallery was broken into. Why questions about keys?'

'Please answer my questions first. Then I will explain.'

'Yes, I locked the door,' said Lena.

'And Sarika went back for her phone.'

'That is correct.'

'And you believe, but cannot be sure, that she locked the gallery door behind her and put on the burglar alarm.'

'Yes,' said Lena. She cursed herself again for not going back with Sarika to check. 'It was the last thing I said. Lock the door. Set the alarm.'

'Could anyone have taken the keys from Sarika after she locked up?'

Lena thought for a moment. 'She had the keys in the morning. On the floor of her room.' Lena paused. Could Kat have taken them and put them back again in the morning? Could Dragg? Lena made a mental note to see what they'd been up to that night. She'd need more evidence before she threw around any allegations. 'The keys were on her floor in the morning. I do not know if that is where they spent the night.'

'And she told you that she would meet you at the police station?'

'Yes.'

'Thank you. The reason I am asking,' explained Blake, crossing her legs, 'is that the lock to the door was smashed, as you would expect in a break-in. But my team have analysed it more carefully. They believe that the door was opened, with a key, before the lock was destroyed. The burglar alarm records show that it was disabled with the code, and set off ten minutes later.' She sat back. Lena looked at her, puzzled.

'Why did someone open the door and then break in?' Lena asked. The answer came to her as the question left her lips.

'We think that whoever broke in had a key,' said Blake, taking the words from Lena's head. 'But wanted to make it look like a break-in.' Blake watched Lena. 'They had the code for the burglar alarm too.'

'And Pietro lost his key?'

'So he says.'

'So it is simple,' said Lena. 'Find the person who stole Pietro's key and you find your painting!'

Blake smiled at her. 'You are clearly not from the murky world of art crime,' she said. 'Nothing is ever simple.'

Lena smiled back at her. 'I can tell you who was still there at ten p.m.,' she said. 'When Pietro had his key. It was the people who wanted most to buy the painting. I do not know surnames, but it was Gertrude, an old lady who drank too much champagne. Patrick, the American man who never put his phone down and was angry later that night. Trudy Weincamp, the artist, but she was asleep downstairs. Malcolm with the purple trousers, but he did not have a canvas when he was being—'

'Could any of them have known the code for the burglar alarm?' interrupted Blake.

'It was written in the office,' said Lena. 'On a Post-it note. Anyone could see.'

Gullins tutted. 'See what I have to deal with?' he said. 'It's no surprise these people get burgled.'

'Thank you for your help,' said Blake to Lena, standing up.

'Pietro Agnoletti was there too. Ophelia Agnoletti, his wife. And Simon Archer, the gallery manager. They all have keys.'

'We have the list. You have been very helpful.'

'So it is not Sarika,' said Lena. 'She would not have stolen Pietro's key because we have one.'

'We're not jumping to any conclusions here. But don't worry, we will find the real culprit.'

'What is your method?' said Lena, keen to find out as much as she could.

'Excuse me?' replied Blake.

'What is your plan to track down the painting?' asked Lena, remembering when she worked with PC Cartwright before. 'Do you have a matrix of your suspects?'

'I'm sorry,' replied Blake. 'I need to proceed with my investigations. The longer the painting is missing, the less likely we are to recover it. The market for art crime is an international one.

I want to find out what happens before it disappears to China and is never seen again.'

Lena looked at her. She might know her stuff about the art world and theft, but it was Lena who had been at the reception. She was the one who had seen the people that night. And she would be the one to solve this.

'One last thing,' said Lena, remembering her angry visitor. 'When will Sarika's flatmates get their computer back?'

'It is evidence,' said Gullins, getting to his feet. 'It will be a while.'

'But you have not found anything on the computer?' said Lena. 'Have you?'

'It's time to go now,' said Gullins. 'Don't waste any more of DI Blake's precious time.' He managed to make the statement sound like an insult to both women.

'We'll be in touch if we need more information,' said Blake. 'And please do let us know if Sarika contacts you. We are very keen to talk to her. If just to eliminate her as a suspect from our investigations.'

Gullins showed her out, again reminding her not to leave the country. He needn't have bothered. Lena wasn't going anywhere. Not until she'd made it so her friend could come home without ending up in prison.

This was an excellent development, thought Lena as she made her way towards Upper Street. Not only was there a new detective investigating, who seemed to know what she was doing, but she also had a nicely whittled-down list of suspects from the gallery reception. The faceless hordes of guests were now only three. One of the people who was there after ten p.m. could have taken the key from Pietro. She just needed their details and a plan. How hard could that be?

★ ★ ★

Lena looked in dismay at the mess she'd made of her room. It was as if her wardrobe had vomited its limited contents over the double bed, also splashing the carpet and the chair. And still she could not find anything that was right for tonight. Fussing over her clothes like this, she suddenly felt like a teenager. Or like Sarika.

She picked up her black dress again and held it to her body. It was tight and a little low cut, displaying her modest cleavage. Too desperate. She'd be more comfortable in her jeans and red T-shirt, but didn't want to look like she hadn't made an effort. Nor that she had made too much effort. She sat on the bed, wishing it wasn't too late to cancel her date with PC Cartwright.

If Timea were here, she'd know what to wear. Perhaps she'd even lend Lena something from her own, more extensive, wardrobe. Lena paused, swallowing back the grief that was creeping up her throat. Crying would get her nowhere. And she'd already applied her mascara.

Abruptly, Lena pulled on a soft green jumper from where it was sprawled across her pillow. Timea had given it to her, saying the colour brought out the green in her otherwise hazel eyes. Today had not been warm, and the evening was cool already. Paired with fitted beige trousers, impractical for cleaning and hence hardly worn, she'd do. She slipped on a flimsy pair of ballet shoes and sprayed herself with Timea's favourite perfume. She was ready.

Arriving at the bar, Lena cursed herself for being early. Now she had to kill time or look overly keen. She forced herself to walk up and down the street, pretending to look in shop windows. She felt she looked shifty, like a shoplifter casing the joint.

'Lena?' She knew the voice, soft and well spoken. She'd recognise it anywhere. 'I thought we were meeting in the bar?' he said.

'You are outside too,' barked Lena. *Szar*, she thought. That sounded so aggressive.

'Sorry,' said Cartwright. A broad smile illuminated his face. 'It's so good to see you.' He leaned towards her for a kiss on the cheek. The right cheek, Lena realised too late, going in the wrong direction. The result was an awkward but oddly thrilling nose bump.

'Sorry,' said Cartwright again. 'Listen, the bar is really busy, more so than I thought it would be on a Sunday, but I suppose people need a drink no matter what day of the week it is.' He paused to draw breath and placed a hand on Lena's arm. She wished she were wearing short sleeves, feeling the tingle only weakly through the material of her jumper. 'Anyway, what I meant to say was how about we go straight to the restaurant and have a drink there, before dinner, if you'd like. I've booked a table.'

'That is good,' said Lena. 'We have much to catch up on.'

'Sarika said it was not her,' said Lena. 'I believe her. But since she has run away, she is under suspicion. As if she could steal a painting.' Lena took a bite of the excellent veal chop and chewed determinedly. They were sitting in the courtyard of a small Italian restaurant set back from Upper Street. Its romantic atmosphere had excited Lena, but now the fairy lights and candles were starting to annoy her. She couldn't see her food properly.

'But then why did she leave?' ventured Cartwright, taking a sip of his wine.

'She is worried that the police will arrest her. But at most she did not properly set the alarm. That is all.'

'At least we know that she is okay,' said Cartwright, fiddling with the salt-shaker. 'Not like . . . before. Oh, I'm sorry,' he said, seeing Lena's face cloud. 'I'm an idiot.'

'You are no idiot,' said Lena. 'I am fine.' She smiled. He'd been the one who had helped her finally bring Timea's killer to justice.

'What are you working on?' she asked, changing the subject. 'Now you are a hotshot from the special project in Newcastle?'

. 'I'm assisting CID on a case now. It's not pleasant,' said Cartwright.

'Go on,' said Lena.

'The victim's wife has already spoken to the papers,' said Cartwright. 'So I can tell you what's public. A man who worked in one of the chippies on Upper Street was beaten up. Really badly. He is in intensive care.'

'Chippies?' queried Lena.

'Sorry, a fish and chip shop. Although they sell pies too. Mushy peas, sausage rolls . . .'

'Do you know who did it?'

'Hoodies should be illegal,' said Cartwright, putting down his fork. 'It is impossible to see the men's faces on the shop's CCTV. We have a good boot-print though. The medical examiner took pictures. It's right on the victim's cheek, poor man.' He shuddered at the memory.

'Will he recover?'

'I hope so,' said Cartwright. 'But the doctors are not certain of it. He has a serious head injury.' They sat in silence for a moment.

Cartwright picked up his fork again. 'I don't want to ruin our dinner,' he said. 'Tell me more about your investigations. I expect you have a plan?' he said. 'And a list of suspects?'

'Of course,' said Lena. She took a sip of wine. 'But it is still on a napkin. Not your fancy computer spreadsheet.'

Cartwright coloured a little. Lena watched in admiration as he delicately used his spoon to wind his spaghetti carbonara around his fork.

'I could help,' he said, popping the spaghetti spiral into his mouth. 'Perhaps I could bring my laptop round to your place and get the data entered?'

Lena sawed at a fatty bit of veal, trying to conceal her pleasure at the offer. 'You do not have to do that,' she said, feeling much less alone already.

'I'd be delighted to,' said Cartwright, a little flushed. 'I haven't seen your new flat. I imagine it is impressively clean.' Lena looked up at him. 'Not that I have imagined your flat, that would be weird. Not that your flat is weird, I'm sure it is perfectly normal . . . just clean.' He shoved a half-rolled forkful of spaghetti in his mouth, coughed and struggled for a moment before instinct took over and he successfully swallowed. His face was red from the exertion.

'I have missed you,' said Lena, placing her hand on his.

Cartwright used his other hand to gulp his wine, rinsing down the last of the errant spaghetti before he replied. 'I have missed you too,' he said. 'It is so nice to see you, Lena.' He reached to pour her more wine and discovered the bottle was empty. 'Another?'

Lena wasn't really a big drinker, but she liked the way this wine was making her feel. She agreed. But somehow, she didn't think it was just the wine that was making her feel warm inside.

CHAPTER 7

'What do you mean there is a warrant out for Sarika's arrest?' shouted Lena.

'It means that we want to arrest her but we can't find her right now because she's run away,' said Gullins.

'I know that,' hissed Lena. 'But how can you think it is her? What about Pietro? Simon? The guests at the gallery who wanted that painting? All are more likely than Sarika.'

She sat back in the chair at the police station. She'd hoped when Gullins had called her in he would have good news, would have found something useful. He hadn't, of course.

Gullins smiled, looking amused at her anger. 'As you know, we confiscated her laptop. There was incriminating evidence and we'd like to talk to her about it.'

'That is not even her laptop,' said Lena. 'It is her flatmate's.'

'But she had access to it, and to the painting. And now she is gone. She has to be our prime suspect.'

'She did not use that laptop,' said Lena. 'Her flatmates did. One of them could have taken the keys from her and taken that painting. Dragg, he went to art school. He would know what to do with a stolen painting. Not Sarika.'

'Sarika is the only one who has run away.'

'But you must have other . . .' Lena struggled to remember the police phrase. 'Strings of enquiry?' Lena was wearing a cotton summer dress that she'd picked in case she bumped into Cartwright again, when she thought this meeting would be easy. Now she felt exposed, compared to Gullins's sturdy uniform. But the room was hot. Sweat trickled down the crevices in his face, likely left by teenage acne.

'Who else is on DI Blake's list?' asked Lena.

'None of your business,' said Gullins, wiping his brow with the cuff of his shirt. 'Where is Sarika?'

'I do not know where she is,' said Lena, feeling like a broken record. 'But you are wasting your time. She is innocent.'

'She is looking pretty guilty from where I'm sitting,' he said.

'She would,' said Lena. 'But she is not.'

Gullins shifted uncomfortably in his seat. A fresh bead of sweat was travelling slowly down his forehead towards his eyebrow. 'We'll see about that,' he said, getting to his feet with a puff. 'Get in touch if she contacts you.'

'Of course,' said Lena, noticing the shallow pool of sweat that had accumulated on the seat of Gullins's chair. 'I look forward to it.'

Although it was almost seven p.m., it was still warm and light, and people filled the tables outside the Upper Street restaurants even on a Monday evening. Lena breathed in the delicious smells, from spicy curries through garlicky pastas to the sweet aroma of grilled halloumi. She glanced at the dishes as she walked by, wondering if Cartwright would choose one of these restaurants if they went out again.

She wanted to talk to Lucia and she needed to get there quickly. The Black Zenith might be busy later, once the beer and music had fed people's appetite for chicken wings and nachos, but the girl should have time to talk now.

Lena turned the corner at Highbury and Islington station on

to Holloway Road. It was starting to look more and more like its posher neighbour, Upper Street, these days, the greasy restaurants and cheap hair salons being replaced, one by one, with cafés selling artisan coffee and vegan milkshakes. Lena peered through the window of one and saw a multitude of men with glasses and beards tapping away on their MacBooks or staring into space with looks of concentration filling their serious faces.

Ten minutes and she had travelled through the Upper Street overspill into the rougher part of Holloway Road. The Black Zenith was set back from the main street. Lena pushed through the door and walked into the bar, temporarily blinded again by the shift from sunlight to darkness.

She nodded to the ageing cowboy, standing in the same place at the bar, as if he'd not moved since her last visit. Lena ignored his 'howdy' and pushed through the swinging kitchen door.

Lucia was grating cheese and humming to herself. She smiled at Lena as she entered.

'I was going to call you,' she said. 'Sarika has been in touch.'

'Again? That is good. Is she okay?' Lena hopped up so she was sitting on the edge of a sparkling clean counter. 'Did she sound like she had somewhere to sleep?'

'She sounded fine. She is staying with a friend.'

Lena jumped back down to face Lucia. 'Who?' she asked. 'Where?'

'I don't know,' said Lucia. 'Here. Try one of these,' she said, pushing a plate of little batter-coated balls at Lena.

'She gave you no idea of where she was?' quizzed Lena, her relief that Sarika wasn't alone quickly being replaced by suspicion. 'What other friends does she have in London?'

'We don't know if she is in London,' said Lucia. Lena picked up one of the balls and took a bite. It was crispy on the outside and filled with delicious creamy rice on the inside. Lucia knew where Sarika was. She could tell. Lena popped the rest of the ball into her mouth before it distracted her further.

'What other friends does she have?' she asked, swallowing her mouthful and enjoying it glide down her gullet. 'I thought she only knew you and the flatmates.'

'She knew more people,' said Lucia. 'That was an *arancino*. I'm trying to get Doug to include it on the menu but he's not convinced. I think people would love it. With a nice *pomodoro* sauce. What do you think?'

Lena took another in answer. 'There is a warrant for Sarika to be arrested,' she said, biting into the *arancino* and watching Lucia's reaction.

The girl looked horrified. '*Dio mio!* I did not think it would get this bad,' she said. 'What can we do to help?'

'They have found something on the laptop. You need to tell the police Sarika did not use it. Kat needs to do the same.'

'The police will not listen to me,' said Lucia. 'And Kat will never volunteer to help Sarika. Not now Dragg is gone.'

Lena looked up. 'Dragg is gone?'

Lucia put her hand to her mouth. 'No, I didn't mean . . . it's just that sometimes he is out all night . . . with work.'

'Dragg is gone and Sarika is gone,' continued Lena, as the pieces fell into place. 'And Sarika is with a friend, you said. But Sarika told me that her only friends were her flatmates. You are here with me now. Kat is not her friend. That leaves Dragg.'

Lucia put down the lump of cheese she'd been grating. 'I promised I wouldn't tell you,' she said. 'I am such a bad friend.'

'No you are not,' said Lena. 'I worked it out. And you know that the best thing for Sarika is for me to find her. You must tell me where she is.'

'I don't know exactly,' said Lucia, relenting. 'But I know it is Brighton. Dragg has friends he stays with down there. I don't have the address.'

'How can I find them? Lucia, I need to know she is okay.'

Lucia looked down. 'There is a graffiti jam on Saturday,' she said. 'Dragg is painting in it. Sarika will probably be there too. She likes him a lot.'

'A graffiti jam?' questioned Lena, totally baffled.

'Dragg goes to them all the time,' explained Lucia. 'It is when there is a bit of wall that someone wants decorated and they invite graffiti artists from all over to do it.'

Lena took another *arancino* and bit into it while she thought. She didn't know much about Dragg, but he didn't seem to be a murderer or a pimp. Perhaps things were not so bad for Sarika. She would have a roof over her head, at least.

But what about when she came back? The police, and potentially prison, were what awaited her.

The graffiti event was five days away. Lena needed to up her investigations so that she had some proper leads for when she went to get Sarika. She thanked Lucia and left for home. She'd buy what she needed on the way.

Lena sat cross-legged on the living-room floor, her fleecy blanket folded under her to make a pillow. She'd be here for a while. On one side of her was a pen, a pad of Post-it notes, a box of pins, some scissors and a few pictures. On the other side a steaming cup of coffee. Directly in front of her, propped against her sofa, was the corkboard. Time to get things straight. She tried to visualise her suspect napkin, accidentally thrown away two days ago when she was cleaning her flat.

Lena took the invitation to the gallery reception in her hand and looked at it. A tiny reproduction of *A Study in Purple* looked back at her, the tadpoles still trying to penetrate that purple triangle. She stuck it to the corkboard with a pin, right in the centre.

Above it she placed a Post-it note with the gallery details, the date it was last seen and Trudy's name. What next?

The keys. They were the vital clue. Whoever had got in had used a key. They had also known the code to the alarm. Lena got her notes and wrote down all the copies of the key she was aware of.

Pietro's first of all. She put his name down. He'd lost his key, or so he said. Lena closed her eyes, trying to remember the guests who had still been in the gallery at that point.

Gertrude, the old lady drinking lots of champagne. She got her own note. Lena remembered her friend mentioning someone that Gertrude knew, who she had called a thief. Was that significant?

The man in the ironed purple trousers, who she had rescued later that evening. Malcolm. She wrote him down, along with a note of when she had last seen him. He would have to have gone back to the gallery afterwards, which seemed unlikely. But then why hadn't he wanted the police called after he was attacked? He'd mentioned Chinese art dealers. Was there a more sinister connection?

The American man on the phone who had given Sarika a glass of champagne. Patrick. She knew his type. Ignore you unless they wanted something. The kind of person you would clean for for years, dusting his television, washing his socks, wiping the dried up *szar* from his toilet bowl. He wouldn't even know your name and would never think to leave a tip at Christmas. Unless you were an attractive twenty-one-year-old girl, and then suddenly he'd offer you booze. He was just the type to steal a painting and not care who got the blame. And she was pretty sure it was him she'd heard arguing on the phone later. Was he having money troubles?

Lena put his name on the board, telling herself not to be so judgemental. Just because she didn't get a good feeling from him did not make him a painting thief.

Those had been the only guests left at the gallery when Pietro had lost his key. She needed full names and addresses to find out more about them.

Trudy had been there still, too. Lena added her, at the same time wondering why she might want to steal her own painting. She'd said she didn't like it – did she want to get rid of it for some reason?

She added Pietro to the list and added the words 'insurance money' after it. They only had his word that he'd lost the key at all.

Sitting back and taking a sip of coffee, she thought about the other keys. Simon had one, so up his name went. So did Ophelia.

Then she added her own key. Sarika had it. She put each of Sarika's flatmates on the board underneath it: Dragg, Kat, Lucia. Sarika could well have told them about the expensive painting in the gallery she'd been cleaning. She might even have done so that night. They all worked late – any one of them could have been up and home when Sarika arrived. One of them could have sneaked into her room, taken the key, stolen the painting and replaced the key by Sarika's bed in the morning. But they'd need the code for the burglar alarm too. Could Sarika have told them? She doubted it. It wasn't the kind of thing you'd drop into conversation.

But then she thought of that crumpled piece of paper she had seen by Sarika's bed. It had her cleaning itinerary on it. Could Sarika have written down the code for the alarm too? Lena took another gulp of coffee and closed her eyes again. Did she remember seeing those familiar numbers on the paper? And if so, did it incriminate the flatmates?

It was possible. Unlikely but possible.

And then there was the laptop. She still didn't know what was on it, but it seemed to be enough to convince the police that Sarika was their prime suspect. She wrote 'laptop evidence' next to Kat and Dragg's name, then after a pause she added it to Lucia's as well.

Lena added a star next to Dragg's name. He had fled too, albeit later than Sarika, and was with her now. He would have contacts from art school that might mean he could sell the painting. Could he be responsible? But why would he be with Sarika? Lena wondered for a moment if the two could have acted together.

No. Sarika was her relative. And her friend.

Lena stood up and shook the pins and needles out of her legs. She went into the kitchen to make herself another coffee and grabbed a couple of chocolate biscuits from the tin. She'd eaten both before the kettle boiled, so took another one to have with her coffee. Heading back to the living room, she sat back on the floor, pushing her long legs in front of her this time.

She stared at the board. It wasn't much to go on, and she was no art crime detective. What she needed was a plan for how to investigate each one of her suspects. She wanted at least to rule some out. And hopefully find a strong lead.

If she could find that lead by Saturday, she'd have a much better chance of convincing Sarika to come home. And the sooner Sarika came home, the less guilty she would look.

Lena popped the last of her chocolate biscuit into her mouth, following it with a gulp of scalding hot coffee.

Somewhere on this board was the culprit. The person who had stolen *A Study in Purple* and let Sarika take the blame. They wouldn't get away with it.

CHAPTER 8

Lena trudged up the stairs to Sarika's flat. It was one in the afternoon, the time Lucia told her Kat was most likely to be at home. She needed to find out what was on that laptop. Now, standing outside the door, that suddenly seemed impossible. Kat would have no reason to tell her anything. She took a deep breath and rang the bell. Perhaps the pressure of Kat's malicious gaze would give her mind the push it needed.

No answer.

She rang again, and echoed the ring with a good thump on the door. She thought she heard a patter of footsteps and peered through the tiny window, its reinforced glass framing everything inside with small grey squares. A flash of pale flesh and black lace swept through the hall from one room to another.

'Kat!' she said. 'Open the door. I know you are in there.' She banged the door again. 'Please.'

The door swung open. Kat was wearing a black fleecy dressing gown and clutching a laptop to her chest. 'What the fuck do you want?' she said. 'I'm busy.'

'You have a new laptop already,' said Lena, trying to enter the flat. 'That is lucky.'

'Borrowed it,' said Kat, squaring up to block Lena's entrance. 'From work.'

'The bar gave you a laptop?' said Lena.

'Other work,' said Kat. 'Someone has to pay the rent.'

'Maybe I can help,' said Lena, an idea finally forming. 'Can I come in?'

Kat paused for a moment. 'You have rent money?'

'Let me in and we can talk about it,' said Lena. 'I have some questions about Sarika before I give you any money.'

'Now isn't a good time,' said Kat, nonetheless sounding more polite now the prospect of money was involved.

'Is Dragg home?' said Lena.

'None of your business,' said Kat, her rudeness resurfacing. 'But you can come back, with the money. Not now. Nine hundred pounds.'

'I am not giving you nine hundred pounds!' exclaimed Lena, too shocked at the sum to even play along.

The door was already closed. Lena walked back down the stairs. What did Kat have in the flat she didn't want Lena to see?

Lena went straight from Kat's to the gallery, thinking about what she had seen. Kat was hiding something on that laptop. Could she be trying to sell the painting online? She thought for a moment. Was that what the police had found on the other laptop? An internet history of dodgy art-selling forums? It must be, for it to be incriminating. But how could she get proof?

In the meantime, she'd get the client list from the gallery. She needed to start the other stream of her investigations. Pietro's missing key.

Lena stood outside the gallery door, peering through the glass. Inside, she could see Ophelia, gazing into a computer screen at the little reception table, a troubled look on her face. A wisp of Ophelia's auburn hair had escaped her messy bun, and was gently caressing her neck, so white it was practically translucent. Lena found herself admiring the beauty in the woman, even as she frowned with confusion at the computer. Ophelia must be nearly forty, but her face was flawless. A benefit of having skin that wouldn't tolerate the sun's rays.

Suddenly Ophelia looked up and laughed. Lena watched as Simon stepped towards her. Apparently Lena had not been the only person admiring Ophelia. He leaned over her shoulder and reached around to take the mouse. Lena put her face to the glass, glad that she had cleaned it recently. She could see every detail of what Simon did. Including the deep inward breath he took as his face neared Ophelia's hair. He even closed his eyes for a moment, and the first happy expression Lena had seen on him appeared, making his face completely different. Softer.

Then it was gone. His eyes snapped open and misery took over. Ophelia stood up and Simon sat down, fixing whatever was the problem on the screen. Lena watched the woman closely, looking for signs that the feeling was mutual. But she saw nothing. No gentle stroke of the shoulder, no longing gaze. Ophelia was simply adjusting an errant but elegant earring.

'So is this as close as we can get to the art now?' drawled an American voice right behind Lena's ear. She jumped. 'Or are we allowed inside?'

Lena turned to see Trudy Weincamp standing behind her. Lena stepped to one side to allow the woman access, then followed her in, glad of the distraction.

'So I see you've put a guard on the door,' she said to Simon, gesturing at Lena. 'But there's not much point now your best piece has gone!' She laughed as Simon looked up guiltily and Ophelia hurried to kiss Trudy on both cheeks. 'Only kidding,' she added. 'That dinosaur is awesome.'

'What are you doing here, Lena?' asked Simon. 'I thought Pietro told you not to come back?'

'Never mind what she is doing here,' said Trudy. 'Let me tell you what I'm doing here. You stood me up.'

Simon looked at her in confusion. 'What do you mean?'

'We had a date. We made it at the party. You were going to show me your stuff.'

'What? I didn't think . . .'

'You thought I'd forget? I may have been pretty out of it but I always remember being hit on.'

'I really didn't mean . . .'

Ophelia clasped her hands together. 'This is perfect,' she said. 'You two are an exquisite match.' Her voice was full of glee. Lena studied her face. She smiled right up to her eyes, oblivious to Simon's pain.

'Hey,' said Trudy. 'If it was the drink talking . . .'

'Of course it wasn't,' exclaimed Ophelia. 'He's just shy, that's all. Simon hasn't been on a date in, gosh, I can't remember how long. It's not healthy for a man in his forties to be on his own so much.'

'Where are you going?' said Simon to Lena. In the confusion, she'd been edging past the clay eyeball towards the office, hoping to pick up the details she needed for her investigations.

'Never mind Lena,' said Ophelia. 'Where will you take Trudy?'

'I don't . . . Lena, you really must leave.'

'I left some things in the office,' lied Lena. 'If I can get them I will be gone. Out of your . . .' Lena searched for the expression. Was it beard?

'Hair,' completed Trudy. She turned her attention back to Simon. 'I was hoping to see some of your work?'

'Simon hasn't painted in years,' said Ophelia, looking puzzled.

'Painters' block?' asked Trudy. 'That's tough. One cure. I can give it to you.' She grinned at Simon, who swallowed uncomfortably.

'Are you painting again, Simon?' asked Ophelia. She clapped her hands together. 'That would be amazing. Pietro will be so happy. When can we see?'

'I'm not painting,' said Simon, abruptly. 'You know that. I must have meant my old stuff. I was drunk.' He turned to Trudy and made a little bow.

'And I thought I was the tipsy one,' said Trudy. 'Good to know it wasn't just me!'

'I apologise for forgetting our date,' replied Simon. 'Perhaps you would allow me to escort you to ...' He glanced at his watch. 'Afternoon tea.' He offered his arm.

'You Brits are so charming,' purred Trudy, taking his arm.

'Ophelia, are you okay with the website updates now?'

'Oh yes,' said Ophelia, looking ecstatic. 'Don't you worry about me. Have fun!'

'After you, Lena,' said Simon, firmly. Lena nodded and exited, turning left down Upper Street. Taking shelter behind a tree, she turned and watched Simon and Trudy proceed down the road. This was an interesting development.

'Thank goodness you're here at last,' said Penelope as she opened the door. Lena glanced at her watch. She'd made good time and was not late, even though Penelope had asked her to come on a different day and time at the last minute. 'What kept you?'

Lena looked at Penelope. She was wearing a low-cut green silk dress, her hair curled and fastened up and her delicate lips adorned with a deep red lipstick.

'You look beautiful,' Lena told her. Penelope's red lips burst into a smile.

'It's our anniversary,' she told Lena. 'I'm meeting Hugo in the City for drinks at the Coq d'Argent and then he's taking me to Le Gavroche for dinner.'

Lena looked past the excited Penelope to the children. Casper was drawing something with felt tip on Crispin's belly. 'The children ... I have plans later ... I am not babysitter,' said Lena in alarm.

'Oh, of course not,' said Penelope, gesturing Lena inside and shutting the door behind her. 'I wouldn't dream of it. Tabitha will be here at eight p.m. to take care of the little monkeys.'

'But it is only six p.m. now . . .'

'I know, I'm running horribly late. I need to be at Hugo's office for six thirty. Here's my phone, be a darling and order me an Uber. There's no way I can get the tube in these heels. I'm just off to find the necklace Hugo gave me for our last anniversary. It's diamonds but it's gone walkies. Keep the kids busy too, will you? Casper keeps trying to put his orange juice in my Louis Vuitton handbag. He's quite determined, no matter how many times I tell him what it costs. And give the kitchen cupboards an extra wipe-down, will you? There's something green and sticky that won't seem to come off.'

Penelope disappeared up the stairs. Lena went into the sitting room and rescued Crispin from his brother. He had what looked like a dinosaur drawn on his belly. She picked him up and carried him to the kitchen sink, filling it with warm water and getting the soft side of a fresh sponge ready for him. He giggled as she dabbed at his belly. Casper began to wail.

'My dino!' he shouted, his voice curdled with snot. 'My brother.'

'Just because he is your brother does not mean you decorate him,' Lena told him. 'I find you paper to draw the dinosaur on and if it is good I will stick it on the fridge.'

'Promise?' sniffed Casper. Lena dried Crispin's belly on a tea towel. He blew her a spit bubble in gratitude.

'Promise,' said Lena. 'Now, help me find the paper. And where are your crayons?'

Penelope's phone beeped. 'Your Uber is here,' Lena called.

'Come up here, will you?' Penelope shouted back. Lena looked at the boys. Casper was lying belly down on the floor, concentrating on drawing some vicious-looking teeth. Crispin had nodded off.

'On my way.'

She gasped when she saw Penelope's bedroom. Clothes were flung everywhere. Jewellery boxes were upturned. Sharp, glistening bits of jewellery sparkled on the bedspread like stars in the night sky. 'What happened?'

'I was looking for my diamond necklace. And it took me a long time to decide what to wear. Here, look, I still can't find it. Am I being blind?'

Lena methodically sorted through the jewellery on the bed. 'This is pretty,' she said, holding up a chunky amber necklace. 'You could wear this tonight and I look for the diamonds for you later.'

'I need to find it.' Penelope waved her hand through the neat piles of jewellery Lena had made, sending them back into disarray. 'It's the only damn chance I have to wear something nice again.' Her lips were trembling like Casper's did and Lena could tell that tears were not far behind.

'When did you last see it?' she asked her.

'Just before the last time you cleaned,' replied Penelope. Lena chose to ignore the implication of that statement.

'Then it cannot have gone far,' she told her. 'You do not want to be late. Here. This one will match your eyes.' She held up a sparkling sapphire pendant. Penelope sniffed, looking a little comforted. 'I will put it on for you,' said Lena.

Penelope obediently turned the back of her neck to Lena. 'It is pretty,' she conceded. 'We bought it on honeymoon in Sri Lanka.'

'Perfect,' said Lena. 'Now it is time to leave. Your taxi is waiting outside. I will tidy up in here and look for the missing necklace.'

When she finally left Penelope's house the buses conspired against Lena and she arrived late and flustered. Cartwright was sitting in a quiet corner of the pub, nursing a glass of white wine. Lena noticed another glass next to him and felt a moment's annoyance. She'd wanted to talk about the case.

'Who is here?' she asked, sitting down with more force than she'd intended.

'What?' said Cartwright. He picked up the glass and handed it to her. Lena looked at it in confusion for a moment.

'Sorry, I hope the wine hasn't got too warm. I wasn't sure what time you'd arrive.'

Lena felt a flash of shame and covered it with a smile. 'Thank you,' she said. Cartwright grinned back at her and they chinked their glasses. Lena took a sip and then put hers down and leaned forwards.

'There is much that smells like fish,' she said.

Cartwright looked around the pub, his gaze landing on a nearby man devouring a plate of scampi. 'If you don't like the smell we can go somewhere else,' he said.

'No,' said Lena. 'Was that not right? Things that smell of fish – that means suspicious?'

'Oh, something's fishy?'

'Yes,' said Lena. 'Very fishy.' She paused a moment, thinking perhaps she shouldn't try to use English idioms.

'Talking of fish,' said Cartwright, 'the poor fish-and-chip-shop owner is still unconscious. And I'm not getting very far, for all my spreadsheets and gadgets.'

He looked forlorn. Lena put her own problems aside for a moment. 'Tell me what is happening,' she said. 'We can think together.'

'The victim is still in intensive care and I have no decent leads. Victims always seem to die when you have no idea who was involved. If you find a person standing next to them holding a smoking gun, that's a sure-fire way to know the victim will pull through!'

'That happened to you?' said Lena. 'Newcastle is a dangerous place?'

'Actually no,' admitted Cartwright. 'I read about the phenomenon. In a book on Baltimore's police.'

Lena laughed and had to stop herself from reaching out to ruffle his hair. 'Tell me all about it,' she said.

'It's horrible really,' said Cartwright. 'Although violence always is, I suppose. I'm piecing it together from CCTV footage at the moment, because my only witness is the victim, and he's far from being able to tell me about it.' He took a sip of wine. 'Well, the camera is a little grainy, and like I said, there weren't any witnesses because it was late at night.'

'What happened?' repeated Lena, taking a deep gulp of wine, instantly regretting her decision. It was warm and vinegary and left her feeling a little sick.

'All the details are online now,' said Cartwright. 'His wife has been appealing for witnesses. It was at The Fish Plaice, a lovely little fish and chip shop. It does brilliant mushy peas but, having been in Newcastle, I like having gravy with my chips. Of course they don't sell that there.'

'You've done your research,' teased Lena.

Cartwright coloured. 'I'd been there before, actually,' he said. 'Sometimes Gullins would go there for lunch and I'd tag along, when he let me. Mr Theopolis, the poor owner, was so friendly. Lovely Greek chap. Anyway, the attempted murder. These men walked in and you can see them giving Mr Theopolis some bother. Leaning over the counter, waving fists around, generally being threatening. One of them spits at him. So Mr Theopolis pulls out a gun . . .'

'. . . so it is one of the aggressive men who is shot? Not the chip-shop owner?'

'Yes, I mean no. They look scared for a moment, then one of

91

the men starts to laugh. He jumps at the counter and swipes the weapon out of Mr Theopolis's hands.'

'That is stupid,' said Lena, at the same time thinking she would do the same if anyone threatened someone she loved.

'But not as foolhardy as you might think,' said Cartwright. 'We recovered the gun at the scene. It was a fake.' He paused. 'Not even a good fake. It could only fire water.'

'But why . . . ?'

'We've interviewed his wife. She is distraught. Apparently the fake gun was her idea. She worried about her husband, working late at night around drunk people, and thought it would be a good idea to have the gun as a deterrent.'

'A gun that fires water?'

'Clearly it was a bad idea,' said Cartwright. 'The footage of the men attacking Mr Theopolis is testament to that.'

'And what leads do you have?'

'Blurry CCTV footage. And there's no witnesses except Mr Theopolis; and it is unclear if he will ever wake up.'

'Did they steal?'

'Only their fish and chips,' said Cartwright. 'Drunk, I expect. Forty per cent of people imprisoned for violent crime act under the influence of alcohol.'

'I have missed you,' said Lena, smiling at him. 'Full of statistics to help solve cases.'

'Not much help now,' said Cartwright, his voice awash with misery. 'Let's talk about something else. What is happening with the painting?'

'I am suspicious of Kat.'

'Sarika's flatmate?'

'Exactly. The police took her laptop and she tried to take mine. There is something not right on there. So I went to her flat. She was in her dressing gown, in the middle of the day.' Lena leaned back again. Cartwright looked at her, his face blank.

'But she works in a bar. Wouldn't that be normal?'

'There was something in there she did not want me to see. And she was holding her laptop to her chest.' Lena mimed the movement, encircling her chest with her arms. Cartwright watched her and then shifted in his chair. 'It was a different laptop, but she was doing something secret with it.' Lena took a deep breath. 'I have a bad feeling about her,' she continued. 'I think maybe she has the painting and she tries to sell it online. But I have no way to prove that. I hope you can help?' She looked to Cartwright.

Cartwright coughed. 'How?' he said.

'Can you find her internet history? See what she has been doing online?'

'I'm not sure how much I'll be able to do . . . it's not my case so I can't go on to the laptop. It could cost me my job.'

'I do not want you to get in trouble,' said Lena. 'But you studied computers, that is right? At university?'

'Among other things,' said Cartwright, looking a little flushed.

'Then you will find a way,' said Lena.

'I can try, I suppose,' said Cartwright. 'I want to help, if I can.'

'You can,' said Lena, smiling at him. Her investigations were starting to feel less lonely.

'I suppose you can't blame the poor girl, knowing what we know about her mother,' said Greta. Lena held the phone a little away from her ear, wishing she hadn't decided to call her mother so late in the evening when a headache was already setting in from the wine. When her mother got excited, the level of her voice rose exponentially. 'And her uncle as well, for that matter. The dirty thief that your father turned out to be. And after I ironed his socks for all those years. That's gratitude for you.'

'What do you mean?' asked Lena, confused.

'He stole from us and the factory. To think that I could love such a man.'

'I know that,' said Lena. 'What poor girl?'

'Sarika of course. Who else?'

Lena paused, trying to work out what her mother meant. 'You mean Sarika is a thief?'

'Of course. We should have known.'

'She took the painting?' said Lena. Her heart felt like it was beating in her ear. 'How do you know? Has she been found with it?'

'What painting?'

'*A Study in Purple.*'

'Stop talking gibberish,' said Greta, sounding cross. 'I'm not sure what she took, but it wasn't that. Some outfit she wanted, it seems. I don't know if it was purple. She couldn't afford it so stuck it up her top. Years ago. That mother of hers wouldn't say a thing about it. I had to ask Dora, she'd been to that village they lived in and remembered it. Quite the scandal. Sarika's got a record and almost went to a young offenders' centre. Expelled from school, too.'

Lena held the phone from her ear and tried to process the information. Sarika had stolen in the past. She wondered if the police had seen Sarika's record back in Hungary.

'Who did she steal from?' asked Lena.

'Some shop or other.'

'And what did she take?'

'Clothes. Keep up.'

'When?'

'About four years ago. Now I think of it, they were meant to visit, weren't they, for Laszlo's fourth birthday and never showed up. I bet that was why. All those extra *kiflies* I baked went rancid and had to be thrown away. It's times like that you could really do with a man like your lovely ex Tomek around. He'd never let food go to waste. Have you seen him?'

'No,' said Lena.

'Does your policeman like *kiflies*?'

'He isn't my policeman,' said Lena. 'Not really.' She wanted to get to less sensitive subjects while she processed this new information about Sarika. 'Has Istvan visited recently?'

'Oh yes, he's quite devoted to little Laszlo. They go to the swimming baths together in town and play chess in the hot water outside. Laszlo usually wins. Such a bright boy.'

Lena closed her eyes, only half listening to her mother witter on. It had been exhausting trying to clean with Penelope's children under her feet. She hadn't got the house much cleaner or found the necklace, but at least both children were still alive and thriving when the babysitter finally arrived, late of course. Lena was pretty impressed with Casper's dinosaur drawing and had affixed it to the fridge door with Blu-Tack. She'd seen pictures of a similar quality going for £800 in the Agnoletti Archer Gallery. Lena felt herself drifting off, dinosaurs and hedgehogs creeping from her subconscious towards her dreams as sleep approached.

Sarika had stolen before. That didn't mean anything, she said to herself. It was completely different. Everyone deserved a second chance.

Yet at the same time, Lena knew that if she had been aware of Sarika's past she never would have hired her. Not for Lena's Cleaners. Honesty, integrity and her professional reputation all placed higher in her priority list than forgiveness.

CHAPTER 9

In general Lena wasn't a big fan of picnics. The prickle of grass on your legs; ants going places on your body where they had no business; the constant worry about knocking over your plastic cup of warm white wine on the uneven grassy surface. Not her idea of a great lunch. Certainly not when there were perfectly good cafés with steady tables, clean plates and useful knives and forks.

But Cartwright looked so pleased with the surprise he'd planned for her. His face lit up when she found him, as promised, on the grass near the lake in Clissold Park. He'd spread out a picnic blanket, had a fancy-looking basket full of sun-heated food and he'd donned a loose pair of shorts for the occasion. 'Your table awaits,' he said, handing her a plastic cup of something warm and fizzy.

Lena smiled back at him and sat awkwardly on the blanket, trying not to flash her knickers at him in the process. She tried to balance her plastic cup on the grass, but soon gave up and clutched it in her hot hand, accepting a paper plate with a piece of quiche, smoked salmon and half an avocado with the other. 'This is lovely,' she lied, balancing the plate on her lap and taking a deep swig from her cup.

'Food tastes so much better outdoors,' said Cartwright, still smiling from ear to ear. He stretched out his bare legs along the blanket, knocking over a small tub of bulbous olives.

Lena couldn't help but stare at his legs. She'd not seen them before; they were always concealed under trousers. She almost gasped at their perfection. Muscular, tanned, and covered in soft blond hairs that glistened like gold in the sunlight. If police uniform were shorts she'd be tempted to commit a crime herself, just to lure Cartwright to her. She popped an olive in her mouth to stop herself reaching out to stroke his legs with her hands. Lena subtly spat the pip into her hand and disposed of it in the grass nearby. Perhaps one day an olive tree would grow there. A homage to Cartwright's legs.

'It wasn't easy, but I've found out what you wanted to know,' said Cartwright. 'About Kat.'

Lena tore her eyes from his legs and looked up. 'You have her internet history? Has she tried to sell the painting?'

'No, I couldn't get into that without compromising myself,' said Cartwright. 'I need to respect people's right to privacy.'

Lena almost choked on her hummus. People who stole and tried to incriminate her family had no rights as far as she was concerned.

Cartwright bit into his quiche, oblivious to her feelings. 'But I think you'll like what I've discovered from my colleagues in vice,' he said. 'They'd been keeping an eye on an unsavoury little website and were watching Kat – for professional reasons, of course. It's all legal at the moment, but they think it could be a nursery for a fully fledged prostitution ring. I downloaded something for you on my personal computer and brought it with me,' he said, reaching to pull his laptop from his briefcase, which he'd been keeping cool under the blanket. 'I'll be pleased to get this off my machine, but I thought you'd want to see for yourself first,' he added nervously, booting up and peering into the screen. 'You can't see very well because of the glare in the park, but I've turned the brightness right up and I think you'll get the idea. Just scoot into the shade of that sycamore tree.'

Lena took the proffered laptop and stared at it. The screen just looked dark. Then she heard a voice blare out. Kat's voice. 'Hello big boy.' A couple nearby turned to look at her, a pram next to them covered in a blanket to protect their offspring from the sun while it napped.

'Sorry,' said Cartwright, hurriedly snatching the computer back. 'Let me turn the sound down a bit. This isn't appropriate for everyone. Not PG-rated, as they say. And it gets worse.'

Lena took the computer back, her interest thoroughly aroused. Peering into the screen, she saw Kat leer back at her, wearing a black silk teddy. She was on the phone, one of the old-fashioned ones with a coiled cable. She was wrapping the coils around her fingers and staring into the camera. All of a sudden she giggled, then her tongue spiked out of her mouth and she licked the handset. 'You're a naughty boy,' she said, in a husky voice. 'Is that what you want me to do?' Her legs opened, revealing her nakedness beneath.

Lena slammed the laptop shut.

'Not my cup of tea at all,' said Cartwright, taking the computer back and putting it into his briefcase. 'But it looks like that's what she's been up to. That's why she was so keen to get her computer back.'

'Do the other officers know about this?' asked Lena. 'Blake and Gullins?'

'DI Blake is brilliant, don't you think?' commented Cartwright. Lena looked at him. What did that have to do with anything?

'She is better than Gullins,' said Lena. 'But that is not to say much.'

'She is the best,' said Cartwright, with more enthusiasm than Lena would have liked him to show for an attractive woman. She felt a prickle of sweat run down her back. At least she hoped it was sweat, not an errant ant. She slapped her own back, just in case.

'DI Blake,' continued Cartwright. 'I can't believe she's in our station. I went to a lecture she did while I was studying at the academy. They are lucky to have her for such a small case. She's recovered some of the world's most valuable lost treasures, you know. Like a female Indiana Jones.'

'So do they know about Kat?' asked Lena, keen to change the subject.

'It's not related to this case,' said Cartwright. 'Although they probably found evidence of it on the confiscated article. Vice set me up with an account. You pay just to watch, and it's a hefty premium if you want to dial in.' He caught Lena's eye and took a sip from his cup. 'It's not the sort of site I usually visit, but at least that's what they told me,' he said. 'More smoked salmon?'

'Thank you,' said Lena. She flicked an ant off her leg. It landed in the hummus.

How could this video help Sarika? It clearly had nothing to do with the stolen painting. But it was a secret. Kat's secret. She was doing it from the flat. The flat she shared with Sarika.

'Sarika is not on the site,' said Cartwright, reading her mind. 'I checked. No Hungarians.'

Lena breathed a sigh of relief. 'Thank you for finding this for me,' she said. She looked to the ant. It had scrambled out of its chickpea prison and was exploring the rim of the container, pausing frequently to sniff its garlicky path. 'It is good to know about this,' said Lena. 'But I do not see how it helps us.'

'You have to kiss a few frogs to find the prince,' said Cartwright, his voice full of cheer. Lena looked at him blankly. 'I mean,' he continued, 'you need to find out all the facts you can and some of them will be useful and some of them will not be.'

'I have some frogs,' Lena told him. 'For a start, I know how to find Dragg on Saturday. And I think he will lead me to Sarika. That is frog number one. Frog number two is my new plan.' Lena smiled at Cartwright. 'I think it is a very good plan indeed. Perfect for catching frogs.'

Lena leaned back and stretched, feeling pleased with both her plan and her mastery of the peculiarities of the English language.

'I can't even look at her,' shouted Pietro. 'Simon, get her out of my gallery.'

'But we have things we need to discuss,' objected Lena. 'I want to help you find out who stole the painting. I have a plan. I have frogs.'

'And I have clients. Clients in this gallery this very minute,' shouted Pietro, gesturing to an uncomfortable-looking couple who were edging towards the door. 'Get out of my shop,' he hissed at Lena. 'Out of my sight.'

'But I can help you find the truth!' she said, moving towards the desk. She could see Ophelia's gallery keys sitting there, brand new since the locks were changed, but with the same feathery key ring.

'You can help me find nothing,' said Pietro.

'I can help you find a buyer for that hedgehog,' said Lena. 'That couple look very keen.' Both men turned to look. The couple disappeared through the door.

Simon stepped forwards and shepherded Lena out of the gallery behind them. 'That's right, Simon,' said Pietro. 'Show her the door before she steals something else.'

He was too late.

Lena clutched the keys in her pocket, feeling the feathers crumple in her sweaty palms. Simon joined her outside the gallery, closing the door behind him. Had he seen?

'This is not fair,' began Lena, trying to sound confident. 'I want to help.'

'I believe you,' said Simon. 'Come on, let's get a coffee while he calms down. You like those ones that put hairs on your chest from Lavazza, don't you?'

Lena gave him an odd look. She had no hairs on her chest and doubted if he did either. But he was right about the coffee she liked, and she allowed him to lead her to the coffee shop around the corner. If he wanted to buy her coffee he had not seen what she had in her pocket.

'Here. You sit down and I'll fetch us both a drink. Then we can talk.'

Lena was surprised. Pietro used to chat away all the time in the gallery, but Simon was taciturn. She assumed he didn't much like her, perhaps didn't much like anyone. Except Ophelia.

Lena settled on a brown leather sofa. She couldn't tell whether she was hot from anger or the weather, but either way her thighs were sticking to the seat. She adjusted her position, trying to draw her skirt to cover more of her legs, resulting in an unpleasant squelching noise. Lena glared at a man who had turned round at the noise.

Simon returned with a tray containing a cup of coffee for Lena, a large slice of millionaire shortbread and a weak-looking tea. Lena took the coffee and looked at the biscuit.

'It's for you, too,' said Simon. 'I'm sorry for how Pietro is behaving.'

Lena took a sip of the coffee, bitter and strong, just how she liked it. She picked up the shortbread and took a bite. As she chewed she felt the caramel calming her down. Another bite and she'd be ready to hear what excuse Simon clearly had for Pietro's behaviour. She looked at him. He was staring out of the window. To hell with it, she thought. She'd eat the whole thing and then talk. At least that way, if he had any accusations to throw at her or Sarika, she could make a quick and angry exit, without missing any of the caramel-y biscuit.

'You know I did not take the painting,' said Lena, swallowing the last mouthful.

'I don't know what happened,' Simon replied. 'But Pietro is a mess. He's worried that the police think it could be him, for the insurance.'

'Was the gallery in trouble?' said Lena.

'No. It's never been profitable, but Pietro's family are extremely wealthy. He's been bailing the gallery out of trouble for years. All galleries should have trust-fund backers. Life would be much easier.'

'Why does he keep it going?'

'He loves it. We both do. We decided to set it up together back in art school, before he married Ophelia. But then it took a few years before we got ourselves sorted.'

Lena took another sip of coffee and sat back in the leather sofa, feeling the softness caressing her back. 'But if he is wealthy, why does he steal for the insurance money?'

'Exactly,' said Simon. 'That's what I keep telling Pietro. He isn't really a suspect. He is just being dramatic.'

Lena scooted forwards on the sofa. It was less comfortable, but she found it hard to hear Simon unless she was close to him. His voice was soft and the café's music interrupted her concentration. 'Pietro does like drama,' she said. 'But you think he will be okay?'

'I'll make sure of it,' he said. Lena saw the intensity that rose to his eyes now and again. 'I wouldn't let anything happen to him. Or Ophelia. We go way back.'

Lena sat for a moment and watched Simon take a sip of his tea. 'How was your date with Trudy?' she asked.

'It wasn't really a date,' he said. 'Just a chat.'

'Was she at art school with you too?'

'No, she visited as a guest artist for a bit. Had a thing with Pietro. It broke him and Ophelia up for a while. But we were all kids back then. They sorted things out and later got married. I still can't believe they've got two children.' Simon looked at the café wall. Lena followed his gaze. A dreary rendition of a beach was hanging there in black and white. He looked back at Lena. 'Did you get what you needed?'

'What?' said Lena, puzzled.

'The things you left in the office. Remember?'

'Oh yes,' said Lena, cursing herself for getting caught in the lie. 'I mean no, I did not get the . . .' She thought for a moment. 'Sunglasses. Could I . . . ?'

'I'll look for you,' he said.

Szar, thought Lena. She'd have to come back when the gallery was closed and use the keys she'd stolen from Ophelia if she wanted to snoop around. Simon wasn't going to let her back in. 'So who do you think took the painting?' she asked him, hoping to get something more from this meeting than a biscuit and a coffee. 'You have a theory?'

Simon took another sip before answering. 'The art world is full of unscrupulous people,' he said. 'But our security is not that scrupulous – the gallery is no Fort Knox. It's not really necessary when most of our art is lower-value items, under a thousand pounds. I have tried to get Pietro to invest in a proper security system, with cameras and all. But he's too much of an optimist to believe we'd ever need them. It would be easy enough for some-one in the know to arrange this theft, especially of our only really valuable work.'

'But why that evening?' said Lena. That question had been bothering her for a while. 'The evening the artist was there, the evening there was a big reception?'

'I'm no art thief,' said Simon. 'I don't know their reasoning. Maybe someone at the reception took Pietro's keys?'

'Who do you think?' pressed Lena. 'You must have an idea?'

'It could have been anyone,' said Simon. He turned his gaze to the window. 'People on the circuit, getting the invitations, paying someone else to do their dirty work. I hear there's a big market for Trudy's work in China.'

Lena looked out the window, wondering what was so interesting. She was surprised he could see anything, the state of that glass. Her special cleaning concoction of vinegar and fresh lemon juice would sort it out. 'I need to prove that my agency is not to blame or Sarika will not come back.'

'I'm sorry that she ran off like that,' said Simon. 'It doesn't look good. But Pietro will come round. He blusters and he has his faults.' Simon looked straight into her eyes. 'But he is the most forgiving man I have ever met. It has only been a week since the painting was stolen. Give it another, maybe two, and he'll give you your job back. Another week and he'll be recommending you all over town.'

'And the police?'

'They don't really think she could have done this, do they?'

'There is a warrant out for her arrest.'

'I didn't know that,' said Simon, taking another sip of his coffee. 'But if she is innocent then she will be fine,' he said. 'Just give it time.'

'That is not good enough,' said Lena. She looked at Simon, who had taken to staring out of the window again. She followed his gaze to a tree this time, blowing in the wind. She decided to take him into her confidence. 'I want to find out who took the painting,' she said. 'I will investigate the suspects.'

Simon looked back at her. 'How do you plan to do that?'

'I need the list,' said Lena. 'The list of everyone who was at the drinks reception. I want to find out which of them has something to hide. I have other suspicions too, but I need to know more about everyone to investigate properly.'

'Are you sure you are just a cleaner?' said Simon.

'Because I am a cleaner does not mean I cannot want justice,' said Lena.

'Well I can't help you,' said Simon. 'That is client data, I'm afraid. There's no way I can share that with you.'

'Just three names then? If I have surnames, not even addresses, then I can—'

'Sorry, Lena.' He stood up. 'I need to get back to the gallery.'

'Okay,' said Lena, her mind racing. 'I understand.'

'It will all work out,' he said. 'As I said, Pietro forgives quickly.'

Lena snorted. 'I have done nothing wrong and he has accused me. I am not sure that I can forgive him.' She stood up.

'That is no way to live your life, Lena,' he said. He held open the door of the coffee shop. 'If you can't forgive, you will never be happy.'

Lena said goodbye and started back towards the bus stop. It was easy for Simon to say that, she thought. When you're a wealthy middle-class English white man who has never suffered a day in his life. She stopped. Something in that sentence didn't feel right. She realised what it was. Something in Simon's eyes. She remembered how he had looked at Ophelia. He had suffered. Plenty.

CHAPTER 10

'Thank you for coming with me,' said Lena to Cartwright, raising her voice to be heard over the din of the A23 traffic and his little car's struggling engine.

'It was lucky. Saturday is my day off this week. There's nothing I'd rather be doing,' said Cartwright with a smile. He wiped his brow and shook the sweat from his fingers. 'I'm so sorry again about the air conditioning. It always plays up in hot weather.'

'It is okay with the window open,' said Lena. It wasn't really. She could feel little beads of sweat escaping from her skin and making a run for it down her back, finally travelling through her T-shirt to their destination. The back of Cartwright's car seat. She hoped they wouldn't leave a mark, a tell-tale imprint of the discs in her spine, crafted in salty sweat.

Lena wound the window down full and let the petrol-infused air batter her face with all it had. She closed her eyes, which stung with the assault. They were off to Brighton to the graffiti event Lucia had told her about, in the hopes of finding Dragg and perhaps even Sarika. Lena was excited to see Sarika, to check that she was okay. But she was also disappointed. She did not have any real leads as to who had taken the painting. She still didn't even have contact details for the clients who could have taken Pietro's key. There was little to help her convince Sarika to come home and face arrest.

She became aware that Cartwright was trying to say something, but Lena couldn't hear it above the violence of the incoming air. Reluctantly she wound up her window halfway and turned to him. 'What did you say?'

'So what is a graffiti jam anyway?' said Cartwright. 'I take it you don't have it with cream and scones?'

'Lucia said Dragg does them often. There is a bit of grey wall that someone decides can be more colourful, and lots of graffiti people come to paint it.'

'I love Brighton,' said Cartwright. 'Do you think we'll have time for a walk along the beach before this graffiti jam? Perhaps we could have some ice cream?'

Lena smiled at him. 'We look for Dragg first,' she said. 'But maybe ice cream later.'

'Maybe fish and chips too,' said Cartwright merrily. 'There's nowhere chips taste better than by the sea. The salty smell and the salty taste and the constant risk of attack.'

'Risk of attack?' said Lena, wondering if this was another odd English idiom new to her.

'From seagulls,' he explained. 'They have real monsters of those birds down in Brighton. If you're eating chips they'll dive at you like doodlebugs. Don't worry, I'll protect you.'

'I protect myself,' said Lena, realising too late the inappropriate sharpness in her voice.

'Of course,' said Cartwright affably. 'You have fought off Yasemin Avci and her Turkish gang and solved your friend's murder. You are quite capable of protecting chips from a seagull.'

Lena smiled, relieved he hadn't taken offence. 'But I am not too familiar with seagulls,' said Lena. 'They are not common in my landlocked country.' She paused a moment. 'So perhaps I will need your help.'

'Well there's oodles of them in the Cotswolds, so you're in experienced hands. The secret is not to let them smell your fear or they attack in a huge pack. One slaps you with its wing to make you let go of what you're eating and then the rest swoop in. Proper organised crime – could teach that gang leader Yasemin Avci a thing or two.' Cartwright laughed. 'Right, we're here. We just need to find somewhere to park. A detective project in its own right.'

After driving around narrow streets and along the wide road by the coast for some time, Cartwright eventually squeezed the car into a tiny spot in a busy car park. They clambered out and Lena breathed in deeply, tasting the salty air deep in her throat. She followed Cartwright, who had started to climb a steep hill on an extremely narrow street. 'It is around here somewhere,' said Cartwright, as they both started to sweat.

Lena sniffed the air again. The sea air had a less pleasant aroma here, and the yelping of seagulls had something more rhythmic underpinning it. She left Cartwright frowning at the map on his phone and followed a stale smell of weed and the sound of hip-hop music through another narrow alleyway. As she wound through the passage, another scent greeted her nostrils. A cleaner, more chemical aroma. Spray-paint.

'Cartwright,' she hissed. 'Through here.'

Another few steps and she emerged from the alley into a square teeming with activity like an ant farm. The large walls had been divided into sections and each was being worked on by a collection of colourful individuals. No one looked around as she entered the square, each entranced by their own patch of wall.

'I can't believe something like this is legal,' said Cartwright. 'It reeks of class B. I could arrest them for possession.'

'We must be focused,' said Lena. 'We need to find Dragg and we need him to help us. We do not need a car full of angry men with spray-paint.'

'You're the boss,' replied Cartwright. 'So can you see Dragg? What does he look like again?'

'He is pale, with dark hair and a dragon tattooed on his neck . . .' Lena looked round. There were pale dark-haired men everywhere, many sporting tattoos. 'Come with me,' she said. 'We search together.'

They started at the right-hand side and began to walk behind the painters methodically. Despite the music and the aroma of drugs, everyone seemed completely absorbed in what they were doing. They were taking it seriously. Some impressive murals were beginning to take shape, each as individual as a fingerprint.

A tall man with baggy shorts and no shirt was painstakingly constructing a walrus using tiny blasts of a spray can, each less than an inch in diameter. He was enclosed by a wall of different cans, each a shade of grey. One the other side, a girl with so much metal in her face that magnets would be a hazard was stencilling the lyrics of a poem and decorating the words with furiously intricate illustrations. Next to her a man was using broad brush strokes of red paint to create the aftermath of an explosion. Further along another man was instructing a girl in an unseasonable woollen beanie hat on the art of drawing fire with a spray can. His arms were encircling her as he guided her hand. Lena looked more closely at the painting. There was a faint pencil guideline at the end of the fire. It was in the shape of a dragon.

'Dragg,' she exclaimed. The man turned around, sending the girl's arm off its stride. A line of red crossed into her neighbour's painting of a giant skull. He swore at her. The girl turned around.

'Sarika?' said Lena. Her hair was blue under the beanie and she had an infected-looking ring through her eyebrow that made her face lopsided and her expression quizzical. But it was her cousin all right.

Lena stepped forwards but Sarika had already darted to the left, upsetting a tin of red paint that splashed to the floor behind her like blood at a crime scene. She scrambled past it and disappeared into the street.

Lena rushed after her, pushing past disgruntled artists as she went. 'You get Dragg,' she shouted to Cartwright as she went. She turned for long enough to see Dragg running the opposite way, Cartwright hot on his heels. Then she put her full attention into her pursuit of Sarika.

The girl was fitter than she gave her credit for. She'd associated lateness with slowness, but she'd been wrong. Sarika could move when she wanted to.

The streets were narrow, busy and filled with the hazards of summertime in a tourist spot. Lena narrowly missed knocking over a wobbly metal table covered in glasses of freshly squeezed juices in unappetising shades of brown. She saw Sarika swerve to just miss a table at the neighbouring café with a chintzy table-cloth and enormous platter of scones. An elderly couple seated at the table swore at Sarika, and Lena saw the woman sneer in Sarika's direction.

Lena knew she could outrun Sarika in the open, but in these conditions it was more like hurdles than a race. Sarika was getting further and further ahead of her, and people were filling the spaces in between like gas particles spreading to fill the space in a jar. It was hilly and getting steadily steeper and Lena felt her glutes begin to ache in objection.

Sarika turned a corner and Lena followed. There were no more outside tables here and the going was smoother. Lena glanced through the window of one of the shops. Row upon row of antique jewellery, glittering in the midday sunlight. A couple emerged from the shop, hand in hand and staring into each other's eyes, blocking Lena's path. The woman held a small bag that Lena presumed contained an engagement ring. It was too narrow to get around them here and Lena had to slow right down or send both flying.

Rohadt romantika. Damn romance.

Eventually she got past the obstacle of lovers.

But Sarika was gone.

Lena continued through the Brighton Lanes, more slowly now as the gradient of the hill increased further, searching for a glimpse of Sarika. She saw a small group of middle-aged American tourists in their shorts and T-shirts study the menu of a tea room with intent. A white man with bright blue eyes, ginger dreadlocks and a guitar was singing Bob Marley while a small gaggle of teenage girls giggled and threw him smiles. No sign of Sarika.

Defeated, Lena attempted to find her way back to where she had come from. It was not so easy. The third time she passed the busker she was ready to give up. She glanced at the menu of the tea room herself, and saw the group of Americans inside, sipping unenthusiastically on cups of weak tea. She found herself wondering where she could get a decent cup of coffee around here. And what on earth she would do now she had missed her one chance of finding Sarika.

Her mind went back to her cousin. She didn't look as though she had showered for a while, and Lena felt herself itching to disinfect the septic metal in her eyebrow. But otherwise, she'd looked well. Happy even. She could certainly run. At least it didn't seem like she had been chained in a basement or locked in a brothel. Perhaps the girl was doing better on her own than Lena had first thought.

Her phone bleated to her and Lena fished it out of her pocket. When she saw it was Cartwright she was surprised by her urge to ignore it. She felt ashamed that she'd dragged him all the way here and failed in her mission to retrieve Sarika. With a sigh she picked up the call. 'What is it?' she said.

'Lena, I've got him,' Cartwright said, his own voice full of elation. 'I've got Dragg. Meet me at the beach, we're by the pier.'

'You have been swimming?' Lena looked at the men, both dripping wet on the pebble beach. They had their backs to her and both were gazing towards the sea. 'In all your clothes?'

111

Cartwright twisted round to look at her and then jumped up. Lena felt a little flutter when she saw how his polo shirt clung to his toned chest. Her eyes found his and she smiled at the victory that filled them.

'Red footprints!' he said. Lena looked at him, wondering if he had gone insane. Perhaps the sea air didn't agree with him after all.

'What?'

'He trod in the paint that you knocked over!' said Cartwright. 'That was a brilliant idea.'

Lena looked at him, unwilling to take credit for a mess, even a useful one. 'I did not spill paint,' she replied, with pride. 'That was Sarika.'

'He tracked it far enough for me to follow his footsteps. Then I was able to catch up with him just as he was getting on to the pier. I tackled him to the ground, using a technique I learned on my attachment in Newcastle. It's called the armbar hammerlock, pioneered by the NYPD.'

'It is called falling into the sea,' said Dragg, with a laugh. He reached into his pocket and retrieved his pouch of tobacco. He opened it and shook the pouch, tutting as seawater came flooding out. He made a futile attempt to shake it dry.

'To the untrained eye that's what it might look like,' said Cartwright, with half a smile. 'But I can assure you, it was the armbar hammerlock.'

'You could have just said what you wanted,' said Dragg. 'Without ruining my smokes. Look, we are sitting here quite civilised now. No need for ruined cigarettes.'

'Smoking is bad for you,' said Lena. 'Like I will be if you do not help us.' She positioned herself between the men and the sea so they were facing her and popped herself down with a jolt. *Szar.* The stones were harder and more jagged than she'd given them credit for. Braving her discomfort, she continued. 'Where is Sarika?'

Dragg shrugged. 'You were chasing her last time I saw you. You tell me.' He reached into his other pocket and withdrew some damp Rizlas from the packet. 'Ruined,' he commented, throwing a handful towards the sea. The papers fluttered to the ground like injured seagulls.

Lena reached out and grabbed them, unable to allow litter on the beach. She had to stop herself telling him off. She must keep herself focused on the task in hand. Getting Sarika back.

'We know Sarika is staying with you,' she said. 'She is here in Brighton, we saw her. She was with you. She knows no one else here.'

Dragg shrugged again. 'Coincidence,' he said.

Lena thought a moment. 'I wonder if your lovely girlfriend Kat will think that too. When I tell her.'

Dragg shifted uncomfortably on the pebbles. 'There is no need for that,' he said. 'Kat is fantastic, but she is not always the most . . . understanding.'

'Where is Sarika, Dragg?' said Lena, pushing her advantage. 'Tell me where I can find my cousin.'

Dragg reached into his pocket again, this time removing a small pouch of weed, which he shook with pleasure. Cartwright looked horrified and went to lurch towards him but Lena gestured him back. 'Thank god for Ziploc bags,' said Dragg. 'I think my stash is going to be okay after all. Perhaps today is not such a bad day.' He looked back at them. 'Listen, I can't tell you where Sarika is. I promised her I would tell no one. You'd just take her to the police anyway, and she'll get done for something she didn't do. You know what they are like. Dirty pigs.'

'That's it,' said Cartwright. He grabbed Dragg's arms and pinned them behind his back.

'What is happening?' shouted Dragg. 'Get off me.'

'It is my job to be always on duty,' said Cartwright, authority filling his voice. 'I'm an officer of the law and I'm arresting you for possession of marijuana and obstruction of justice. You do not have to say anything, but it may harm your defence if you do not mention when questioned something which you later rely on in court. Anything you do say may be given in evidence. Do you understand?'

Dragg grunted assent.

Cartwright looked at Lena, who gave him an approving smile. 'Sorry, Lena,' he said. 'That line of questioning didn't seem to be going anywhere. Let's take him back to see Gullins and Blake. We'll see if they can't be more persuasive.'

'I am innocent,' said Dragg. 'Let go of me.'

'Good plan,' said Lena, ignoring Dragg's objections. 'He will have some questions to answer about what is on that laptop. I am sure of it.' She helped Cartwright lift Dragg to his feet and they clutched one arm each as they trudged over the stones towards the walkway, ignoring the looks from bemused passers-by. Both men were still dripping wet. 'Unless he wants to tell us where to find Sarika?'

'Okay,' said Dragg. 'I'll tell you.'

'Stop! Let him go!' Lena felt a judder and Dragg went flying backwards, knocked over by a flurry of blue hair which landed on top of him. Suddenly the question of Sarika's whereabouts was academic.

'Sarika!' exclaimed Lena.

'He didn't do it!' Sarika kissed Dragg's wet head and then rolled off him to face Lena and Cartwright. Dragg groaned. 'He didn't steal the painting. What was on his laptop, the evidence they found. I can explain it all.'

'Sarika, be quiet,' said Dragg, still prostrated on the floor. He moved to get up and yelled out in pain. 'I think you've broken my back.'

114

'He didn't steal that stupid purple painting,' continued Sarika, unperturbed. 'He was only on those art theft forums to take what was rightfully his. His people's. That London museum has no business holding those statues from Crete. He was only going to take them back to where they belong.'

'You were planning to steal the Elgin Marbles?' said Cartwright, his voice filled with incredulity.

'Of course not,' said Dragg. 'There's lots of smaller, lighter things you British have stolen. And I wasn't really going to take them. It was a fantasy.'

Dragg groaned again and abandoned his attempts to get up. Lena and Cartwright looked at him in astonishment. 'See?' said Sarika. 'He is innocent. We both are. You need to let him go.'

'There's no chance of that, I'm afraid,' said Cartwright. 'Both of you need to come with me. I'm taking all of us back to London. We'll see what my colleagues at the station have to say about this.'

After some faffing about who would sit where, Lena pushed a still damp and sore Dragg into the front seat and climbed into the back next to Sarika. The men soon started to steam like hot coffee as the seawater evaporated in the heat of the car. It left a sparkle of salt on both their clothes that looked like glitter in the sunlight.

'Running away was the worst thing you could do,' Lena told Sarika as soon as the seatbelts were fastened. 'Do you know the suspicion you are under? I have been so worried about you. Plus Lena's Cleaners has been fired from the gallery. Our name is like mud. Worse than mud. Like *szar*.'

'I'm sorry,' said Sarika, sullen. 'I had to go. The police would never believe that I'm innocent. Not with my record for theft.'

'A record?' said Cartwright. 'This gets better and better. Did you know that each year over 500,000 crimes are committed by people who have been convicted before, in the UK alone? I'm sorry, Lena, but this cousin of yours deserves to be a suspect.'

'See?' said Sarika. 'Even your boyfriend thinks I am guilty.'

'No he does not,' said Lena, kicking the back of Cartwright's car seat. It was padded and made her aggression futile, annoying her further. 'And he is not my boyfriend.'

'An Eastern European will not get justice in this country,' added Dragg, turning awkwardly in the front seat to address Lena. 'Nor a Greek. It is not possible.'

'It is quite possible,' replied Cartwright. 'Her Majesty's justice system is second to none. Without prejudice.'

'Then why is your girlfriend fired from this so-called gallery if she did nothing wrong?' said Dragg.

Cartwright beeped his horn at a surprised motorcyclist. 'Bloody road hogs,' he muttered.

Lena looked out of the window. A cow looked back at her, catching her eye for a moment before the car whizzed past, leaving it behind for ever. 'I will not let anything bad happen to you,' she said, turning back to Sarika. 'I will look after you.'

'There is not much you can do to look after her if she goes to prison,' reasoned Dragg, shifting backwards again to look at the women. 'How will you protect her then?'

'You are no help,' Lena hissed. 'And tell us more about what the police found on your laptop. Why were you on those forums?'

'I'm very interested in that too,' chimed in Cartwright. 'Planning to steal artefacts from a major gallery and smuggle them out of the country?'

Lena saw Dragg shrug from the front seat. It made the creature tattooed on his neck wriggle as if it were preparing to take off. 'That is a dream only,' he replied. 'You British stole it from my island. I want to steal it back. That is justice. But it is impossible. Too difficult.' He sighed. 'Maybe one day, but not now.'

'It is a good thing we caught this one,' said Cartwright, talking to Lena through the medium of the rear-view mirror. It reminded her of being at the hairdresser's. 'As well as the drugs, he is planning a theft. Of government property, no less. He is not someone I would want around my cousin. Especially if my cousin already had a criminal record.'

'That was years ago,' said Sarika. She turned to Lena and spoke in Hungarian. 'It was just an outfit I wanted that my mama wouldn't buy me. You know how mean she can be.' She took Lena's hand, gripping it in her own, like Timea used to when she was that age. 'Lena, I'm so sorry. But Dragg was doing nothing wrong. Neither was I. I know it looks bad for me, especially since I ran away. But I can't go back to London now. I can't go to prison. It would kill my mother. It might kill me.'

'Do not be so *melodrámai*. Melodramatic,' she translated. 'It will not come to that.' But Lena found herself squeezing her cousin's hand as she turned back to the window.

Staring out at the passing fields, rolling hills covered alternately in grasses, crops and trees, Lena thought about what the girl had said. It would not be easy for Sarika back in London. The police would question her, and it would not just be her lovely Cartwright. It would be Gullins, full of smug aggression and prejudice. Not to mention Blake's cleverness. Sarika would be no match for them. With no painting she would have nothing to bargain with. Unless Lena could find it . . . but she had no real leads at all. Sarika's flight put a seal on her apparent guilt. It seemed the girl was unlikely to place suspicion on Dragg. Lena saw the way she looked at him, like a puppy gazes at a new tennis ball.

With no other suspects, what would happen? Sarika would be charged and, after running away once, she would not get bail. So even if she was not convicted, she would spend time in custody. Lena turned from the window to look at Sarika. She could tell from her gentle shakes that the girl was trying to swallow back tears.

Dragg was right. She couldn't protect Sarika if she were in a cell. Just like she couldn't protect Timea either, not when it really mattered. She could investigate, she might even find out what had really happened to the painting. But all the time Sarika, innocent Sarika, would be in custody.

'Stop the car,' she ordered.

'What?' said Cartwright, indicating towards the hard shoulder. 'Why?'

'We need to let them go.'

'Absolutely not,' said Cartwright, speeding up again. 'How can you even suggest that?'

'Give me more time,' pleaded Lena. 'They can stay with me, just until we have more evidence. Then they will turn themselves in. I promise.'

'No,' said Cartwright, his voice firmer than Lena had heard it before. 'Sarika is wanted by the police. I have already arrested Dragg for possession of illegal class-B drugs and he has admitted to planning, if not executing, a serious theft. It is my duty to take them to the police station.'

'Just a week,' said Lena. Sarika had taken her hand and was squeezing it.

'We will stay in Lena's flat,' said Sarika. 'We promise.'

Cartwright took his eyes off the road for a moment and looked at Lena. 'You cannot guarantee they will not abscond,' he said. She looked at him blankly. 'Run away,' he clarified. His eyes flicked back to the road, but not before Lena noticed they no longer resembled water. They were like steel.

'Fine,' she said. They sat in angry silence, Cartwright marking out time with an urgent tapping of his fingers on the steering wheel. Lena caught a flash of something on the dashboard.

'You are almost out of petrol,' said Dragg.

'I am aware of that,' snapped back Cartwright.

'You won't make it all the way back to London with that much petrol.'

'Thank you, Jeremy Clarkson,' said Cartwright. 'Luckily for me there is a thing called a petrol station just ahead.' He took the turning. Lena saw Dragg and Sarika exchange a look through the rear-view mirror.

'Lena, they are in your custody while I fill up and pay,' said Cartwright. 'Come sit in my seat at the front. I will put the child locks on. There is a machine to pay right here. I will not be long,'

'You can trust me,' said Lena. He clambered out and Lena took the driving seat. They all heard the locks click into action.

Sarika immediately leaned forwards to Lena. 'You need to let us out,' she said. 'I can't go to prison. Please, Lena. Please.' Lena shot a glance at Cartwright. He was filling the petrol tank, with that special expression men reserve for petrol pumps, spraying with a hose and urinating. He began to fiddle with the machine. It spat out his card. Cartwright leaned to the window and gestured. He would need to go inside and pay at the till.

Lena didn't believe much in fate, but this seemed as though it was meant to be. 'Wait till he is inside the station,' said Lena, her mind made up. 'Then make a run for it. Different directions. I will try to follow one of you, but you will be too fast for me.' Sarika enveloped her in a massive hug from behind. 'Stop,' Lena said. 'We do not want him to see.'

'Thank you for doing this,' said Dragg. 'I will look after her.'

'This is not the end,' warned Lena. 'What is your address in Brighton?'

'What do you need that for?' asked Dragg.

'You have one week,' said Lena. 'This is not permanent,' she told them. 'It is just so that you are not in prison while I find out what really happened to the painting. I hope that PC Cartwright will still help me. He is a very good policeman.'

'Oxymoron,' said Dragg.

Idióta, thought Lena. He had no right to call Cartwright an ox or a moron. Cartwright was worth fifty Draggs.

'If I cannot solve the case then you must come back. You cannot live as fugitives for ever. Remember you are innocent. I just need to prove it. Sarika, the address.'

The girl looked at Dragg and reluctantly muttered the address. 'That had better be the truth,' said Lena. 'I need to be able to find you again. Sarika, I am trusting you. Promise me.'

'I promise,' said Sarika. Lena looked at her, concerned she was lying. But what else could she do? She could hardly imprison the girl in her own flat. Cartwright would be sure to come there. Lena laughed grimly to herself. It was times like this a basement would come in useful. And not just for storing old mops and broken vacuum cleaners.

They all looked back innocently as Cartwright peered through the window, then walked towards the shop. He disappeared inside.

'Go,' said Lena, unlocking the doors. They did. She paused, watching them run. The petrol station was at the end of a winding road sloping down from the motorway that cut through fields and a collection of trees. With a brief head start they should be able to conceal themselves.

Slowly, she climbed out of the car. Dragg ran awkwardly after his fall but still moved fast. She couldn't even see Sarika. Cartwright emerged from the shop, blinking in the sunlight.

'Stop,' she cried out, for Cartwright's benefit, and began running in the direction neither had taken. 'Cartwright, they have escaped. Follow me.'

'I can't believe you let them get away,' said Cartwright. They had eventually given up the chase and were back in his car.

'It was not my fault,' said Lena. She looked at Cartwright, his hands tightly gripping the steering wheel.

'Tell me again how it happened?' he said.

'I think your child locks were faulty,' said Lena. She hated lying and was grateful that Cartwright's gaze was firmly on the road ahead.

'The locks are working fine now,' replied Cartwright. 'What happened next?'

'They jumped out and ran in different directions.'

'And you couldn't catch either of them? Even though Dragg had hurt his back?'

'He is fast,' replied Lena.

'I caught him earlier,' said Cartwright. 'And I have seen you run. You are quicker than me.'

As the traffic slowed, Cartwright turned to look at her. She could see disappointment shining in his eyes like a grey day reflected in a puddle. She tried to keep his gaze but found her eyes drawn down to the gearstick. 'I do not like to be lied to, Lena,' he said. 'Especially not by you.'

Lena could not think of a reply. Instead she stared into the suburban sprawl as they headed back into London. At least she had a plan of what to do next. But it was not a plan that she could share with PC Cartwright.

At ten p.m., Lena let herself into the gallery with the key she had stolen from Ophelia and typed in the code to prevent the burglar alarm blaring out. Thankfully they hadn't thought to change the number. The gallery was deserted – the events of the week cancelled due to the disappearance of *A Study in Purple,* the star attraction. Lena closed the door behind her and crept through the darkness. She wondered if it was still breaking and entering if she had a key, albeit a secretly borrowed one. She didn't much want to be caught and find out. The glass front of the gallery would make the ground floor like a fishbowl if she were to switch on the light. She paused for a moment, mentally recreating the layout of the gallery. The last thing she wanted to do was bump into that spiky hedgehog or knock the glass foot from its podium. Confident she had the lie of the land, she crept forwards, finding a clear path to the little office.

Once there, Lena used the light on her phone and began to rummage through the papers strewn like confetti over the desk. There was a bill for the electrics, then an overdue notice for the gas, and an angry letter from an artist's agent complaining of a lack of payment. Lena took a quick photo of each with her phone. She ignored the pile of unopened envelopes, likely more of the same. Looking at the lateness of all the invoices, Lena was glad she had insisted on cash up front for her work. She moved an old local newspaper to one side, glancing at the headline. 'Chippie in intensive care over cod fillet.' She read the stand-first. 'Islington now a dangerous plaice.'

But she hadn't found what she was searching for. She moved to the overloaded desk tidy and froze. There was a noise outside. She tapped her phone to turn off the light. Then she recognised singing. It was just a few boys enjoying their Saturday night. She sighed with relief and hurried up her progress, moving to look through the pile of papers lining the desk chair.

She found it. The list of guests from the gallery reception. It had only been ten days ago, but felt like a lifetime to her already. She carefully took a picture of each page and replaced it where it had been. She saw a dirty teacup and fought the urge to wash it up. She needed to get out without leaving a trace.

Lena switched off the light and crept back out to the gallery. She stood in darkness, getting her bearings again. As she did so, she looked at the wall where *A Study in Purple* had hung. The white wall shone by the light of the moon, coming in through the skylight. The wall looked empty, blank. Although she hadn't much cared for the painting, Lena was sad to see the square shape it had left behind; a square of brightness against the faded wall. They'd need to find a larger picture to cover that space, or repaint the wall, perhaps in a different shade of white, as Simon had wanted.

She was surprised at how dirty the wall had become. Perhaps she wasn't as good a cleaner as she thought. There was such an obvious square of cleanness under the painting. She walked towards it, her professional interest piqued. Under her careful gaze and by the light of the moon, she thought she saw two echoes of paintings. Almost exactly the same size, but not quite. Lena looked around, then shone the light on her phone at the wall and examined it carefully.

Two paintings had been here, of slightly differing sizes. How had she never noticed? And what did it mean?

It wasn't that unusual, decided Lena, padding across the room. The shop sold many paintings; another could have hung here before her time.

Lena looked through the glass at the street beyond. No one was walking past. She had what she came for and slipped out, carefully putting the burglar alarm on as she left and locking the door. She couldn't have another painting going missing. Not on her watch.

Lena caught the night bus back to her flat. The bus was quiet at this time, not turning into pandemonium until later. A couple of Chinese students were chatting animatedly. A night worker stared out of the window, seemingly fascinated by what the dark street held. A drunk man in a suit slipped into and out of sleep, his head rolling like a pendulum. Lena looked at the list of people who had attended the gallery reception. She studied the names, emails, phone numbers. And addresses. Mentally she tried to visualise her three suspects. Here was Gertrude, the older lady who'd been indulging liberally in champagne. She lived in Barnsbury. And here was Malcolm, the man she had rescued in the alleyway, but seemed so keen for the police not to be involved.

Which one was the American on the phone? There were two Patricks on the list. Pieterson and MacGregor. Pieterson sounded Scandinavian in origin and the man had been tall with blond hair. She couldn't be sure, but it was a good place to start. She closed her eyes, recreating in her mind how each had behaved that night. Who had been near enough to Pietro to swipe the key from his pocket? It was hard. Pietro was a tactile man – always hugging people. He worked the room, socialising with everyone. It would be much easier, decided Lena, if Simon's key had gone missing. He had spent the evening glued to Trudy's side and did not seem much of a hugger.

Lena smiled to herself. She loved her new idea. It was a perfect way to multitask. And now she finally had the details she needed, she could put it into action.

CHAPTER 11

'Well this is a treat. References first, though. Pass them through.'

Lena didn't usually make a habit of carrying references, but Gertrude had been insistent on the phone the day before. Lena pulled out the papers. Gertrude kept the chain on the door, but her hand reached through the opening to grab them, like a frog's tongue flicking out to catch a fly. The door shut abruptly.

Lena stood outside the door, unsure of what to do. Gertrude sounded thrilled with the idea of a free two-hour cleaning session when Lena rang her to say she had won her imaginary competition. Lena had been pretty thrilled with the idea herself. A chance to snoop around the houses of the gallery guests who had still been there when Pietro's keys were stolen. She hardly expected to find the painting, but there might be some clues. And potentially it was a way for her to get herself a few new wealthy clients. Only the innocent ones, of course. Gertrude was first thing Monday, but she had already lined up Patrick for later in the week. Malcolm was proving more elusive.

But now, standing outside the door of this pebble-dashed mews house in Barnsbury, Lena started to question the brilliance of the idea. At first she thought that whichever guest refused her offer would be the one most likely to be guilty and perhaps she could give that information to Inspector Blake. But that wasn't enough. She needed to find more. And as a cleaner, she would have the perfect excuse to look into every cupboard, every corner where something could be hidden. She just hoped she'd be able to uncover a clue.

Just as Lena was wondering if the lady had forgotten all about her, the door reopened. 'You check out,' said Gertrude, sounding like she still had suspicions. 'So you'd better come in.'

Lena entered. The house was even smaller on the inside that it had looked from the street: the opposite of a Tardis. Gertrude shooed Lena past and relocked and bolted the front door, popping the keys in her apron pocket. Lena tried to get a look at the keys but there were lots in the bunch. This women was security conscious. Was one of them Pietro's?

The decor was as Lena expected: the ubiquitous chintz of a house decorated in the seventies. It smelt of mothballs and loneliness. She followed Gertrude into the kitchen. 'You said I needed to provide the cleaning products,' said Gertrude. 'Here you are.' Lena stepped past her and opened the cupboard under the sink. 'I've marked the level of the bottles,' said Gertrude. 'So don't go thinking you can syphon them off.'

'Never!' said Lena. She'd met some suspicious people in her time, but this was ridiculous. This woman was deranged. 'I start upstairs. You have vacuum cleaner?'

'Of course. I don't live in the 1800s, you know.'

Lena took the vacuum from the cupboard Gertrude indicated, grabbed a duster and made her way upstairs. Gertrude followed close on her heels.

Lena went into the bedroom. Pink, as she expected, with curtains featuring delphiniums, daisies and rhododendrons, with the odd butterfly fluttering amongst the flowers. There was a profusion of satiny cushions on the bed. The room was tidy and sparse, but greyed with a thin veil of dust. Lena withdrew her own special anti-dust concoction made of olive oil, apple cider vinegar and a few drops of lemon essential oil mixed in an old plant-spray bottle and set to work.

'I'm not paying extra for that stuff,' said Gertrude, watching her from the doorway with her arms crossed.

'No,' said Lena. 'It is my own special mix. And it will leave a fresh smell behind.'

'I'm not buying it from you either,' said Gertrude. 'Don't try your sales pitch here.'

'You should go downstairs and have a rest,' said Lena. 'I will do the work.'

'No thank you very much,' said Gertrude, renewing her stance. 'I am quite happy watching you from here.'

Lena carried on cleaning, feeling incredibly self-conscious with Gertrude's eyes following her around the room like those of the Mona Lisa. She carefully dusted the selection of ornaments on the mantelpiece. There was a little china dog, a cat companion for it seated on a fluffy pink pillow, both common enough in this type of house. But something seemed off. No photos.

'You do not have photos of your family?' asked Lena, hoping to turn the conversation to the nephew she had heard mentioned at the reception. The one released from prison.

'Rotten gold-diggers,' said Gertrude, merrily. 'I'd rather not look at their money-grabbing little faces.'

'It is sad when we are separated from family,' continued Lena. 'My mother is in Hungary,' she told her. 'But we speak on the phone often.'

'Such a rip-off, these phone companies. Paying a fortune to speak to people. If they want to speak they should come and visit. Then they want biscuits, tea, money. Family. I can do without them all.'

'But when my mama comes to London to visit it is always so good to see her,' said Lena, thinking again of the nephew Gertrude had mentioned back at the reception. 'When you have been apart from someone for so long. Often it is not by choice. Almost like they are locked away from you.'

Gertrude repaid her with a grunt.

Lena continued to dust. 'I am sure no one wants to be a financial burden to you,' she said, remembering what Gertrude had said at the gallery. 'After all, you are on a pension. They must all have their own sources of income?'

'You vacuum,' said Gertrude. 'When you are done cleaning up here, I have something to show to you.'

'This house will be the most clean it has ever been,' said Lena. 'You will want to have your family visit just to see it sparkle.'

'Modest, aren't you?' said Gertrude. 'Wanting a tip, I expect.'

'No need,' said Lena. 'Free service for the competition winner.'

'Humph,' said Gertrude. 'Nothing is ever free.'

Lena dusted, vacuumed, changed the sheets, watered the plants and scrubbed the bathroom top to bottom. Gertrude kept her beady eye on her the whole time. Looking under the bed, Lena saw a long pole with a hook on the end. 'That's none of your business,' said Gertrude, when Lena turned to her with a questioning eye. When Lena was finished, she stood up straight and surveyed the sparkling top floor.

'What do you think?' she said, smiling at her work.

'It is clean,' said Gertrude. 'But you are a cleaner. What do you want, a medal?'

A thank you would be nice, thought Lena, but she kept her mouth shut.

'Follow me,' said Gertrude. 'I'll show you the living room.'

Gertrude's living room was painted off-white, like the spiced buttercream on a *Eszterházy* cake. But what drew Lena's eye was the multitude of framed postcards on the wall, each a tiny reproduction of a painting.

'Some art collection, eh?' said Gertrude. 'Impressive, isn't it?'

Lena leaned forward to peer at the postcards. 'Very nice,' she said, feeling confused.

'I own all of those,' said Gertrude.

'I can see that,' said Lena, wondering at the things people could make themselves brag about. 'It is an impressive collection of postcards.'

Gertrude laughed. 'Yes, no one will steal the postcards,' she said. 'Little do they know.'

'Know what?'

'That would be telling,' she said, fiddling with a chain around her neck. 'Right, time for you to clean the kitchen. I'm not paying you to stand around chatting.'

'You are not paying me at all,' muttered Lena, under her breath.

Back at home, Lena gave her orchid another polish with her duster. It was the first and only present Cartwright had ever given her and she loved it. She knew she should really leave the plant alone while she waited for Cartwright to arrive. Already the orchid had abandoned a large shiny leaf to her overzealous hand as she wiped off the dried echo of a splash of water. She'd hidden the leaf deep in her organic waste caddy, her shame concealed by avocado skin and flaccid carrots.

But she wanted to be able to show that she could take care of something. Nurture it through life. Lena blinked the old-fashioned sentiment away. She was pleased that Cartwright was still prepared to help her, but she would not fawn over him.

By the time Cartwright rang the bell, she'd worked herself into a very feminist frame of mind to make up for what she perceived as her earlier weakness. He was lucky to be allowed into her flat at all, let alone eat the *kiflies* she'd baked, hard little dry crescents of slightly burnt nutty pastry that they were. She'd make no apologies, she decided. A *kiflie* was a *kiflie*.

Lena swung open the door. Cartwright looked at her, clutching a potted plant. 'You seemed to like the last one,' he said, bowing slightly as he presented her with the orchid. It was resplendent in full bloom, with delicate flowers dotted with rich purple, like a *túrógombóc* dumpling stuffed with plums. Lena omitted a small gasp of delight. 'But I thought it must be dead by now,' Cartwright added.

'Why would it be dead?' said Lena, her pleasure replaced with indignation. She gestured to where the plant sat, its remaining leaves glowing but sadly bereft of flowers. 'I know how to look after the orchid,' she declared.

'That's not what I meant,' said Cartwright. 'My mother breeds orchids in one of her greenhouses, and I know how hard it is to keep them alive without special care. That's all.'

Lena felt dreadful. She wished she could push Cartwright out of the door and start all over again. But if she did so there was no guarantee he'd come back in. She could tell his disapproval over Dragg and Sarika's escape still lingered over her like cigarette smoke. 'Sorry,' she said. 'It is lovely and I very much love orchids. And thank you for coming. I was not sure that you would come after Brighton.'

Cartwright shrugged, but Lena could still see doubt in his eyes. 'Innocent until proven guilty,' he said. 'If it's good enough for Her Majesty's justice system, I suppose it has to be good enough for me.'

Lena smiled at Cartwright, gesturing to him to take a seat. 'Cup of tea?' she offered, feeling like a true-born Englishwoman.

'Thank you,' said Cartwright. 'That would be just the ticket.'

Lena went into the kitchen, using the clatter of the cups and the boiling of the kettle to pull herself together. Smiling and holding a tray with a cup of tea, one of strong coffee and a small plate of the most salvageable *kiflies*, she re-entered the room.

Cartwright took one and gave it a tentative sniff. 'I made them myself,' said Lena. She watched as he bit in and chewed. She reached to offer him another as he made approving noises but stopped herself. If she wasn't careful she'd turn into her mother, always pushing food into other people's mouths.

'Delicious,' said Cartwright, taking a healthy swig of tea. 'Very . . . Hungarian-tasting.'

Lena smiled. 'You have tried food from Hungary before?' she said.

'No,' admitted Cartwright. 'But this is how I imagine it. Nutty.'

Lena felt the urge to attempt to make him a goulash then and there. She swallowed it back down. Maybe she was turning into her mother?

'Your flat is lovely,' said Cartwright, taking his tea.

'Yes,' said Lena. She was pleased with it. 'Hardly room to swing a cat though,' she said, proud of the expression she had learned from her neighbour.

'Talking of cats, you should come and visit Kaplan now he is back with me,' said Cartwright, still attempting to chew the last of the *kiflie*. 'I'm afraid he's fattened up quite a lot while Mrs Everest looked after him when I was in Newcastle. It turns out she had a hairless cat when she was a child and has really taken to him. I don't think she really wanted to give him back. He looks like a little baby elephant now. Without the trunk, of course. Or the tusks, although his whiskers are really rather impressive these days . . .' Cartwright paused. 'Anyway, we're here for a task.' He pulled his laptop from its leather case. 'You are going to tell me all about your suspects and I am going to put them into my spreadsheet and see if we can work out some probabilities. Now we know that Sarika is safe, albeit AWOL, it's time to piece together this mystery of who took the painting.'

Lena switched seats so she was next to him on the little sofa and could see his screen. Their legs rested against each other comfortably, sending little shivers of pleasure up Lena's thigh. Cartwright opened the laptop and a spreadsheet sprung up. 'I've already inputted the formulae,' he said. 'So we just need to populate the suspects.'

Lena smiled. 'I have missed you,' she said.

Cartwright smiled back at her. He leaned forward and Lena closed her eyes ready for a kiss.

'Right,' said Cartwright. Lena opened her eyes. He'd leaned over to grab his tea and was now typing away with his other hand. 'Let's build a matrix for you.'

'Oh,' said Lena. 'I will get my board.' She stood up to cover her disappointment and went to fetch it from the bedroom.

'The painting is in the middle,' she told him.

'And the people with the keys are around the edge,' continued Cartwright, admiring the board. 'Blake told me the gallery door was opened with a key.'

'You have been talking to Blake about this?' asked Lena.

'Of course,' replied Cartwright. 'It is her case. And I have a lot of respect for her. I think she might be the best policewoman I have ever met.' He smiled again.

'The guests who were still there were Gertrude, Patrick and Malcolm,' continued Lena, her voice firm. Cartwright began entering their names.

'And Pietro and Trudy,' she continued. 'They were there. Simon had his own set of keys. I did too. Sarika had mine that night but one of her flatmates could have taken them from her room. Dragg, Kat or Lucia.'

Cartwright entered them all. 'Theft is very different to murder,' he said, his fingers still tapping the keyboard as if they were performing an intricate salsa routine. 'Motives are different, and therefore the profile of the criminal is different.' He smiled. 'DI

Blake will know all this. I wonder if I can ask to assist on the case, officially. Perhaps I'll ask her over lunch one day.'

Lena shoved the tray of *kiflies* in his direction. 'Eat another,' she commanded.

'Perhaps in a moment,' replied Cartwright, too deep in thought to notice her expression. 'Anyway, thieves. You might find an otherwise law-abiding person, driven to extremes, committing a murder. But it is unlikely that such a person would suddenly plan a theft. Steal something, yes; over 300,000 people shoplift every year in the UK. But it is mainly little things that they take, on the spur of the moment.'

'I have never,' said Lena, a little appalled.

'Me neither,' said Cartwright. 'But people do. There is a difference between opportunistic shoplifting and a theft like this. It has been planned. The thief has targeted the most expensive painting in the gallery and left everything else behind. He, or she, knew what they were doing.'

'So they know about art,' said Lena.

'Yes. Or someone told them.'

'That could make it anyone who has been in the gallery. They can all see the price.' The enormous price, thought Lena.

'Plenty of people would know, but we need the right type of person to want to steal it. Statistically it is most likely to be some-one who has committed a robbery before. Maybe even stolen a painting before. What do you know about their histories?'

Lena paused. Sarika was the only one who she knew to have a record of stealing. 'I find what I can,' said Lena, eventually. 'I will give free cleaning to the three clients there when the keys went missing. To look around their houses. I pretend that they have won a competition.'

'I'm not sure that is legal,' said Cartwright. 'But I have to admit, it is a clever idea.'

'I have done one already,' said Lena. 'Gertrude Humbledon.'

'And? What did you find out?'

'Not much. But she hates her family. She thinks that everyone is going to cheat her. She's paranoid. She followed me the whole time, thinking I was going to steal from her. And she was funny about some things she had in the house.' Lena explained about the postcards of paintings and what Gertrude had said about owning them all. Cartwright listened.

'She sounds like a psychopath,' said Cartwright. 'I've been researching their behaviour.'

Lena looked at him blankly. 'You think she is a murderer? She must be seventy years old.'

'I know that this is not a murder, but this is textbook. Antisocial behaviour. Lack of empathy. Egotistical. I'm not saying she is this severe, but do you remember the Clissold Park murderer? He'd kill his victims, photograph them and cut off an appendage – a finger, a toe, that kind of thing. Then he made a grisly shrine to them in his attic. You must remember; it was all over the press in the nineties.'

'Not in Debrecen,' replied Lena. 'But what does this have to do with Gertrude?'

'Don't you see?' said Cartwright, warming to his subject. 'Perhaps she is doing the same thing with paintings. She could be keeping them somewhere, but puts the postcards on her mantel-piece as a souvenir. She doesn't think she can get caught for that, but she can look at her ill-gotten gains whenever she wants! Classic profiling. Not a serial killer, but a serial art thief!'

Lena looked at him doubtfully. 'Maybe,' she said.

Cartwright sat and thought. 'I suppose it does seem a bit extreme,' he said. 'And I don't know if the profiling maps across different types of crimes like that. And you say she is seventy? It would be a tall order for her to break into a gallery and run off with the painting on her own.'

'She did mention a relative,' said Lena. 'Who she called a thief. I think he was in prison. I tried to find out more but she would say nothing.'

Cartwright's fingers sped over his keyboard. 'Let's see about that. Humbledon, you said the surname was? Google will know all about it. Ah, here we are.' Lena leaned in to get a closer look at his screen. 'David Humbledon, sounds right?' Lena nodded. 'Committed a string of burglaries and spent two years in prison. Was due out three weeks ago.' He grinned. 'We need more information. You have to go back, clean again,' he declared. 'But it could be dangerous.' Cartwright thought a moment. 'Maybe I should come and help you. It's not strictly procedure, but I can't see it getting me in too much trouble. It's like volunteering at the weekend.'

'I think she will be suspicious if I clean again, and she will not pay.'

'I'm sure you can work it out.' Cartwright sat back down and began typing merrily on his laptop. 'Anything we find will not stand up in court, of course, but it will give us a steer.'

'Maybe you can look in the police records,' said Lena. 'See what her nephew stole?'

'I can't,' he said. 'I've no reason to be snooping around there, and we don't want me to attract the wrong kind of attention from Blake.'

'I am sure you can work it out,' snapped Lena.

'I'll do some more research around psychopaths instead,' said Cartwright. 'Perhaps I can work out more about her character. I've got a brilliant book about profiling at home. I've always wanted to give it a go myself. Will be great fun if they are in it together. Like a familial Bonnie and Clyde.'

'This is no game,' said Lena, watching his excitement escalate. 'We need to help Sarika. I do not want her in prison.'

'No, of course not,' said Cartwright. 'Right, let's focus. Perhaps we can rule some people out, that would help. We need to find out if anyone has an alibi. Have you asked Kat and Dragg?'

'No,' admitted Lena. 'And I think it will be hard to get alibis for that time at night.'

'Perhaps Kat was online?' said Cartwright. 'That would take her out of the equation.' He made a note to himself. 'I'll check on the website.'

'Maybe I should check,' said Lena, not liking the thought of Cartwright looking at a naked Kat.

'I have an account now,' said Cartwright. 'It's no trouble.'

Lena shoved the tray of *kiflies* at him again.

'Pietro and Ophelia are married,' said Cartwright, waving away the *kiflies*. 'So they might be able to give each other alibis?'

'Unless they are in it together,' said Lena.

'And we are forgetting the most important person,' said Cartwright, breaking her reverie.

'What do you mean?'

'Sarika. Is there a chance she could have been with someone? A boy, perhaps?'

'No,' said Lena. 'She was thinking of meeting Lucia, but Lucia told me she was still at work so Sarika went home. To bed. Alone.'

'She couldn't have spent the night with Dragg?' said Cartwright. 'She seemed pretty besotted by him?'

'I know,' said Lena. 'But then he was with Kat. I do not think Sarika would do something like that. So sneaky.'

'She doesn't seem to have the best morals to me,' said Cartwright. 'We know she is a thief. We know she runs from the law. We know that she has stolen her flatmate's druggie boyfriend.'

Lena looked up at him sharply. 'It sounds like you think that she is guilty,' said Lena.

'I don't think we should rule it out,' said Cartwright. 'Especially since she ran away a second time.'

'She did not steal the painting,' insisted Lena.

'An open mind is all I ask,' said Cartwright. 'All options are still on the table.'

Lena looked at the table, fighting the urge to throw the uneaten *kiflies* at Cartwright's self-righteous face. 'I don't think it would do much good anyway,' continued Cartwright. 'Even if Sarika and Dragg were in bed together. He's not exactly a reliable alibi. I can't see Amy Blake believing a word he said. Not after his internet history.'

He typed something else into his laptop and then looked up, oblivious to Lena's anger. 'There is another possibility,' he said. 'A bit far-fetched, I'll give you that. But organised crime is often involved in art theft. Art is a great currency for criminals, a good way to make payments between gangs.'

'You are obsessed with gangs,' snapped Lena, thinking back to Timea's murder.

'There's been more activity recently,' he said, not listening. 'At this stage, we shouldn't rule out any possibilities, no matter how blue-skies they may seem. Remember Yasemin? Her Turkish gang could be back in town.'

'I think it is not likely,' said Lena. 'But more likely than Sarika being guilty.'

'I'm not so sure,' replied Cartwright.

Lena stood up. 'Thank you for your help,' she said. 'But I am sure you are busy. I do not think we need to see each other again until we clean for Gertrude.'

'Okay,' said Cartwright, looking confused as he got to his feet. 'Thanks for the biscuit.'

'*Kiflie*,' replied Lena, closing the door behind him.

CHAPTER 12

'I knew it,' said Gertrude, through the door, the chain still on. 'One free clean and now you're going to hassle me for the rest of my days.'

'But you have not yet had your windows cleaned,' said Lena. 'It is the second half of your prize. Did I not tell you that we would come back today?' she bluffed.

'Who is he?' said Gertrude, her suspicious eyes peering through the crack at PC Cartwright, dressed in overalls and holding a bucket.

'He is my assistant,' said Lena. 'I do the insides of the windows and he goes up the ladder to do the outsides.'

Lena cast a glance at Cartwright. He'd turned a little green. 'You didn't mention anything about climbing ladders,' he whispered.

'Shush,' whispered Lena. 'We are almost in.'

'And there is no charge?' said Gertrude. 'Are you sure?'

'None,' replied Lena.

'And you'll leave me alone after this? No trying to sell me stuff. I know what you lot are like. Going door to door selling your dishcloths.'

Lena decided not to think about what Gertrude meant by 'you lot'. 'This is the last part of your prize. If you want me to do any more work for you I will leave you my card, but I will not contact you.'

'Don't hang around out there then,' said Gertrude, opening the door. 'Get to work.'

Lena walked through to the kitchen and Cartwright followed, carrying the bucket, a squeegee mop and a worried expression. Lena put the hot tap on and waited for the water to warm.

'I pay for my water, you know,' said Gertrude, watching her.

'Hot water is much more effective,' said Lena. 'You want us to do a good job?'

Gertrude grunted and left the room.

'I'm not sure about this,' said Cartwright. 'You really should have told me your ladder plan.'

'You were there when we borrowed it from my friend Roland, the window cleaner. You put the ladder on your roof rack to get it here!' said Lena. 'What did you think it was for?'

'Couldn't we have shampooed carpets or something?'

'Her windows are filthy and she loves watching the neighbours through them. I knew she would say yes to this.'

Cartwright stood for a moment in silence. Lena put her finger under the running water and then snatched it away again. It was plenty hot. She put the bucket underneath the tap and filled it up, adding a good squirt of her homemade vinegar, lemon juice and baking soda concoction.

'You do want to go ahead?'

'Of course I do,' said Cartwright. 'It's just . . .' He paused. 'I've done lots of research on what to look out for and I'm not sure I'll be able to see well enough if I'm outside. Trying to balance. On a wobbly ladder. Miles from the ground.'

Lena laughed and patted him on the arm. 'We will job-swap,' she said, hoisting the heavy bucket out of the sink. 'I will go up the high wobbly ladder and you can clean the inside of the windows.'

Cartwright breathed a sigh of relief. 'If you don't mind, I really think that would be better,' he said. 'It's not that I don't want to, just in terms of looking for evidence . . .'

'Do not worry,' said Lena. 'Not everyone spent their childhood climbing trees like me!'

'What are you two plotting?' said Gertrude, re-entering the kitchen. 'You'd better not be eating my fish paste.'

'Do not worry,' said Lena. 'We are not interested in your pastes. We come to work only.'

'Get on with it then,' she said, gesturing to the windows. 'They won't wash themselves.'

'Classic psychopath behaviour,' whispered Cartwright to Lena. 'Paranoia, lack of empathy . . .'

'We are looking for a missing painting,' replied Lena, her voice quiet. 'Not bodies chopped up in the gutters.'

'We will start at the top of the house and work down,' Lena told Gertrude. 'That is the best way. If there are any drips we can catch them when we do the ground floor.'

'I'll be watching you,' said Gertrude.

'I know,' replied Lena. She handed Cartwright the bucket and walked out. 'Meet me upstairs,' she said to him. 'I will get the ladder set up.'

'You don't want me to hold the ladder?'

'You stay inside to look around,' said Lena. 'I'll be fine.'

'I don't like to be rude about the older generation,' said Cartwright, cradling a brandy in the empty pub down the road. 'But she was a horrible lady.'

Lena inspected her glass. She could see the ghost of the previous drinker's lipstick lingering. She put the glass down again. 'She is not my favourite person,' she agreed. 'But did you see anything suspicious?'

'It was hard to do anything with her beady eyes constantly on me,' said Cartwright. 'And you are right. There's something creepy about those framed postcards. I can't quite put my finger on what it is . . .'

A man entered, grunted an order at the barman and put some money in a fruit machine. The pub was filled with jangly music.

'You suspect her?' asked Lena, raising her voice to be heard.

'Very possibly,' said Cartwright. 'She wasn't a classic psychopath, though. Normally you'd expect them to be charming, superficially at least. If there's one thing you can't accuse Gertrude of, it's being charming. But I don't think that means she isn't a little unhinged, and a thief. Innocent until proven guilty, of course, but there is something not right about her.'

'I tried to get a photo of the postcards, through the window,' said Lena. 'I thought you could look them up and see if they are paintings that were stolen.'

'Brilliant idea,' said Cartwright. The fruit machine agreed, its tune reaching a crescendo.

'It did not work. I got a photo of my reflection in the glass.' The moment of fruit-induced excitement subsided. Lena heard the man swear and insert another collection of coins.

Cartwright smiled. 'I wish I'd taken a photo,' he said. 'But she was watching me so closely I couldn't put my hand in my pocket to get my phone without her swooping in on me. That kind of paranoia can be typical of thieves. They think because they are dishonest that everyone else is too. Perhaps she has the painting hidden. The problem is, we've no idea where.'

'We might have some idea,' Lena countered. She sipped her gin and tonic.

'How? I've been in every room in the house. I couldn't see anything but ornaments, mothballs and those damn postcards.'

'Not every room in the house,' said Lena, thoughtfully. 'There was a tiny window, right on the roof, at the back of the house.'

'I didn't see anything.'

'You can see it from the top of the ladder,' said Lena. 'And she was more nervous when we were up the stairs. She kept looking up. I saw a trapdoor in the ceiling on the landing. She had one of those poles with a hook to open it, under her bed.'

'You think she's got stuff hidden in the attic?'

'I am sure of it,' said Lena.

Cartwright took another sip of his brandy. 'There's no way we'd get a warrant to search the place,' he said. 'Even if I could reveal what we'd done so far. We don't have enough evidence.'

'We do not need a warrant,' said Lena. 'We have a ladder.'

'This is a terrible idea,' said Cartwright, for the umpteenth time. 'It's too dangerous. I can't let you do it. What if you fall?'

'Do you want to go up instead?' whispered Lena. 'I can stay down as the lookout if you prefer?'

Cartwright adjusted the black baseball cap he was wearing and parked the car around the corner from Gertrude's house. It was almost midnight. 'I'm not sure the ladder would take my weight,' he said. 'You're sure no one will see us?'

'I checked out the garden before,' said Lena. 'No houses overlook it. We can leave the car here and walk down the driveway. I left the garden gate unlocked. You carry the ladder.'

They unloaded it from the car and crept along the pavement. The street was deserted at that time of night. Lena led the way down the driveway and opened the gate. The hinge released a squeak of objection. Cartwright winced. 'Do not worry,' hissed Lena. 'No one will hear that.'

'I'm not worried,' replied Cartwright, with dignity. 'But remember, we are only here to look. No breaking. No entering. If you see the painting, you take a photograph that you leave anonymously at the station. No one can know I was involved in this.'

'Agreed,' replied Lena. She went into the garden, feeling the unmowed lawn soft beneath her feet. 'Extend the ladder and rest it on this wall,' she whispered. 'The window was around this part of the roof.'

Cartwright did as she said, giving the ladder a few good shakes to make sure it was steady. 'Perfect,' said Lena. 'You stay here and keep watch. I go up.'

'I will hoot like an owl if I see anything,' said Cartwright. Lena smiled as she climbed the ladder, a torch in her pocket. There were no owls in Islington, as far as she knew. In fact, she hadn't heard an owl hoot since she'd last visited her village back in Hungary.

The ladder didn't reach quite to the window, so Lena grabbed the guttering and hoisted herself up. She glanced down and saw Cartwright's worried face watching her. Treading gently and quietly, she scrambled up the slated roof and peered into the dormer window.

This window had not been cleaned in years. Perhaps never. She switched on the torch and shone it down. All she could see was the mixture of grimy, dried-up rainwater and dead, semi-fossilised insects coating the glass. She had no chance of seeing through.

Lena felt around the frame with her hands, looking for a way to open it. Unsurprisingly, there was none. She was loath to break the window – she had promised Cartwright that nothing would be broken. Plus it would make too much noise. Looking more closely, she could see the glass was reinforced with a crisscross wire, like they used for chicken coops. She couldn't break it if she wanted to. She had another idea.

'Cartwright,' she hissed.

'What is it?' he whispered back.

'Fetch the bottle of my special window cleaner from the car,' she said. 'And two rags.'

'Do you need to clean everywhere you go?' he said.

'Just do it. I cannot see through the window. It is too dirty.'

Lena stayed where she was, wiping the window as best she could with her sleeve. As she thought, it was hopeless. Years as an insect graveyard had made the grime stick, the creatures unwilling to give up their final resting place.

'I've got it,' said Cartwright.

'Bring it up,' said Lena.

'What?'

'Hurry. If you climb up part of the way you can pass it to me. Otherwise I have to come down on the roof and back again. It makes too much noise.'

Lena heard Cartwright take a deep breath. Extremely slowly, he began to climb the ladder. Partway, he stopped. 'Perhaps we can get a warrant after all,' he said. 'I've been thinking, that might be a better idea.'

'You said it was impossible,' whispered Lena. 'And we are here now. Just a few more steps and you pass me the bottle.'

'Okay,' said Cartwright. He took on two more rungs and stopped. 'That's it,' he said.

Lena looked down. She eased herself around so she was lying on her front facing him and held out her arms.

'Pass it to me,' she said.

Cartwright reached in his pocket for the bottle then held it out to her. She couldn't reach. 'Just one more step,' she said.

Cartwright took it and wobbled. The bottle was in his hand so he couldn't steady himself. He let out a small scream.

Lena grabbed his other hand. 'You are safe,' she said.

'I know,' said Cartwright, passing her the bottle and both rags but keeping hold of her hand.

Lena smiled at him, and squeezed the clammy hand she held in her own. Then she froze. 'Did you hear something?' she said. They both stayed there in silence, Cartwright clinging to the ladder with one hand, to Lena with the other.

Silence.

'My imagination,' said Lena. 'You go down. I take it from here.'

Cartwright didn't need to be asked twice. He was on the ground in a fraction of the time it had taken him to get up. 'You let me know if you need anything else,' he said, sounding more confident now the earth was once more under his feet.

Lena twisted herself back round and got to work on the window. Her special blend cut right through the dirt and she wiped at it vigorously with one rag until it was coated with tiny insect bodies, then she switched to the other to get the last of the grime off.

Lena felt a moment of pleasure at how clean the window had become. Then she pulled her torch from her pocket again and shone light into the room, pressing her face against the window. Her cleaner left the glass smelling like her mother's *csalamádé* – a pickled summer salad.

At first all she could see were bare wooden floorboards. Then she angled her torch to the walls and gasped at the beauty. The reds and oranges of an autumn in the Transylvanian hills, captured in a rectangular frame. She moved the torch to the next painting. A man looked back at her, his moustache gleaming and his eyes lively as he sat on horseback. Lena turned the beam to the next painting. A church, its stone glowing with the soft light of sunset.

'What do you see?' called up Cartwright, his voice soft but urgent.

'Beautiful paintings,' said Lena, turning her head to project her voice down to Cartwright without making too much noise. 'The postcards from downstairs. The real things are up here, just like we thought.' She turned to look back at the paintings, searching for *A Study in Purple*.

She felt something slip down her leg and heard it clatter on to the tiles. The bottle of window cleaner. It bounced once. Twice. Then fell to the ground.

'Ouch,' exclaimed Cartwright. 'Argh! It's splashed in my eyes.'

'Are you okay?' she asked, peering down at him.

'I'm blinded,' he said, blinking furiously.

'It is the lemon juice,' said Lena. She turned back to the window and put the beam on each painting in her search for *A Study In Purple*. 'It will sting but you will be okay.'

'A light!' said Cartwright.

'See, you are fine,' said Lena. 'Your vision is back.'

'No!' said Cartwright. 'There is a light on in the house. You need to get down.'

'I have not found *A Study in Purple*,' said Lena, furiously waving the beam around the room. She caught a glimpse of purple but it was in the near corner, almost directly under her. She couldn't angle herself to see it any better.

'Now, Lena. Get down now. Another light has come on. We need to go.'

Lena obeyed. She stepped back on to the ladder and clambered down, jumping the last few rungs. She grabbed the ladder and started to collapse it. The light in the kitchen in front of them came on.

'We need to get out of here,' said Cartwright.

'Grab the other end of the ladder,' said Lena. 'Then we run.'

'Did she see us?' asked Lena, once they were safely back in the car and driving away.

'I don't think so,' he said.

'We could go back,' said Lena. 'I saw something purple but could not see it well enough.'

Sirens sounded in the distance. 'No chance,' said Cartwright. 'That siren could be the police on their way here already. We need to get as far away as possible. I'm taking you home.'

Lena leaned her head back against the headrest and shut her

eyes for a moment. Had that been *A Study in Purple*? It must be. She smiled.

'I will call the station,' said Cartwright. 'Just in case. They need to search that house.'

'But they will know we were there,' said Lena.

'I'll call anonymously,' said Cartwright. 'And I'll pretend to be a neighbour who saw someone trying to break in. That should do the trick.'

CHAPTER 13

For once, Lena rang the bell at Penelope's house and didn't feel dread inside her. In fact, nothing could dampen her mood after yesterday. Not even the screams of an angry Casper that greeted her through the front door.

She'd found *A Study in Purple*. Or as good as. An old lady who had expressed an interest in the painting, declared herself on a pension, with an attic full of expensive art and a relative fresh from prison for theft. It took all Lena's willpower not to summon Sarika back immediately, but she forced herself to wait until they had confirmation. It couldn't be long now.

'Crispin has a cold,' said Penelope as she opened the door, handing the snotty baby to Lena. 'In June of all times. It's that damn baby yoga class I take them to. A hotbed of germs. If I don't watch out I'll catch it next, and that's the last thing I need. Don't just stand there, come in.'

Lena entered the house holding the sickly baby at a slight distance from her. He sneezed and Lena felt her face covered in a delicate little shower. She smiled anyway, stepped over Penelope's handbag, put the baby back in his Moses basket and went into the kitchen for a paper towel. It wouldn't be long before the police found the painting. Cartwright had impersonated a concerned neighbour and called the police last night, reporting strange men lurking on Gertrude's roof. With any luck they'd do a thorough search of the house and find the secret attic. If that didn't work, Lena would get Blake and Gullins up there herself. Even if she had to drag them.

'Come on you,' she said to the baby, picking it up, basket and all. 'It is a beautiful day outside and some fresh air will do you good.'

'I've got to do a conference call,' shouted Penelope as she left. 'One of my old clients is having a PR nightmare. I'm consulting. I'll be at Le Péché.'

Lena ignored her and stepped into the garden. The rose bushes were in full bloom. Lena suspected they had a gardener who also did his share of childminding. Casper looked up at her from his seat at the bistro-style table, dirt all over his face as he drew yet another dinosaur, this one surrounded by roses, pink this time. His *leitmotif*, thought Lena, remembering what she'd learned at the gallery. She shook her head. She'd spent too much time with Pietro.

'That is very good,' she told him, peering more closely at the crayon drawing. Little clocks and gadgets she couldn't decipher punctuated the roses. 'Is it your garden?'

'There are no dinos in our garden, silly,' Casper replied. He stuck his tongue out at Lena.

'Watch your brother,' said Lena, feeling her good mood start to be replaced with a headache. She went back inside to start cleaning the kitchen.

The front door opened and Penelope burst back through. 'Can't find my phone,' she said by way of explanation. 'Where is it?'

'Have you looked in your bag?' said Lena. 'That front pocket where you keep it?'

'Of course I have,' snapped Penelope. 'Would you phone it, please?'

Lena fetched her own phone and selected Penelope's number. Both women waited in silence.

'I bet it's still on bloody silent after my morning meditation,' said Penelope. She looked at Lena, an ominous glint in her eye. 'A lot of stuff has gone missing recently,' she said.

Lena shrugged, refusing to rise to another implied accusation. 'Perhaps you should be more careful,' she said coldly. 'With your nice things.'

That was it. Penelope crumpled and sank to the hallway floor. 'I'm so sorry, Lena,' she said. 'I know that sounded like I'm accusing you. Of course I'm not. It's just it's all too much.' Lena paused for a moment, then sat on the floor next to Penelope and put her arm around her. Penelope pushed her head into Lena's shoulder and began to sob.

'My husband comes home later and later every night,' she said, her voice thick with tears. 'I think it's to avoid me. It's only so long before he finds some pretty young thing with a flat stomach and no children to start up with. My boss doesn't think I should come back to work at all. He says being a mother is a full-time job. But I miss the office, the journalists, even the clients. I love PR.' Penelope wiped her nose on her sleeve, as Lena had seen Casper do earlier. 'I miss Timea. She was so sweet to me. You are lovely too,' she added quickly. 'But she loved being with the children. Maybe more than I did.' Penelope covered her mouth as though she wished she hadn't said that. Lena hugged her closer.

'Can you get help?' she suggested gently. 'To look after the children?'

'Whenever I suggest getting help with childcare, my husband suggests his mother should come to stay with us.' Penelope shuddered. 'I can't have her in this house, judging me all the time, thinking I can't cope.' She looked up at Lena. 'And she would be right. I can't. Losing my phone, that's going to be the last straw for my job. My boss already hates me doing these keeping-in-touch days with the office. Missing this call, that will be it.'

Lena stroked Penelope's hair. From her vantage point on the

floor she could see an errant crayon, hiding underneath the sofa. Purple.

Suddenly it made sense.

Lena gave Penelope a quick kiss on the top of her head, then lurched forwards and grabbed the crayon. She stood up. 'Come with me to the garden,' she said.

'I told you, I've got to find my phone,' grumbled Penelope, slowly clambering to her feet. 'It's not going to be outside.'

Lena grabbed the picture Casper had done last week from its place on the fridge door and studied it more carefully. A dragon, purple roses, a tiny clock and a star. She handed it to Penelope who took it without looking and followed her outside.

Crispin was lying in his cot in the shady spot of the garden where she'd left him. 'Look at the picture,' she told Penelope. 'See what it tells you?'

'That you are having a meltdown too,' said Penelope, looking at Lena with concern. 'But what can you have to be stressed about?'

Lena rolled her eyes at that comment. She approached Casper, who was carefully drawing the teeth on the dragon with his yellow crayon. Next to the pink roses he had drawn a tiny clock and a little star again. Another gadget had been added alongside. Lena looked more closely at it.

'Is that your mama's phone?' she asked him. He looked up at her and beamed, nodding over and over. Penelope snatched the picture from the garden table.

'Let me see that,' she said. Casper reached out and tried to tear the picture back from his mother's hands, but she held it too high for him to reach.

Lena put her hand on Penelope's back. 'Casper can explain it to us,' she said. Penelope allowed Lena to take the picture back and put it on the table. 'That clock,' she said, pointing to it. 'Is that your mama's watch?'

Casper nodded, less sure of himself now, watching his mother's expression. Penelope knelt down next to him.

'That star,' said Penelope. 'That's a diamond, isn't it?'

Casper nodded. 'Clever mummy,' he said, smiling again. 'Looking at my pictures.'

'Perhaps I don't do that enough,' said Penelope. 'Perhaps I am not the only one finding it too much?'

Lena walked over to the rose bush. The blooms were a light shade of purple, like Casper's blueberry yogurt. And the lost purple crayon. Penelope followed her. Lena knelt down.

Hanging from one of the bush's lower branches was a pendant, the diamonds catching the sunlight and projecting it back as myriad tiny rainbows. Lena reached out and delicately unhooked the pendant from the bush, handing it to Penelope.

'I go inside to clean,' she said. 'But I think Casper will show you where to find the rest,' she said. Casper ran over, nodding again so furiously that Lena thought he would make himself sick.

'Find Mummy's phone first,' said Penelope, her voice soft. 'I will make a little call here in the garden while you sit on my lap and draw me another dragon.'

Lena watched as Casper scooped the phone from under a large rock, wiped the earth off on his trousers and handed the phone to his mother. She kissed him on the cheek and lifted him back to her lap, handing him the purple crayon as she dialled.

Lena began doing the dishes, feeling her earlier good mood return. She'd figure out a way to get Penelope the help she needed. As soon as she'd confirmed *A Study in Purple* was back with its rightful owners and Sarika could come home.

CHAPTER 14

'It is nice to see you,' said Lena, walking into a café the next day.

PC Gullins looked up from his plate of breakfast: eggs, bacon, sausage and beans, all swimming in grease. 'What the hell are you doing here?' he said. 'I'm on my break.'

'You are not hard to track down,' said Lena. 'I want to know if you have any progress on the case? It is two weeks now.'

'I don't think I exactly owe you an update,' said Gullins, concentrating on his eggs once more. 'You don't own the painting.'

'I need to know if Sarika has been proven innocent yet. Off the ...' Lena searched for the expression. 'Crook,' she said triumphantly.

'Hook,' said Gullins. 'Well, then Sarika herself can track me down like a crazy stalker while I'm trying to eat my breakfast.' Gullins shovelled a forkful of sausage into his mouth and chewed angrily. 'Oh no, wait, she's run off.' Lena sat down opposite him and ordered a coffee from the curious waitress.

'Coffee is terrible here,' said Gullins.

'Coffee is terrible everywhere in this country,' replied Lena. 'But at least it is not tea.' Gullins picked up his mug and took a deep slurp. 'This country was built on tea,' he said. 'What's the rush, anyway? I suppose you heard from that hotshot boyfriend of yours about the burglary the other night? I told him there were a few paintings there and now he keeps going on at me about it too.'

'Well?' She looked around and leaned forwards. She could smell the greasy aroma of bacon fat floating in the air. 'Was one of them *A Study in Purple*?'

Gullins looked at her for a moment and then burst out laughing. Lena felt herself sprayed with tiny indeterminate chunks of his breakfast. 'I didn't even find a cup of tea!' he said. 'All the way to that old lady's house and not a cuppa. Not even a biscuit. Rude old biddy. Had a nice collection of paintings, though, since you seem so interested. No burglars to be seen.' He looked at her, suspicion in his eyes.

Lena returned his gaze and feigned surprise. 'Anything you recognised?'

'Not a dickybird.'

Lena had no clue what that meant, but guessed it was in the negative. She tried not to let disappointment cloud her face. Or her judgement.

'But how did she afford all that? A pensioner?'

'I didn't mention anything about her being a pensioner,' said Gullins. 'I know you two lovebirds are up to something.'

'I do not know what you mean,' said Lena. 'I just wanted to know how an old lady affords the paintings.'

'It's none of your business. Perhaps she got a payout from her husband's life insurance when the poor sod passed away. Nothing there was stolen property. She showed me the receipts. All legit. Likely the old bird didn't trust the banks so invested in art.' Gullins scooped up the last of the baked-bean juice with an emaciated scrap of white toast. 'So leave the policing to the professionals. Okay?' Gullins put a crumpled five-pound note on the table and stood up to leave as Lena's coffee arrived.

She took a sip. He was right – it was terrible.

But not as terrible as the news she'd just had. Gertrude didn't have the painting. At least not in her house. Lena piled sugar into the coffee, stared at the ghost of Gullins's breakfast on the empty plate and forced herself to think. It seemed Gertrude was innocent. She tried to swallow her disappointment along with her coffee. There was a bright side. It was one suspect eliminated. It meant Lena could focus her attention elsewhere.

She had to close in on the people who knew the most about the painting. Time to swallow what pride she had left and grovel to Pietro.

Lena decided to visit the gallery after closing time when Pietro would be upstairs on the gallery sofa, drinking tea and updating his Twitter or Instagram.

To her surprise, the gallery door was not locked. Hadn't he learned anything from being burgled? She peered inside but couldn't see anyone. Lena tutted to herself. If this was what their security was like, no wonder the gallery had been robbed. Lena stepped inside. She could hear voices, the tension in them obvious. The sound was coming from upstairs. Lena crept further forwards, straining to hear what was said. As if she was powering the conversation with only her will, the volume rose.

'It won't take long at all,' she heard Pietro say. 'As soon as the insurance comes through, you'll get your money. I promise you.'

'That is too late.' Lena didn't recognise the other voice. There was a foreign lilt to it that was familiar to her but she couldn't quite place it. She closed her eyes. Yes she could. He was Turkish. *Szar.* She hoped he wasn't from Yasemin Avci's gang. The last thing she needed was that diminutive but angry woman coming back to Islington.

'It's out of my control,' said Pietro. Lena could hear panic rising in his voice.

'Not my problem,' said the man.

'Please put that down,' Pietro pleaded. 'Its wings are very fragile.' Lena thought of the collection of porcelain butterflies upstairs. They were so delicate it seemed they would chip if you so much as looked at them too hard.

She heard a crash.

'Butterfingers,' said the man, with a laugh. 'You should be more careful. Apparently this stuff is valuable. Now this one, this one looks pretty.'

'Leave *La Bella Mariposa* alone!' said Pietro. 'I told you – you'll get your money.'

Lena had heard enough. She threw herself up the spiral staircase, taking the steps two at a time. She burst in on the men, grabbing the large tortoiseshell porcelain butterfly from the intruder's hands before he even knew what was happening.

'Get out,' she shouted at the man. 'Get out of this gallery before I call the police.'

'Nice bit on the side,' he replied, regarding Lena coolly. 'Does that pretty redhead wife of yours know?'

'Lena! What are you doing here?' said Pietro, his voice shaking.

'I mean it,' said Lena, her phone in her hand. 'I call the police now. Destruction of private property.'

The man stood up and faced off to Lena. He was shorter than her but stocky, and he looked powerful, his muscles rippling beneath his T-shirt like a tiger about to pounce. 'Don't you threaten me,' he said. 'I could eat you up, spit you out and still have room for a nice tray of *baklava*.'

Lena pulled herself upright and stepped closer. She was a head taller than him. 'Sorry, I forgot,' she said. 'You can smash porcelain butterflies with a flick of your wrists.'

'Lena!' exclaimed Pietro. He turned back to the man. 'I'm so sorry,' he said. Pietro looked around, panicked. He picked up another of the butterflies. 'Here, take this, a gift for you, Erjan. Lena, apologise.'

Erjan looked at them both and laughed. 'Keep your bugs,' he said. 'Like the lady said, I've got bigger things to smash.' He looked straight at Pietro, who averted his gaze, suddenly finding a speck of dust that worried him on the butterfly.

'Get out,' said Lena.

'You have two weeks,' said the man to Pietro. 'Two weeks. After that, it won't be the butterflies your girlfriend here will be scraping off the floor.'

He stomped down the stairs. Both of them watched him go. Lena followed the man to the door and bolted it from the inside as soon as he was gone. Then she went to the kitchen and fetched a glass of brandy for Pietro. On second thought she grabbed the bottle too. He was stroking the butterfly's wing when she returned. She took it from him and handed him the brandy. He took a sip and then cradled the glass in his shaking hands. They sat together in silence.

Finally Pietro spoke. 'I'm in trouble, Lena,' he said.

'I can see that,' she replied. 'Drink your brandy. Then you need to tell me what is going on.'

'I was to be the business brain,' said Pietro, eventually. 'And Simon was going to be the artist.'

'You were the business brain?' said Lena, unable to keep the incredulity from her voice.

'Of course,' snapped Pietro. 'I know lots about art and I come from a successful family business. It runs through my blood.'

'So you provided the money,' said Lena.

'Well yes,' confessed Pietro. 'That was the plan. I invested the start-up capital to get the place up and running, and Simon was meant to paint. He was the talent. He'd sold some pieces already,

157

straight out of art school. He was going to be hung in the Summer Exhibition! But then he went and lost his mojo. He's barely painted a thing since the gallery opened. So we had to start selling other artists' work, on commission, while we waited for him to get inspired again. It's been almost twenty years and no joy. We've both resigned ourselves to just selling work by other artists. '

'When did the gallery open?'

'It was just before I got back together with darling Ophelia,' said Pietro. 'That's when I got the first decent-size chunk of my trust fund. Simon's lucky I kept him on at the gallery, you know. We were going to be partners originally and he'd provide the paintings to cover his share, but when those didn't show up I made him the manager and put him on a salary instead. He's surprisingly organised, for an artist. Ex-artist, I suppose. He can even sell a bit, even if he does hate the social occasions we put on. He's got a nice intensity the women seem to like. And the men, for that matter.'

'Which does he . . . ?' Lena struggled for the words.

'Women, I suppose, are more his thing. Never seems to be that interested in either. One of these arty asexuals. All the rage these days.' Pietro sighed. 'If only he'd paint a bloody picture. That would solve all our problems. He's better than Trudy, you know. Or could be.'

'All your problems?' said Lena. 'But I thought you were rich?'

'I am,' he said. 'That's the heartbreaking thing. But it is tied up in trusts. I get a chunk every five years.'

'And the chunk is gone?'

'I run a business. I invest. Art dealing isn't easy, you know.'

'Simon told me you bailed out the business with the trust fund.'

'I did. But *A Study in Purple* was a big expense. It's a year till I get another instalment, and we have bills. Lots of bills. So I borrowed from the bank, just to tide me over until we sold *In Purple*.

But then we didn't. I can't understand it. I thought it would get snapped up. It's a masterpiece. The bank wouldn't lend me any more. Then Mehmet, who owns that lovely Turkish restaurant across the road, suggested a company he knew. Loans for business people. Professionals, but less particular than the banks. More forceful too, as it turns out. In over my head. You've just met their bailiff. As you can see, now I'm in a bit of a jam.'

Lena paused, watching as Pietro took another sip of brandy. Had Pietro taken the painting? Stolen it from his own gallery out of desperation? For a moment she felt angry at him for putting her through this, for putting Sarika through it. Then she looked at him, shaking in front of her like a butterfly being cast about in a stormy wind.

'So you arranged for *A Study in Purple* to go missing,' she said gently. 'To claim the insurance.'

Pietro looked at her for a moment, confusion clouding his face. Then indignation took over.

'Absolutely not!' said Pietro, slamming his glass on the little coffee table. Brandy slurped over the edge, forming a small puddle on the table. Lena fished in her bag for a tissue and mopped up the mess before the alcohol could leave a permanent mark. 'I did no such thing.'

'But you said . . .'

'I simply called in a favour to get Trudy here. We were pretty close for a while, met when she came to give a lecture at our art school, must have been almost twenty-five years ago. Damien Hirst was the new noise back then. Everything was about the psychological effects art has on the viewer, dissolving the distinctions between life and art.'

Lena felt her impatience rise. Was she going to get a lecture on art of the 1990s?

'Well, Trudy and I dissolved a few distinctions between student and lecturer, let me tell you! Ophelia wasn't too pleased, although we weren't married back then. Took me four years to win her back.'

'And what is going on now?' said Lena, looking at him closely.

'Not much to it. I heard Trudy would be in the UK for the Summer Exhibition and got her lined up to be an attraction at the gallery. It would have worked, as well. I had three seriously interested parties for the painting that night. You saw them. Three people who would have paid me a damn sight quicker than the bloody insurance company.' He took another swig from his brandy glass. 'It's the worst thing that could happen to me, that blasted painting being stolen.'

Lena refilled Pietro's glass and thought about whether to believe him. He smiled at her.

'Thanks, Lena,' he said. 'I do feel a bit better now I've talked to someone about this.'

'Simon does not know?' said Lena. 'He must see the accounts.'

'God no. He knows the gallery struggles but still thinks I can bail us out whenever I need to from my trust fund.'

'And Ophelia?'

'She has no idea we have any problems at all. All she does is mingle with the clients and put pictures on the website. I can't let her down. And the children. Both at boarding school. Thank goodness they have a separate trust or I'd have to send them to a state school.' He shuddered. 'God, I wish I'd never borrowed from those scoundrels. People in the art world are always borrowing money and taking forever to pay it back. It's how we work! I should have known not to get involved with them as soon as I went to their office. It was above a Turkish barber's shop, you know. Men getting their ear hairs singed off with matches while they drink coffee sludge and home-brewed liquor and chain-smoke. But I was desperate. I told myself it would be okay. Once I sold the painting I could pay them back.' He looked at her, his eyes filled with fear.

Lena sat back. She wasn't sure if she believed he had had nothing to do with *A Study in Purple*'s disappearance or not. But having him on her side could only help the investigation.

'It is a difficult situation,' she said. 'But there is good news too. He gave you two weeks to pay. We will make that time count.'

CHAPTER 15

Lena walked up to the grand Georgian house, complete with pillars and a portico. She tipped up a sad window box to look beneath, as instructed. Its plants had long since departed from the land of the living. Four surprised woodlice immediately started to panic at the sunlight, running in all directions. A centipede coolly made its way beneath a dead leaf, and a key gleamed up at her as promised by Patrick, the gallery guest who had constantly been on his phone that night. She picked up the key, carefully replaced the window box and unlocked the front door. She called inside the house and waited a moment for a reply, but it was hardly necessary. Lena could tell it was empty. She was pleased. Cartwright had a day off and had agreed to come with her. She was looking forward to being together while they cleaned and looked for clues.

She gestured to Cartwright, waiting in the car. 'It is clear,' she said. He jumped out with a smile.

'Excellent,' he said. 'I've been looking forward to this. Good old-fashioned detective work – like Sherlock Holmes. And not a ladder in sight! You've met this man already. What's he like?'

Lena made her way through to the kitchen. 'He spent the whole time at the gallery on his phone. He did not say thank you when I filled his glass, and he flirted with Sarika but wore a

162

wedding ring. He was having an argument on the phone later, outside the gallery. I think it was over money.'

'He sounds lovely.' Cartwright followed her through. They both looked at the kitchen. 'I can see why he took up your offer,' he said.

Lena looked around, her heart sinking at the way this man lived. It was a large kitchen, with a grand range cooker, granite worktops the colour of the ocean and a smart solid wood table with four chairs. But it was a disaster area. All the baking trays were filthy, with what looked like remnants of a combination of fish fingers, chips and pie crusts still clinging to them. There were dirty frying pans containing what might have been juice from various steaks. Empty ready-meal packets lined the counter. There was a fruit bowl with what could once have been an orange, but was so mouldy it looked more like a curled-up furry grey rat.

'I do not want to be sexist,' said Lena. 'But this is what happens when a man lives alone.'

'This is not what my kitchen looks like!' declared Cartwright.

'Really?' said Lena.

'Not at all,' said Cartwright. 'In fact, perhaps you'd let me cook for you sometime soon? I'm pretty handy with a leg of lamb.'

Lena felt herself flush with pleasure. 'I would like that,' she said. She felt her colour intensifying and began moving around to conceal the cause. 'Now, we must get to work.' Lena handed him a pair of rubber gloves and looked around for a job for him. 'You start collecting mouldy food,' said Lena. 'I saw an organic waste-bin in the front garden, tipped on its side under some leaves. I do not think he has ever used it, so it might have moss growing on it. Can you get it?'

'I thought maybe I'd just have a look around first,' said Cartwright. 'See if I can find that painting?'

163

'If you can find the painting in this house I will eat that fuzzy orange,' said Lena. 'We need to clean first.' She watched his face fall. This was his day off, and he was the only person who was on her side. Plus he was going to cook for her. 'I will clean up the old food,' she relented, looking around for a less revolting job for Cartwright. 'You can water the plants while you look for clues.'

The plants were a lost cause, but Cartwright didn't seem to notice, merrily emptying the jug Lena filled with water into the dehydrated pots. Lena couldn't imagine who would let plants in their care get in such a state, thinking with affection of her small but growing orchid garden. 'Any guesses about what this man is like?' she asked him, while at the same time trying to scrape fish-finger breadcrumbs off a baking tray with a dubious-smelling sponge. The breadcrumbs clung on stubbornly. 'You can tell much about a person from their kitchen.'

'*You* can,' replied Cartwright. 'I remember when you could tell Yasemin was a gangster from those pizza boxes she left lying around.'

'You can too,' said Lena, with a smile. 'You are the fancy police inspector.'

'Constable,' said Cartwright, colouring a little. 'You start.'

'Patrick is single now, but clearly this used to be a marital home,' said Lena. 'His wife must have left him. All the meals are for one.'

Lena ran hot water to fill the greasy frying pans. She squirted in a bit of washing-up liquid. They both watched the tiny bubble that escaped the bottle meander up to the ceiling. Then unceremoniously pop to nothing.

'He likes art,' Cartwright added, gesturing to a watercolour hanging above the dining table. Lena looked at it more closely. It depicted a crisp green apple sitting in a bowl with a bunch of bananas, a bit of discarded orange peel in the foreground. She leaned in closer to read the signature, scrawled in the bottom right-hand corner.

'I need to see more of the house to work out the rest,' said Cartwright. 'I'm not as expert at kitchens as you.'

Lena smiled. 'I will get these pans soaking,' she said. 'Then let us explore. Here, you can carry this tray, you will find it useful. The kitchen is full of pans but no plates. Those will be scattered around the house. In front of the television mainly, I guess.'

Lena was right. She collected plates strewn around the otherwise lovely living room and piled them on to Cartwright's tray. They also found a number of mugs of half-drunk coffee and empty wine glasses, some of which had been used as ashtrays.

'This man is disgusting!' exclaimed Cartwright.

Lena looked at the living room. There were various scrunched-up socks lying around like soft cricket balls, and a messy mountain of shoes, still lying upturned where they had been kicked off. But the walls were painted a delicate shade of green that reminded Lena of the lichens that grow in the Transylvanian hills. The curtains depicted wisteria, clambering up from the floor to the ceiling, dappled with leaves that matched the wall colour. There was a watercolour in this room too, hung in the far corner. It showed wildflowers messily arranged in a glass vase: daisies, poppies and Queen Anne's lace. A butterfly was in the top left corner, the tip of one wing almost escaping the confines of the painting. 'That's beautiful,' said Cartwright, his eyes following her gaze.

'I prefer orchids,' said Lena, and then blushed fiercely at betraying herself. She didn't want Cartwright to know how much she treasured his gifts.

'It's not very masculine though,' said Cartwright. 'I think this man is only recently separated.' Lena nodded.

'He probably cheated,' said Lena, her voice full of disapproval. 'He is perhaps a man who spent too much time at the office and not enough with his art-loving wife. Even at the gallery, he was always on the phone.' She thought for a moment. 'But I do not know what he was doing at the gallery, if he is separated. Maybe he tries to win her back?'

'I don't think that will help us determine if he stole the painting,' continued Cartwright, focused for once. 'I'll have a snoop at his papers. There might be some kind of trail there.'

'I will clean,' said Lena, feeling unable to concentrate on anything else while the heap of shoes stared mournfully at her. 'Then I will help you.'

Cartwright busied himself shuffling through desk drawers in the dining room. Lena did a quick audit of the rest of the house. There were three bedrooms, but two sat perfectly clean and unused, a lonely contrast to the rest of the house. The master bedroom made up for it in filth. Dirty clothes covered the floor. There were empty packets of men's underwear sitting on top of piles of dirty ones: this man had been buying new pants instead of washing the ones he had. Lena collected a pile of laundry and carried it down to the washing machine in the kitchen. She was starting to feel sorry for Patrick. He'd looked so together at the gallery, masterfully addressing a minion on the telephone. At home his life was a mess.

Divorce didn't feel right to her, but he was certainly not living with anyone at the moment. She went back upstairs to look for evidence of a woman, but was distracted by the state of the yellowing sheets, emitting a musty odour. She stripped the bed. The sheets would go into the wash next.

Cartwright popped upstairs. 'I've found some bank statements,' he said. 'A lot of money has left this man's account recently.'

'Patrick,' said Lena. 'His name is Patrick.'

'Yes, well, Patrick withdrew almost twenty thousand pounds last month. And a similar amount the month before.' Lena looked at him thoughtfully. 'Paying for people to steal the painting, perhaps?'

'That is a lot to spend on a robbery for that painting,' said Lena. 'How much could he get for it on the black market?'

'Probably not much more than twenty per cent of its value. Maybe that is just one painting in a series he is stealing,' said Cartwright. 'Have more gone missing, from other galleries?'

'Ask Detective Blake,' said Lena.

'Good idea. She is bound to know.'

Lena shrugged. Cartwright's phone went off. 'That's my supervisor,' he said. 'I need to go. My victim, Mr Theopolis, has regained consciousness.'

'That is brilliant news,' said Lena. 'I will finish here. Thank you for your help.'

'I really think we are on to something,' said Cartwright. 'I have tomorrow morning off too, perhaps I can help then?'

'Tomorrow morning I meet Trudy Weincamp, the artist,' said Lena. 'I do not want to scare her with a policeman. But I can see you later to tell you what she says?'

'I get off at four,' said Cartwright. 'It's a date.'

They looked at each other awkwardly for a moment, the 'date' word echoing between them. Lena wasn't sure if their previous meetings had been dates or not. But this one seemed to be. 'Well, goodbye,' said Cartwright. He leaned in and pecked Lena on the cheek. She felt a dazzle of electricity.

'Goodbye.' Lena watched him leave. From the back he was a perfectly formed upside-down triangle, with broad shoulders, muscular arms, narrow waist and a perfect bottom. Lena sighed a little. If he wasn't going to make it clear where they stood, perhaps she would have to make a move herself. She closed her eyes for a moment. If only he wasn't quite so polite, he'd lean in, wrap those muscly arms around her . . .

Lena opened her eyes and glanced at her watch. This house wouldn't clean itself, and its occupant certainly wasn't going to do it. She went back downstairs and looked at the sad pile of shoes.

She'd seen a little tin of polish in one of the kitchen drawers. Patrick might not deserve clean shoes, but the shoes themselves would certainly appreciate it. She picked up a *Racing Post* newspaper from where it had been abandoned and made a protective cover with it on the floor. She set to work, breathing in the refreshing chemical scent. Polishing shoes always helped her think. And she had plenty to keep her mind busy.

CHAPTER 16

Trudy was staying at a hotel so Lena couldn't exactly offer her cleaning services, but she'd called her anyway earlier in the week to try to arrange a meeting. To her surprise, Trudy was happy to oblige and suggested breakfast on Saturday at her Shoreditch hotel.

Lena got the bus down, alighting at Shoreditch High Street. She watched a group of revellers stumble along the dirty pavement, clearly still on an adventure from the previous night's clubbing. The man clutched a large plastic bottle of beer, glitter twinkling in his beard. The girls both had pink hair and were passing a bottle of vodka between them. They greeted Lena with gusto as she glanced at her watch. Eight a.m. How did they have the energy?

Things were much more civilised inside the hotel. The lobby was cavernous and adorned with uncomfortable-looking furniture shaped like lips and an ear. Lena banged her head on a low-hanging light sculpture before an extremely attractive member of the reception staff in a tight-fitting suit came to her rescue. He guided her to the dining room, where Trudy greeted her with an enthusiastic wave and a kiss on the cheek that smelt of cigarettes.

'Sorry about the unsociable hour,' said Trudy, once they were settled. She waved at the waiter. 'Two coffees, pronto. And eggs Benedict. What do you want to eat, Lena?' Lena felt flustered for a moment then ordered the same, her menu unopened. She couldn't remember the last time she'd eaten out at breakfast. It felt like such an extravagance when spreading toast with *túró* cheese was so easy at home.

'I'm booked at the Royal Academy all day and then have drinks and dinners into the night,' Trudy continued. 'I jam-pack my schedules while I'm here so I can get all the publicity out of the way at once and then get back to my studio in New York and start actually painting.'

'Thank you for making the time for me,' said Lena. She looked at Trudy. The artist's close-cropped hair seemed a brighter shade of pink today and her blue eyes were twinkling in her tanned face.

'I need pleasure with my business,' said Trudy, with a smile. Lena fiddled with the fork in front of her, making sure it was at an exact right angle. 'No need to feel uncomfortable,' laughed Trudy. 'I'm just messing around. What can I do for you?'

Lena paused for a second, and then decided to tell Trudy everything. 'Sarika, my assistant, went missing at the same time as your painting. I do not think she stole the painting. But the police do. I try to find out who took it to clear Sarika's name so she can come home. I hope that you can help.'

Trudy paused for a moment, digesting the information. 'I'm sure if you think your friend didn't do it, then she didn't,' she said. 'But I don't see how I can help.'

'Was there anyone behaving oddly at the reception? Did anything seem not right?'

'Everyone behaves oddly at those things,' said Trudy with a laugh. 'And I was out of it. Everyone knows I like a drink, but I hadn't felt like that since I took quite a cocktail of drugs at that festival in Texas. Your vodka must be stronger over here!'

'Did Patrick talk to you?'

'Who?'

'Patrick Pieterson. Blond, rude, and on his phone most of the night.'

170

Trudy laughed. 'Oh yes, I remember him. The other American. Seemed rich.'

'Anyone else stand out?'

'Apparently there were a few people interested in the painting,' continued Trudy. 'God knows why.'

'What do you mean?'

'I remember how I felt when I painted it. I was full of love, the kind of love that makes you excited, like you could conquer the world. Of course, the bastard dumped me a couple of months later. I was on women only for a few years after. But I didn't know that would happen at the time. I thought I'd captured love on that canvas. The joy. But I must have had too many pills. I did like pills back then.'

'You do not feel the same about the painting now?'

'Maybe I'm being harsh on it,' said Trudy. 'I'd had a lot of vodkas that night. Maybe that was the problem.' She gestured to the waiter again. 'Where's that coffee?' she said. The waiter looked flustered and disappeared. 'I can't get used to the service in this country. Don't they know I need caffeine?'

'What do you think of Pietro?' asked Lena as the worried-looking waiter deposited the coffee at their table.

'He's hot,' said Trudy, with a sparkle in her eye. 'Even after all these years. I expect he told you about our little fling. Why? Are you interested?'

Lena choked on her coffee. 'Never,' she said, feeling appalled at the idea.

'What do you think of Simon?' asked Trudy. 'I've seen some of his early works and they are brilliant. We've been out a couple of times, you know. He's hot too. More my type than Pietro. The quiet ones are normally the most fun.' She winked at Lena.

Lena looked back, not sure what to say.

'I wonder if I could help him get his inspiration back,' said Trudy. 'I'd sure like to try.'

The food arrived, a welcome clatter of plates with a delicately stacked mountain of muffin, eggs and bacon, encircled by a swirl of hollandaise.

'I love it when there is art everywhere,' said Trudy, admiring her plate. Lena had already picked up her knife and fork ready to tuck in, but put them back down to admire the food. 'You don't have to be an artist to be an artist. You know what I mean? Lots of people have artistic souls.' Lena looked at the egg. She could see, even without making an incision, that it was perfectly cooked, the yolk hot and runny. 'I can tell, just from looking at people,' continued Trudy. 'You're an artist.' Lena looked back at Trudy in surprise. She had been dreadful at school art classes. 'You hide it well,' added Trudy, gesturing to Lena's red T-shirt and loose jeans. 'But you've got an eye for detail. A special view of the world. I think you see things others don't.'

'I see my eggs getting cold,' said Lena. Trudy laughed and they both tucked in.

'What did you make of the other guests at the gallery?' asked Lena, keen to find out what she could before Trudy finished her breakfast and disappeared.

'Boring. Only you and Simon interested me. Oh, and Pietro of course. I've always liked him. Can't say I find that wife of his very interesting, although even I have to admit she's pretty.'

'Was anyone asking a lot of questions about the painting?'

'I don't think anyone even really looked at it,' said Trudy. 'They never do at these things. It's more about the champagne than the art.'

'But three people made Pietro an offer.'

'That's different entirely. They want to be able to say that they met the artist, fell in love with the piece. It's a story to impress their friends. They'll probably never really look at it. It was on the wall for ages and no one wanted to buy it, then I turn up and it's a different story. It makes me sad sometimes, when I think about what I poured into it.' Trudy took another bite of her breakfast. 'But artists need to eat,' she said.

'I hear you are famous,' said Lena politely.

'But did you like *In Purple*?'

Lena paused. 'I do not know much about art,' she confessed. 'And I do not like much of what is in the gallery. That hedgehog especially.'

Trudy laughed. 'Pietro does have some weird tastes. Still, we had fun together a while ago and I said I'd help.'

'Do you remember when Pietro last had his keys at the reception?' asked Lena, aware that any memories from Trudy were a long shot. 'He got them out to open a wine bottle. There were only a few of us left at that point. Did you see them again later?'

'Bit foggy on the details,' said Trudy. 'Drink and jetlag don't mix.'

Lena scooped up the last of her egg with the remaining fragment of muffin. 'Do you know anyone who would buy *A Study in Purple* if it was stolen?'

'Oh, tons of people,' said Trudy. 'There's quite a demand for my work on the black market.' She smiled and took her final bite of muffin. 'It's due to my edgy image. Now, I'm sorry to eat and run, but I need to get going or I'll miss my nine a.m. slot. They are remarkably exacting about timings at the Royal Academy, considering we are all artists. Put breakfast on my bill,' she called to the waiter. 'Pleasure hanging out with you, Lena,' she said. 'Let's do it again.' With that and another smoky kiss on the cheek, Trudy was gone.

Lena drank the remains of her coffee. She remembered what Ophelia had said about Trudy. Calling her ugly. Trudy might not have Ophelia's beauty, but she was far from ugly. Was Ophelia still angry about what had happened all those years ago? Lena closed her eyes and felt the eggs she'd eaten start to warm her belly. Was it possible that Trudy and Pietro had rekindled their romance?

After Timea's murder, Lena knew more than she wanted to about the most dangerous emotion there was.

Jealousy.

'I'm so sorry I couldn't come earlier,' said Cartwright, his voice out of breath but his eyes gleaming like marbles in the sunshine. 'Mr Theopolis, the chip-shop owner, is talking.'

'That is excellent,' said Lena. 'I am happy for him.'

'And what's more, he's told us a little about the suspects. He's still quite confused and keeps going on about how to make fish batter, but he also gave us a few details that we couldn't see on the CCTV.'

'Then I am happy for you,' said Lena. 'Come in.'

Cartwright stepped into Lena's apartment. She was pleased to be able to display the still-flowering orchid in all its glory on her spotless windowsill. He sat down on her sofa and she went to the small kitchen area to pop the kettle on. She'd bought Earl Grey teabags specially.

'I want to hear everything about your case,' said Lena. 'And my case too. I have new leads. Pietro has serious money trouble. And I think there is something going on with him and Trudy. You always say that most crimes are committed by lovers.'

'That's not what I say,' said Cartwright. 'I said that over half the women who are murdered are murdered by partners or ex-partners.'

'Exactly,' said Lena. She carefully poured boiling water on the teabag. She watched as it infused the water with an insipid shade of brown.

'Listen,' he said. Lena watched him. His eyes were closed. 'I meant what I said the other day. I would really like to make you dinner. To cook for you at my house. But no talking about work. Would you like to come?' He opened his eyes and looked into her own. Lena felt her heart expand until she thought her chest would burst.

'Okay,' she said, coolly. 'That sounds nice.'

He grinned back and the two stood in silence, smiling at each other like fools.

Cartwright broke the silence and changed the subject, as if thinking Lena might be about to change her mind. 'You'll be pleased to hear I have found out more about Patrick.'

'Really?' said Lena, taking the drinks over to the sofa and inviting Cartwright to sit beside her. 'So what did you find?'

Cartwright pulled out his laptop and angled the computer screen so she could see it too. 'He's a company director, so it's all in the annual report where he works. He's had a number of substantial bonuses in the last five years. All six figures. But he's been depositing the money as quickly as it comes in. In an account in Mexico.'

'How did you find out about Mexico?'

'I've spent time with cyber-crime,' he replied. 'My research wouldn't stand up in court, but it's useful for us.'

'Whose account?'

'I haven't found that out yet. But he's also flown back and forth at least once a month.'

Lena sat and thought. 'So what do you think he is up to?'

Cartwright grinned from ear to ear. 'I know it sounds unlikely, but I have a potential theory. It would be big.'

'It always is,' said Lena, and then blushed furiously.

'I think,' continued Cartwright, unperturbed, 'that he could be part of an international drugs cartel.'

Lena stifled a laugh. 'That seems unlikely.'

'You'd be surprised how many gangs like that are behind art theft. Normally on a grander scale than this, but it's possible. Art is often used as currency. It's easy to transport and doesn't need to be laundered in the same way as money. He could be using it as part-payment to the Mexicans.'

Lena frowned at him. 'I did hear him say something on the night of the reception. About transferring assets. But it does not mean it is a drugs gang.'

'No, look,' he said, directing her to his spreadsheet. 'The formulae don't lie. He is our number one suspect.'

'Two days ago that was Gertrude,' said Lena.

'That was unfortunate,' admitted Cartwright. 'But this time it's really adding up. And we didn't even need to climb any ladders.' Cartwright took his teacup in his hand and took a sip. 'Best tea I've tasted made by a Hungarian!' he said.

Thanks,' said Lena, feeling out-of-proportion pleasure at the compliment. 'Now, tell me what Mr Theopolis said about the *Ördög* monsters who attacked him?'

'There's not much to go on,' said Cartwright, having another sip of his excellent tea. 'They had their hoods up, like we saw on the CCTV. But he thinks one of them had red hair. Apparently he could tell from his eyebrows, and, I quote, "his skin was the colour of cooked cod".'

Lena laughed. 'I like that description,' she said. 'And the other one?'

'He was shorter, but we knew that already. And apparently he had a big black beard.'

Lena didn't laugh this time. 'Two men?' she said. 'One with a beard and one with ginger hair and skin the colour of a cooked fish?'

'Yes, that's right. Why are you so interested?'

'Two men, you said.'

'That's right,' replied Cartwright, looking puzzled.

'And what night was it?'

'Wednesday the fifteenth of June.'

'The night the painting was stolen.'

'Yes,' said Cartwright. 'But that isn't significant, surely? The two hardly seem connected.'

Lena's mind whirred. 'I saw two men attacking a third man that night. Remember?'

'Yes, you told me,' said Cartwright. 'You don't think . . . ?'

'One was ginger,' said Lena. 'The other had a beard.'

CHAPTER 17

Lena's head was full of men with beards and ginger hair as she went through the revolving doors into University College Hospital on Euston Road. She glanced at her watch; she had ten minutes until visiting time started and she could talk to Mr Theopolis. Cartwright had told her he was still in a bad way, so she decided to steel herself with a coffee from the hospital canteen.

The greasy smell of chips was overpowering and Lena was tempted. But even she had to admit they didn't really go with coffee, so she chose a chocolate muffin encased in plastic instead. Giving her coffee a doubtful sniff, she turned around to find a place to sit. Then she froze.

Tomek, her ex. Sitting in a seat by the window. Facing towards her. Holding the hand of a nurse, his face the picture of loving devotion. Lena stared at him for a moment too long and he caught her eye. For a second they both hesitated. Lena was wondering if she could get away with pretending not to see him. He was probably thinking the same thing.

'Lena,' he said, dropping the nurse's hand and standing up, evidently deciding he could not pull off not having seen her. 'It is good to see you. And looking so well.'

Lena accepted an awkward hug, feeling the familiar warmth from his belly press into her own. She'd always loved his softness.

'You are not unwell?' she said, gesturing to their surroundings.

'Not at all,' he replied. 'Better than ever. Come meet Emma.'

'I remember you,' said Lena to Emma. 'You were Tomek's nurse when he was sick.'

'Kidney stones,' said Emma, with a smile. 'That's how we met.'

Lena stood and looked at them for a moment, wishing she could be absorbed into the linoleum floor. They were sharing an enormous plate of chips, the appetising fragrance assaulting her nose and causing her stomach to rumble rebelliously.

'Join us,' said Tomek.

Lena hesitated. It was the last thing she wanted to do. 'I can only stay a minute,' said Lena. 'I have to make a visit.'

'That policeman is okay I hope?' said Tomek, tucking into the chips with gusto. 'You are not here to visit him. Cartman, wasn't it?'

'Cartwright,' said Lena. 'It is not him. We are not . . .' She paused. 'We are working on a case together,' she said, finally. 'I have come to interview a victim.' Lena tried to make it sound official in the hope that it would curtail any further questions as to what was happening with her relationship. She wouldn't know how to answer if she wanted to.

'How exciting,' said Emma, also helping herself to a chip. 'I didn't know you were in the police.'

'I am not,' she replied. 'I was . . .' She thought. 'A witness. Maybe.' Tomek raised an eyebrow at her, then turned his attention back to the rapidly diminishing tower of chips.

'We see the victims of some terrible crimes here,' said Emma. 'Beatings, shootings. Just yesterday two men came in in an awful state. Both bike riders; bumped each other somehow on their bikes and it ended up in a huge fight where they seem to have tried to kill each other. I didn't know a saddle could be used as a weapon like that.'

There was silence while Lena tried to imagine how the saddle had been used. Tomek shuddered. 'How is your mother?' he said, changing the subject. 'And little Laszlo?'

Before Lena could answer, Emma chipped in. 'And then that poor chip-shop owner,' she said, ignoring them and continuing on her theme. 'What those men did to him is disgraceful.'

'Mr Theopolis?' said Lena. 'He is who I have come to see.'

'Do you know what happened to him?' said Emma. 'Thank goodness he can't remember much, poor little dear. Such a sweet man too. I'm not allowed favourites here, of course, but he might be my second favourite patient ever. After Tomek, of course. Tomek is the sweetest.' Emma leaned in and gave Tomek an affectionate kiss on his salty lips. Lena found that she momentarily forgot how to breathe.

She stood up. 'I should go. Family are all well, thank you. Lovely to see you both.' She turned and walked away.

'Lena, wait,' called out Tomek. Lena turned, wondering what fresh ordeal lay in store for her now. 'You forgot your muffin.'

'You have it,' she said. 'I am not hungry.' She saw a flash of joy pass over Tomek's face. She breathed deeply. He deserved to be happy. And not just the kind of happiness brought by a muffin.

'Do you want mushy peas?'

'No, Mr Theopolis,' said Lena for the third time. 'I want to talk to you about the men who attacked you.'

'Oh.' Mr Theopolis rested his head back down on the hospital bed. He had a drip running into his right hand, and a selection of wires taped to his chest. A machine next to him made a panicked beeping sound every few minutes. He closed his eyes.

'I'm sorry about this, Lena,' said Cartwright. 'He was more lucid earlier.'

Lena took the sick man's hands. 'I know it was awful, what they did to you,' said Lena. 'I think I saw them too, that night. Attacking someone else. What do you remember about them?'

Mr Theopolis opened his eyes and looked mournfully at Lena. Cartwright told her he was in his fifties, but to Lena he looked much older. His skin, though olive, had a ghostly pallor under the surface. Grey and black hairs peppered the lower half of his face.

'They wanted kebabs,' he said. 'But I don't sell kebabs. I sell fish and chips and mushy peas and battered sausages and pickled onions.'

'Is that what made them angry?' said Lena.

'Fish and chips and mushy peas,' repeated Mr Theopolis. 'It's what my wife and I agreed. Back in Greece I was a fisherman, when I was a boy. So when we came here we decided to open a fish and chip shop with the money she inherited from her parents. My wife doesn't like the smell of the kebab meat. But fish. Fish you can buy fresh and whole. You know when fish is good. Battered and fried with chips and ketchup. Do you want vinegar?'

'No thank you, Mr Theopolis,' said Lena softly. 'Do you remember what the men looked like? The men who wanted kebabs?'

'Drunk,' said Mr Theopolis. 'You expect a bit of that, in a chippie. But not too much. Not like in a kebab shop. Mainly it is families, coming after work to get their treat meal. The best fish in London, I serve. Cod. Not as good as the sea bream from the Aegean, but tasty and fresh.'

'Anything else?'

'Grouper and whiting and mullet. Even swordfish in the Aegean. So beautiful and so warm there. I miss it, sometimes, even now. We're going back there to Milos to retire. Just a few more years and we'll have enough money saved to live out our days in the sunshine. Back home.'

'Anything else about the men?' asked Cartwright.

'Don't get me wrong, I love this country. But I miss the feeling of sun heating the fresh sea salt on my back. The taste of a freshly caught swordfish on my mother's griddle. Don't you?'

Lena leaned back in the plastic hospital chair and smiled at the urgent black eyes looking up at her own. 'There are no seas where I am from,' she said. 'But I do miss my mother's cooking. Her chicken *paprikash* is the most delicious thing in the world.'

'You should taste my wife's cooking,' said Mr Theopolis. 'Her lamb.' He raised his free hand to his mouth and kissed his fingers. Then he looked at Lena, puzzled. 'We don't serve lamb,' he said. 'Cod and chips? Mushy peas?'

'No thank you, Mr Theopolis,' said Lena. She leaned forwards and gave him a kiss on the cheek before getting up to leave. She exchanged a glance with Cartwright. 'Soon, I hope.'

Lena sat next to Cartwright in the stuffy interview room. 'Don't these windows open?' she said, feeling herself starting to glimmer with sweat.

'Sorry,' said Cartwright. 'Security. But we're almost there.'

He fast-forwarded the grainy tape. Lena watched as the men charged into the chip shop as if in hyper-drive. 'Stop,' she said.

'The best shot of their faces is later,' said Cartwright. 'And this bit is not pleasant.'

'I want to see what happened,' said Lena. Cartwright obediently rewound the tape. They both leaned forwards to peer at the grainy black-and-white footage on the small TV screen.

Lena watched. The CCTV was set up from inside the shop but you could also see passers-by on the street. She watched as a man limped along the road as if his leg were in plaster. Then two men pushed past him, nearly knocking him over. They swaggered in, their backs to the camera, their hoods up. One gesticulated aggressively at Mr Theopolis, the other held back. Was that how they'd been with her? Was there anything familiar about them?

She focused back on the screen. One of the men jumped up on to the counter. She watched as Mr Theopolis backed away. Even through the awful quality of the footage, she could tell he was terrified. One hand covered his face. The other reached for something behind the counter.

The gun.

Everything seemed to go into slow motion. The man on the counter put up his hands. The other man edged slowly backwards. Mr Theopolis stood stock-still, the gun pointed at the man closest to him.

Suddenly the man on the counter tipped his head back and began to shake. Lena peered closer. 'We think he is laughing,' said Cartwright. Then the man swung his leg and kicked Mr Theopolis full in the face.

Lena jerked backwards.

'Mr Theopolis had a bruise the shape of that man's boot-print on his cheek,' said Cartwright. Lena watched as Mr Theopolis crumpled to the floor immediately. He was out of view. They could just see the man's back, shaking with the force of his kicks. The other man came around the back of the counter and watched.

Lena forced herself to carry on watching. 'The poor man,' she said.

Finally the men stopped. Grabbing a bag and filling it with fish and chips, they finally left. Lena breathed a sigh of relief. 'Wait,' said Cartwright. One of them re-entered, grabbed the ketchup bottle, squirted some into the bag and then chucked the bottle over the counter. After he did so, he looked right at the CCTV for the first time. Cartwright pressed pause. Lena found herself looking straight into his pale, dilated eyes. You wouldn't be able to identify him unless you knew who you were looking for. And she did.

'That is him,' she said. 'That is the man who attacked Malcolm Paulter after the gallery reception. I am sure.'

CHAPTER 18

The building was fronted by dirty glass, and the logo, a bold purple affair in the shape of a triangle, was peeling off the immense window. Lena leaned in and peered through the grime. This wasn't what she'd expected.

She'd been trying to reach Malcolm Paulter since she took his details from the gallery. She had planned to offer him the same free clean as the other two, although she felt that really he should see her without the pretence. She'd saved him, and his ridiculous trousers, from those thugs. He had barely thanked her. But, as things turned out, he didn't answer his phone or return her calls. Taking matters into her own hands, she'd caught the Victoria line down to Warren Street to investigate the address she had for him herself. Not only could he hold clues as to what had happened to *A Study in Purple*, he could also be a witness to help her identify the men who had attacked both him and Mr Theopolis.

It was an office, not a residential property: that was clear. But that was not what surprised Lena. It was the state of disrepair. She took the corner of the triangular logo and peeled it back further, revealing clean glass underneath. She looked through the clean patch, using it like a telescope to gain access to the secrets within.

There were triangular purple patterns stencilled over the walls and an enormous version of the sticky logo from the window, enlarged to at least three metres long and made of Perspex, overhanging an empty desk. It was Monday morning, but there was no sign of Malcolm. No signs of life at all.

Lena stood back. Malcolm had wanted the painting for the reception of his office, so he said. He had been at the gallery when the keys were stolen. He had loitered in an alleyway afterwards and had refused to call the police when he was attacked. Now she knew that he had given an address that he had long since abandoned. Did he have money troubles? Money troubles that an expensive painting could solve? What was his connection to the Chinese clients he'd mentioned? In her head he was climbing his way up her suspect list more quickly than Cartwright could scramble down a ladder. She just needed to find him.

Lena was shocked out of her reverie by her phone ringing. She picked it up and listened in alarm to the voice at the other end.

'I come now.' Lena hung up the phone and ran back to the station.

Lena stood on the tube, clutching one of the poles. There were seats but she was too nervous to sit down. She'd known it was going to happen. The warrant was out. There was only so long Sarika could hide. Lena half wished Sarika had fled the country. Then at least she could have put off this ordeal. Or avoided it completely, if Lena had found the painting by then.

The tube lurched to a sudden halt and Lena pivoted to stay balanced, gripping the pole as if to squeeze the life from it. What reassurance could she offer Sarika? She was a long way from finding out what had happened to *A Study in Purple*.

Lena stepped out of the carriage and hurried to climb the long escalator at Angel station. Having Sarika back would have its advantages. If she couldn't work out who had taken the painting, perhaps there was another way to prove Sarika innocent. She could talk to her at least, find out if the girl herself could give her any clues.

* * *

Lena sat in the waiting room. She felt like she'd spent half her life in this room recently, watching worried people, angry people, crying people and drunk people wander in and out, some of their own free will, others not so much. She'd tried to reach Cartwright to see if he could help, but his phone was switched off. He must be busy with Mr Theopolis at the hospital, she thought.

'Got her,' said Gullins, lumbering towards Lena.

'Detective Blake told me,' replied Lena. 'Can I see her?'

'If you must,' said Gullins. 'Follow me.' He led her along a corridor Lena was starting to know well. But it would all be new to Sarika. Lena hurried after Gullins, finding him surprisingly light on his feet for once.

Lena saw Blake first, sitting at the table, her face full of concentration. Sarika's back was to her, but she swivelled round at the sound of the door. Her mournful expression turned to delight. '*Hála Istennek*. Thank god it is you, Lena.'

Lena embraced her cousin. Her body felt delicate against her own. She pulled away and looked around the room. A tired-looking man blinked up at her. 'Your lawyer?' questioned Lena. He nodded his assent.

'Sarika is innocent,' said Lena.

'The police picked her up in Brighton,' said Blake. 'Vandalising a bus stop.'

'What?' exclaimed Lena. 'That cannot be true.'

'It is not,' said Sarika. Lena breathed a sigh of relief. 'We were creating art.'

Lena sank into a chair.

'Look on the bright side, Lena,' said Gullins, clearly enjoying himself. 'Better creating art than stealing it.'

Lena looked at him. 'So you know that she did not steal the painting?'

Detective Blake replied. 'That is not what PC Gullins meant,' she said. 'We are still investigating what happened before we decide whether to charge Sarika. Her co-operation will be most welcome.'

Sarika turned her face away. 'Of course she will co-operate,' said Lena, confused by Sarika's reaction. 'You will,' she told the girl.

'I won't,' said Sarika.

Lena grabbed Sarika's hands. They were damp, hot and slippery, like freshly boiled *nokedli* dumplings. 'What is wrong?' she said, in as gentle a voice as she could manage. 'Why will you not help yourself?'

Sarika leaned into Lena and whispered in Hungarian into her ear. 'They want me to tell on him,' she said. 'Betray Dragg. But I won't.'

'You said that he hadn't done anything wrong either,' said Lena. 'So there is no harm in telling the truth.'

'Speak English,' said Gullins.

'We're in love,' said Sarika, ignoring him. 'He is going to break up with Kat now he is back.'

'I'll kick you out if this continues,' warned Gullins.

'Sarika needs to co-operate with us,' said Blake. 'Perhaps you could talk some sense into her?'

'Give me five minutes,' said Lena. Blake and Gullins left the room.

'You won't be together if you go to prison,' said Lena, wishing she could shake sense into the girl like salt on to *szalonna* bacon. She shot a look at the lawyer, hoping for help. He had closed his eyes for a moment. Lena coughed loudly and he jumped a little, then looked more alert.

'Our time in Brighton was magical,' said Sarika with a smile. 'I think I might have some talent as an artist. He thinks so too. He's never seen a newbie do so well. But they will try to set him up for the theft of *A Study in Purple*, because of what's on the laptop. I won't let them.'

'Sarika!' said Lena. 'It's not Dragg who'll be in trouble if you're not careful. You could go to prison. You need to be honest with the police. Did you have an alibi at least?'

'He painted me. A mural, bigger than life-size.' Sarika looked dreamily in the distance and Lena felt the urge to slap some sense into her. Suddenly Sarika turned to face her. 'I will not betray Dragg,' she said. 'I will go to prison for him, if I need to.'

'If he didn't do anything, he won't be in trouble.'

'You heard what he said. There's no justice for immigrants in this country. You need to find who really did this if you want to help me. Please.'

After the mess Kat had made of Lena's home, Lena felt no compunction about storming straight into Kat's flat as soon as the surprised woman opened the door.

'What do you think you're doing?' shouted Kat as Lena pushed past her. 'I'm busy.'

'I bet you are,' said Lena, looking at the robe hastily pulled around Kat's impressive figure. She went into the living room and found the laptop. She peered at it a moment and realised she was on a webcam. Her own face gazed back at her from the screen. Immediately a message appeared. Lena read it. '*Ooh a fresh one*,' it said. '*Get em out*.' Kat appeared behind her and a flurry of messages appeared, all of them inviting the women to do various things to each other. Lena snapped the laptop shut.

'You're costing me good money,' said Kat, trying to sound tough but with a tremble in her voice. 'That's £300 you owe me already. More if I lose subscribers.'

'You are not getting any money from me,' said Lena. 'But there is something that I want you to do for me. You need to tell the police the truth. That Sarika has never used your laptop.'

Kat laughed. 'And why would I do that?'

'Does Dragg know about your little sideline?'

Kat laughed harder. 'Who gives a fuck what that little shit knows,' she replied. 'He's fucked off to Brighton with that thieving cousin of yours. Now get the hell out of my way so I can get back to work before these perverts switch over to Babes R Us.'

Lena paused, holding the laptop out of Kat's reach. She'd hoped the threat of revealing what Kat was doing to Dragg would be enough. Clearly not. 'Does your family know?' asked Lena, remembering what Lucia had told her about the siblings Kat supported.

'I have no family here,' said Kat, her laugh dying on her lips.

'Not here,' said Lena. 'Back home. Russia, I think?'

'You will never find them,' said Kat, looking unsure.

'You and Dragg used to Skype them together,' said Lena. 'Your little sisters adore him, or so I'm told. He can contact your family. Does your father know what his eldest daughter is doing on the internet?'

Kat sank to the sofa. 'You wouldn't,' she said. 'You wouldn't dare.'

'I do not want to,' said Lena. 'What you do is your business.'

Kat looked up, her face softening like butter on hot *lángos* dough. 'It is not easy,' she said, 'trying to earn money to keep the children back home fed and clothed. I have three little brothers and four little sisters. I hate doing it. But they depend on me. I am buying them a future.'

Lena sat down next to her. 'I know it is hard. My friend Timea used to work all the hours to send money home for her little boy.' She took Kat's hand. It was surprisingly smooth. 'If it helps, I think what you are doing is noble.'

Kat smiled at her. 'So you will not tell?'

Lena looked straight into the woman's eyes. 'I need to protect my family too. Sarika is in custody for a crime she did not commit. You need to tell the police that Sarika never touched that laptop. That is what it will take to buy my silence.'

CHAPTER 19

Lena didn't much fancy going back to the hospital, but she told herself that it was very unlikely that she'd bump into Tomek again. Plus now she had her date with Cartwright to look forward to. Dinner at his house, no work talk. That was unequivocally a date. The beginnings of something she'd been longing for.

Cartwright wanted them to give Mr Theopolis the good news together. After they'd established that the men she saw and the men who'd attacked Mr Theopolis were one and the same, she'd been able to identify them from police files. Cartwright set about tracking down Malcolm Paulter's home address and phone number so he could corroborate, but it wasn't needed. The bearded man confessed, claiming it was his friend who had delivered the worst of the beating. CCTV footage confirmed this, but both faced a serious sentence.

The aroma as she entered the hospital this time was of baked potatoes and beans. Lena walked past the café without glancing in, heading straight to the main lobby. Cartwright was waiting for her there.

'This is the best bit of the job,' he told her, smiling. 'Telling the victims that their attackers will be brought to justice.'

'I am glad to help,' said Lena. She was. 'Does the confession mean that you do not need Malcolm Paulter as a witness?'

'They didn't confess until after I was able to track down his home phone number,' said Cartwright, handing her a piece of paper. 'I can't officially give this to you, you understand.'

'Give me what?' said Lena, pocketing the paper. She'd call Malcolm later and see what she could find out.

They walked up the stairs together, leaving the lifts for the wheelchair-bound. The lino was blue and reminded Lena of the colour of the Hungarian skies above her village at midsummer. She looked at Cartwright. It was also the colour of his eyes. She thought about telling him so, but couldn't think of a way to say his eyes matched the hospital floor without him thinking her strange.

Mr Theopolis was sitting up in bed when they arrived. Mrs Theopolis's hand gripped his. She stood up when they arrived and kissed Cartwright on each cheek before hugging him close. She did the same to Lena.

'Look who has come to see you,' she said to her husband, sitting on the bed next to him and taking his hand again. 'It is PC Cartwright and his associate.'

'Lena Szarka,' said Lena.

Mrs Theopolis smiled at them both. 'I am so glad to have him back with us. All I could do was sit here watching him or go home and clean the house. I've polished the cutlery three times now.'

Lena smiled back, recognising a kindred spirit. 'I like to polish shoes best when I am upset,' she said.

'That is good,' replied Mrs Theopolis. 'Good nesting for a woman when their man is sick. Men cannot do the same.' She cast a glance at Cartwright. 'When I was in hospital with my women troubles, poor Nikolas let the house go to ruin. I don't think he washed a dish the entire time. Men. Not so resilient as women.' She sighed. 'But I do not know what I would do without him.' She used her spare hand to take hold of Lena's and squeeze.

'I have good news for you, Mr Theopolis,' said Cartwright.

'You are giving me another grandson!' cut in Mr Theopolis, an enormous smile on his face. 'It is about time too. Your mother and I were starting to despair of you.'

Cartwright was speechless for a moment. 'He has been like this all morning,' said Mrs Theopolis. 'Come on, tell us your news. I think he understands, somewhere in his mind.'

'Thanks to Lena, we have found the people who attacked you. We have a confession and they will be brought to trial for GBH.'

Mr Theopolis reached out with his free hand and grabbed Cartwright's. He shook it heartily. Cartwright smiled, relief flooding his face. Mr Theopolis pulled his hand until Cartwright's head was just next to his own.

'I never liked that old battle-axe you married,' he told him, in an exaggerated whisper. 'Your new wife is much prettier. Lena, did you say her name was? Is she German?'

Cartwright coughed and looked to Mrs Theopolis. She nodded at Cartwright to play along.

'Hungarian,' said Cartwright, looking confused.

'Well, hang on to her,' Mr Theopolis advised him. 'She looks like she knows her way around a fishing boat. We'll take you both out tomorrow, in the *Xenia Dream*. Are calm seas predicted, Xenia, my love?'

'They are, my love,' replied Mrs Theopolis, dabbing her eyes. 'And bright sunshine too.'

'It's always sunny here,' said Mr Theopolis. He rested his head back on the pillow and breathed a long, contented sigh. The machine next to him beeped alarmingly and a nurse ran over.

'If you're not family you need to leave,' she said. 'Give him space. I'll fetch the doctor.'

Lena and Cartwright left, leaving Mrs Theopolis clutching her husband's hand as the medical staff busied themselves around him.

'I hope he will be okay,' said Cartwright to Lena. She didn't answer. She had a bad feeling. It seemed to her that those men weren't just going to be charged with GBH. They would be charged with murder.

Lena lifted the dismal window box at Patrick's house to retrieve the key. This time there was only a solitary woodlouse, which promptly curled itself into a shiny ball and rolled down the windowsill in response to the sudden sunlight that greeted it. Lena made sure it was clear before she replaced the box.

She'd been surprised when Patrick had called and asked for her to clean again, with pay this time. He seemed to have given up on his house, so she couldn't imagine how he'd appreciate the gifts a cleaner could bestow. Stepping inside, she saw the mess was terrible again. How had he managed that in just over a week?

He'd put all the pots of dying plants in the hallway, turning it into an arid forest of misery. Lena picked her way through to the kitchen, noticing the trail of dead leaves. Inside, the contents of the cupboards were spread over the counters and all the cabinet doors were open. For a moment, Lena wondered if this were some kind of burglary gone wrong. She inspected the counters more closely. He hadn't left the money to pay her where he said he would. Clients often forgot, thinking it was okay to wait till the following week. When she worked at the agency, this wasn't too bad. A harsh word from the manager, but she'd still get her pay cheque as usual. Now it made life much more difficult, especially when she had Sarika to think of as well.

Lena sighed and went into the living room, which she was surprised to see filled with bouquets of flowers, hastily arranged in an assortment of vases. She went back into the kitchen and began to clean the empty cupboards while she thought.

Cartwright had told her about the vast sums of money leaving Patrick's account. Lena hadn't been too surprised at that. What seemed like a lot of money to Cartwright and herself could be a drop in the pan for a wealthy man like Patrick. He could simply be trading stocks or investing in something or other in Mexico.

Lena brushed a few old walnuts out of the back of the cupboard. They looked like desiccated mouse brains. Maybe he was moving house? She felt herself fill with suspicion. Was he making a run for it? Perhaps whatever was going on with the gang had gone wrong and he was cutting his losses.

Lena began putting plates back into the now clean cupboard. But why have her in to clean, partway through the move? She would often get jobs deep-cleaning a place before new tenants moved in, but rarely when people were still packing up. And this was not a rented property, she was sure. It felt too permanent.

Was he sprucing it up to facilitate a quick sell? That would explain the flowers. Lena had seen TV shows about such things. Put some flowers and a scented candle in a clean house and it will trick people into buying more quickly, not realising that the flowers and fragrance would be long gone before the house became their own.

Lena felt her suspicions growing. Patrick had been at the gallery but had not been interested in the art. Money was flowing out of his account to somewhere in Mexico. He was preparing to leave, to sell his house quickly and get out. Maybe Cartwright's theory about gang involvement was not so far-fetched.

She picked up her phone to call Cartwright, and was surprised to see his name already on the screen. He was calling her.

'Patrick is up to something,' she began. 'I think that he is trying to make a quick run-away.' She waited to hear Cartwright's enthusiasm on the other end of the phone. He'd be thrilled at the breakthrough.

Silence.

Then the sound of a deep inhale.

'Lena, it's bad news. Mr Theopolis is dead.'

CHAPTER 20

Lena had finished at Patrick's house in a daze, finding comfort in the monotony of cleaning. She hadn't known Mr Theopolis well, but she could tell he was a good person. A person who didn't deserve what had happened to him. Without thinking, she made her way to the gallery.

Keeping busy. That's what she had to do. Mrs Theopolis was right.

The gallery door was locked and the main light was off, but she could see a gleam coming from the little office, like sunlight through the trees. She rang the bell and waited.

She saw a Pietro-shaped shadow emerge from his office. He peered at her through the glass front of the gallery before switching on the light. 'Thank goodness it's you,' he said as he opened the door to her. 'When I heard the bell I thought it might be the bailiff again. Lena, you look dreadful.'

'Has he been back?' asked Lena, ignoring the comment on her appearance. 'I thought he gave you two weeks. It has only been five days.'

'No he hasn't, but every time I hear a sound, I jump.' Pietro gave her a mournful look. 'I'm not sure he's the sort of person to stick to his timeline.'

Lena looked around the gallery. 'You have not sold anything,' she said. 'Would that not help raise the money? You could have a special promotion?'

'It wouldn't be enough,' said Pietro. 'Most of the pieces are still owned by the artists. I'd make commission, that's it. And there's nothing here as valuable as *In Purple*. That was the only one I owned outright.'

'Have you tried asking your relatives for money?'

'They've been tapped before. Not interested now. And I couldn't tell them how much trouble I've got myself into. I'd die first.' Lena looked at him. With this pride it was very possible that he would. 'The trustees aren't interested either,' he said. 'They won't release the next batch of my inheritance for eighteen months. All my hopes rest on the damn insurance company.'

'Not all your hopes,' said Lena. 'I have some leads to find the painting.'

'You do cheer me up,' said Pietro. 'I haven't laughed for days.'

'There is no joke,' said Lena crossly. 'I have investigations.'

'Following the trail of dust are you?' said Pietro, still laughing. 'Found some clues in the vacuum cleaner?' He looked at the thunder on Lena's face and stopped laughing. 'Sorry, Lena,' he said. 'I know you are trying to help. Let's have a cup of tea.'

'No, thank you,' said Lena. 'But please turn on the light. I want to have a proper look at where *A Study in Purple* was hanging.' Pietro obeyed, locking the door again at the same time. He retreated back into his office.

Lena surveyed the wall. She could see the slightly brighter square of white where the painting had been hanging. Leaning forwards, she noticed again the echo of where a slightly different-size painting had been. Running her fingers along the wall, she felt its subtle texture like the peel of a tangerine. Every now and again her fingers found a slight crevice, made where the frame had struck the wall. Lena leaned forwards and gave the wall a sniff. Not useful. Just the chemical aroma of old paint. But as she leaned forwards, she noticed something, lodged under the clay eyeball. Lena got down on her hands and knees to peer more closely. It was a tack, the kind that was used to keep paintings within their frames. Lena withdrew a paperclip from her backpack and unwound it from its established shape until it was straight. Then she used it to ease out the tack from its hiding place. Finally she was able to grab it. Lena had cleaned behind *A Study in Purple* many times. She recognised the distinctive pattern of rust on this tack, shaped like an elephant's trunk. This tack had been on *A Study in Purple.*

Lena thought about it. It was unlikely that the tack had come off when the painting was removed from the wall. She herself had lifted it in the past to clean behind it and it had stayed firm. But what if the painting had been removed from the frame?

It was possible, thought Lena. More than possible. Likely. It would be much easier to take the painting without the frame. But then the frame would have to be abandoned somewhere, and the police had found nothing. She knew that Detective Blake would have had the area searched. Cartwright would have told her if the frame had been found, and it couldn't have been left far from the gallery.

But the tack would mean nothing to the police. Only to her.

Of course. Suddenly Lena was sure. She just needed to find the evidence.

'I don't mean to hurry your investigations,' said Pietro. 'But I'm going home now and I don't want to leave you here on your own.'

Lena opened her mouth to object, but Pietro, apparently sensing her anger, interjected. 'Not because I don't trust you. I don't want you to be here if that Turkish thug comes back.'

'I am not afraid of him,' said Lena.

'I've no doubt,' said Pietro, with a laugh Lena didn't appreciate. 'But we don't want you two making a mess of each other in the gallery. I couldn't afford the overtime my cleaner charges.' He winked at her.

'I just want to check something in the basement first,' said Lena, hurrying down the stairs before Pietro could stop her. Was the frame hidden here somewhere? Could the police have missed it – one amongst so many, and all the same?

She could hear Pietro's footsteps following her down. Then they stopped. 'Can you hear that?' he whispered, then hurled himself down the remaining steps and switched off the light. Lena froze. Both listened.

The sound of a key in the lock, and the door squeaking open. 'It's him,' said Pietro. 'Let's hide.'

'Does he even have a key?' asked Lena, watching Pietro trying to conceal his generous frame behind a slender easel.

'Ophelia's went missing,' said Pietro. 'He must have taken it. Oh, the thought of his dirty hands, rummaging around in her handbag . . .'

Lena decided there was no good time to tell Pietro that she was the one who had stolen Ophelia's key.

'Come over here,' insisted Pietro. 'There's room for you to hide too, if we pull this thing into the corner.'

Lena followed him and squeezed herself behind it. 'I really do not think . . .' she said.

'Shush,' said Pietro. 'Perhaps he'll just help himself to a painting and leave.' They listened again. Someone was rummaging around upstairs. Then footsteps. Footsteps coming down the stairs.

The light beamed on. 'Pietro?' said a woman's voice. 'I can see your stomach sticking out from behind that easel. What on earth are you up to?'

'My love,' said Pietro, stepping out to greet Ophelia. 'Thank goodness it's you.'

'Who is that with you?' said Ophelia. 'It's Trudy, isn't it?'

Lena stepped out. Ophelia turned to Pietro. 'What is our cleaner doing in the basement with you, with the lights out?'

'I can explain,' said Lena. 'We thought you were—'

'Someone else,' said Pietro, shooting her a look. 'A . . . an artist trying to sell his work. Dreadful stuff, but I find it so hard to say no. So we hid down here. To avoid him.'

'With the door locked?' Ophelia's usually elegant voice was reaching a disheartening screech. 'Perhaps you didn't realise I had a new key cut after mine went missing.'

'We wanted him to think we were shut,' said Pietro. 'So he'd go away. I know, let's go for champagne at Fromage d'Or, just the two of us.' He led his wife up the stairs. 'Come along, Lena, time for us all to leave.'

'I would like to finish cleaning down here first,' said Lena, hoping to seize her chance to search for the frame.

'No need,' he said.

'You promised nothing like this would happen again. Ever. What's going on with that cleaner?' said Ophelia.

'Nothing is happening,' said Pietro. 'Out we go.'

Lena was itching to search downstairs, but she left with Pietro and Ophelia. Even if she found what she was looking for, it would not tell her who the thief was. But it would be a clue. She watched Pietro and Ophelia walk down the street, Ophelia refusing to take Pietro's hand. She pretended to go in the opposite direction. When they were out of view she hurried back, glad that she had kept Ophelia's key.

Feeling furtive, Lena let herself back in and locked the door behind her. She crept down the stairs. As always, there was an assortment of bubble-wrapped paintings and sculptures that hadn't been sold but didn't fit the current exhibition. Apparently they were not 'tormented' enough.

Lena opened the far cupboard. Inside, there had to be fifty frames of various shapes and sizes, but all in Pietro's favourite ebony. When paintings were sold, some were taken with the frame and others not. Simon hated waste and hoarded these in the hope that another painting would come in at the correct size. Perhaps one day he intended to paint canvases to match the shapes. Lena took them out one by one, sorting them into piles by size. She closed her eyes and visualised *A Study in Purple*, rooting through her memory for its dimensions. She found ten frames that were about the right size.

Closing her eyes again, Lena ran her hands along the wood of each frame. They were warm to the touch and she could feel the grain against her skin, as unique as a fingerprint. She repeated this with six frames, not finding what she was feeling for. But the seventh, there it was. A dent. Lena went upstairs and grabbed the mop, bringing it back down with her. She held the handle against the frame. The dent fitted perfectly, like a key in a lock. This was the dent the mop had made when Pietro knocked it over before the reception. This was the frame that had held *A Study in Purple*.

Lena replaced all the frames carefully. She needed time to think about what this meant. She knew she was one step closer to finding the painting, but she wasn't sure in which direction she was heading.

CHAPTER 21

Malcolm of the purple trousers was resistant to Lena's suggestion of a free house clean. She wasn't surprised, after he'd given that derelict address to the gallery. But she refused to take no for an answer and insisted that she clean his home that very day, before he had a chance to hide any evidence. It had now been exactly two weeks since the gallery reception and she had no time to waste.

Had he been in any state to do anything with the painting after being attacked? Lena felt that moved him down the suspect board. But, then again, he hadn't wanted the police called. He must have something to hide. Could he have been working with associates? Did he take the keys from Pietro and pass them to someone else? Perhaps that was what he was doing down that dingy alleyway behind Upper Street. And why give that empty office address instead of his home?

Lena tried to calm her suspicions as she rang the bell and waited outside his house. Jumping to conclusions would get her nowhere. His house was small but impeccably smart. The door was painted a bright purple, two lavender bushes were pruned to be perfect spheres on either side. A welcome mat was centred outside the door. 'Home sweet home', Lena read. There was brilliant green grass in the small front garden. Impressed by the colour, she knelt down to feel it, and discovered that it was fake. Less messy than the real thing, thought Lena admiringly, deciding that it might make a welcome addition to her tiny balcony.

Malcolm opened the door. 'Miss Szarka, thank you for your kind offer. After everything you have done for me already.' He leaned forwards and kissed a startled Lena on each cheek, then pulled her in by her hand.

'My pleasure,' said Lena, trying to regain her composure at this welcome. She looked around, but the interior did nothing to settle her. The hallway floor was coated with a thick carpet in papal purple, and the walls were lilac velvet. There was a second door-mat inside, this one covered in a pattern of purple petunias. Lena gingerly wiped her feet.

'Take your shoes off, there's a dear,' said Malcolm, already wash-ing his hands in the kitchen. 'And welcome to my humble abode.'

'Yes,' said Lena, a little dazed. 'Where shall I start?'

Malcolm led her into the kitchen. 'It's such a mess,' he exclaimed. 'I've been so busy at work. My agency is my life, you know. Copywriters, designers, account people are like the children I never had.'

Lena paused. 'The agency is the address the gallery has?'

'Oh yes.'

'Because I went there.'

Malcolm looked at her, a little paler. 'We've upsized,' he said. 'Moved to much bigger premises.'

'Really?' said Lena. 'I do commercial cleaning as well,' she said. 'Where is the office?'

'It's more of a virtual office really,' said Malcolm. 'Physical offices are so twentieth century. That's what I meant when I said we've upsized. Now the worldwide web is our home.'

Lena looked around, considering this information. The bur-gundy cabinets shone like garnets. The purple splashback was spotless. She realised what she had on her hands. One of those clients who cleaned before the cleaner. She found these people endearing: they didn't really want a cleaner, but were willing to pay for the praise. Always insecure, craving approval. She gave it, readily.

'Your house is so clean,' she said. 'I am impressed.'

Malcolm flushed with pleasure. 'You are the professional,' he said. 'I just do what I can. Before and after work.'

'You are in advertising?'

'Owner, President and Executive Creative Director,' said Malcolm. 'My good friend at the gallery reception was a potential new client. Very big in margarine.'

'You keep your cleaning products under the sink?' said Lena, ready to get started.

'Of course.' Malcolm proudly opened the cupboard to reveal myriad bottles, lined up in order of height, each turned to a neat 45-degree angle. 'I hope you'll find everything you need.'

'What a tidy cupboard,' said Lena with dismay, trying to memorise what it looked like now so she could recreate it herself. Malcolm looked delighted.

'I'm working from home today,' he said, disappearing into the living room. 'I often do now, if I'm not out with clients. So if you need anything, just shout.'

Lena looked around the kitchen. It was too spotless. She couldn't work out anything to do that wouldn't leave it less clean than it currently was. Perhaps the drawers could do with a clean inside, she thought, opening one. It contained gleaming cutlery, perfectly sorted. She tried the fridge. A line of ready-cooked meals from a health-food shop confronted her, sorted in order of colour. She gave up and went into the living room.

Malcolm sat on the white leather sofa with two enormous purple cushions on either side of him. Lena looked around. There was a bright lamp just next to her, highlighting the brilliant cleanness. 'Watch out for Terence,' he said, without looking up. 'He likes to hang out under the lamp.'

Lena looked down. A scaly monster peered back up at her. She stepped back in alarm.

'Don't worry, he rarely bites,' said Malcolm. 'He can get under your feet though.' He called to the lizard. 'Come on Terence, leave the nice cleaning lady alone.' Terence remained where he was, indifferent to Malcolm's encouragement. 'Komodo dragons are more affectionate than people think,' explained Malcolm. 'And the dead chicks are no trouble to store in the freezer. Keep them in an airtight bag and really you have a terribly hygienic pet. No fur. I hate it when fur gets everywhere.' He shuddered.

'You can get hairless cats,' said Lena, thinking guiltily of Kaplan, who she had yet to visit.

'Don't be absurd,' said Malcolm. 'That's against nature.'

'Your kitchen is so clean,' said Lena. 'I will go look to see if there is anything I can do upstairs.'

'It can always be cleaner,' called up Malcolm after her.

Lena decided to have a quick look for clues as she ran a hoover around the house. He certainly enjoyed art. She spotted a number of small paintings lining the staircase and studied a few. Abstract purple cats, a green dog, a baby with enormous purple eyes staring at her as if about to cry.

The bedroom was as she expected. Pristine. Not a wrinkle on the bed linen, and covered in purple, lilac and burgundy cushions at perfect right angles to one another. She opened a door to find neatly sorted socks in individual compartments. She lifted one pair out and admired them. This was a man who ironed his socks. Even Lena drew the line there.

'Oh no,' said Malcolm, who had crept up behind her. 'Put it down.' She obeyed, placing it back in the drawer. 'No,' said Malcolm. 'You touched it. It needs to be washed.'

'My hands are clean,' said Lena. 'And it is a sock.'

'Perhaps this was a bad idea,' said Malcolm, starting to sound alarmed. 'I really don't like other people touching my things.' His eyes were beginning to fill with distress. 'I am grateful for what you did, for saving me, but maybe you should go?'

Lena wasn't ready to leave. She hadn't found out enough. 'I will make you a cup of tea?' she said.

'Great idea,' said Malcolm. 'But I will make the tea. You sit in the living room. Terence will look after you.'

Lena followed him back down the staircase. 'Do you have coffee?' she asked.

'Only tea,' replied Malcolm. 'We don't drink coffee in this house. Earl Grey only.' He went into the kitchen, leaving Lena in the living room. 'That's okay?' he said.

'Sure,' replied Lena, steeling herself for a cup of hot insipidness. English people and their tea.

She sat down, careful to make sure Terence was not nearby. He watched her from the far corner, basking in the heat of the electric lamp. Lena looked around the room. Fake purple flowers sat on the mantelpiece above the fireplace. Flames licked up, but they looked wrong. And it was the summer. She leaned forwards. They were on a screen.

'That looks cosy,' she said, as Malcolm placed a teacup and saucer in front of her.

'Terence loves to watch a fire,' he replied. 'But this is much safer than a real one. Real fires can be so dangerous.'

'And messy,' said Lena, starting to think that this house wasn't weird at all. Perhaps it was perfect.

'Oh, I know. My dead mother, god rest her soul, insisted on a real fire. That was back home in Ireland. My brothers would push me into the fire every Sunday.'

'*Rohadékok!* That is terrible. Were you hurt?'

'What? No, you've misunderstood! Only in the summer. Not when the fire was lit. But I would get covered in soot. Filthy soot.' Malcolm stood up and left for the kitchen. Lena heard him run the tap and wash his hands again. 'Biscuit?'

'Please,' said Lena. She saw Terence look over at her. Suddenly he scuttled towards the sofa.

Malcolm came back with a plate of uniform biscuits, each with three purple smarties on top, arranged in a triangle. 'I make these myself,' he said. 'My special recipe.'

Lena grabbed one and looked down. Terence was scratching her trainer with his clawed foot.

'Terence, I've told you that it is bad manners to beg,' scolded Malcolm, breaking off a piece of biscuit and neatly sliding it along the floor towards the lizard. Terence scurried towards it and snapped it up with his surprisingly adroit pink tongue.

'He's such a comfort to me,' said Malcolm.

'He is very . . . tidy,' finished Lena, watching as he scooped up every crumb. She took a sip of tea. Tea reminded her of when she was ill as a child and her mother made her drink it, withholding her usual milky coffee. The biscuits, however, were flavoured with vanilla and excellent. She polished off the one in her hand and reached for another. Terence scuttled back to her foot and looked up expectantly.

'Go ahead and feed him a piece,' said Malcolm. 'He probably won't bite, if you're quick. And I've got plenty of disinfectant and bandages, just in case.'

Lena threw a piece of biscuit across the room with more force than she'd intended. Terence raced after it like a dog chasing a ball. She took her opportunity to segue the conversation in the direction she wanted.

'You must have used the bandages, after the gallery reception,' she said. 'Were you badly hurt?'

'Thank you so much for your assistance,' said Malcolm. 'I really am terribly grateful.'

'I wish you had let me call an ambulance,' said Lena. 'Or the police.'

'No need,' replied Malcolm. 'I am well stocked up here to take care of myself.'

'But the men should be punished. It is justice.'

'Justice is an abstract concept,' said Malcolm. 'And I really needed to get home. Terence was waiting. The blood was dripping on to my beautiful lilac trousers. Not to mention the dirty mess I'd been pushed into. I would have burned my clothes, had it not been such a fire risk. As it was, I had to throw them all away.' He looked to Terence. 'My favourite trousers,' he added, mournfully.

Lena looked at him, wondering whether there was more to it than that. 'It is hard,' she said, reaching out to touch his hand. 'To be clean in this world.'

'Indeed,' said Malcolm. They shared a moment of understanding. Then Malcolm took his hand away and went back into the kitchen. Lena heard him running the tap again and washing his hands.

Perhaps there was such a thing as too clean, after all.

Lena sat in the police waiting room. It had an unpleasant aroma of stale sweat today, more so than usual. She wasn't surprised. The sun had made Islington like an oven. As she'd walked through Islington Green, she'd seen usually conservative Londoners rolling up their trousers and removing their shirts, lying prostrated around the tiny stretch of grass as if victims of battle. Tomorrow they'd be an assortment of shades of angry pink, bad-tempered and painful to the touch as they crowded themselves into humid tube carriages.

The police had held Sarika here for two days already. Surely they had to let her go soon? Lena cursed herself for her own stupidity that first day after the painting went missing, two weeks ago now. She shouldn't have gone to the police station alone. She should have waited for Sarika to shower and escorted her there herself. Running away had been the worst thing the girl could have done. That made her look much more guilty than the fact she had been the last person in the gallery, or the nonsense that was on Kat's laptop.

Lena stood up when she saw DI Blake approaching. The policewoman was wearing a smart beige linen dress that fitted loosely around her taut figure. She managed to look cool and breezy, even in these conditions. Lena breathed in, trying to absorb some of the coolness. Instead she got a mouthful of Blake's perfume and was filled with memories of *mákos kenyér*, blue breadseed poppy fields back home. *Szar.* Even the scent of this woman was perfect.

'I see Sarika now?' said Lena, feeling her English worsen whenever she spoke to this lady.

'I would like a quick word with you first,' replied Blake. She shepherded Lena into a small room inside the station, without waiting for a reply.

'Kat talked to you?' asked Lena, once Blake had shut the door.

'Yes,' said Blake. 'She told us that Sarika never used her laptop. Please, take a seat.'

Lena sat down in the chair, its plastic hot against her skin. 'Then you have one less piece of evidence against Sarika,' said Lena. 'If you let her go I will keep my eyeball on her,' she said, confident she was using this expression correctly. 'Make sure that she is where she is needed to be.'

'It's not that simple,' said Blake, pouring herself a glass of water and offering one to Lena before sitting down. 'Although it is strange that Kat should voluntarily come in and change her story like that. I hope that no one has been interfering in the case. Tampering with witnesses is a crime.' She looked at Lena. Lena gazed back with what she hoped was a blank expression.

'Perhaps she felt guilt for lying,' said Lena, her eyes on the plastic cup of water in her hand. She took a sip. It was warm as bath water.

'In any case, the material on the laptop was never key to the case against Sarika. It just added to the story. But having spoken to her, I do feel that she does not seem to have the expertise needed to successfully execute this crime.'

Lena felt relief flood over her and took a celebratory sip of the warm water. 'She can come home with me?'

'However,' continued Blake, 'I cannot base my actions on my personal opinions alone. Facts are facts. The painting went missing and Sarika was the last person to be at the gallery. She had the keys. She has a criminal record for theft. She fled the next day. I would not be doing my duty as a police officer if I allowed my chief suspect to walk free, knowing as we do that she is a flight risk. I mark my success upon whether I recover the stolen goods. In this case too much time has passed. It is likely that the painting has been sold and is on its way abroad by now. There is a strong market for Ms Weincamp's work in China.'

'And if you cannot get the painting back?'

'It does not look good for your friend. I believe I have enough to charge her. My main problem is that I've been unable to establish enough information about my other suspects.'

Lena smiled. 'Why did you not say?' she said. 'I have plenty of information on everyone. Who do you want to start with? Patrick Pieterson. He was still there when the keys were stolen. And he is planning to leave town . . .'

'No,' replied Blake. 'I am not interested in the gallery guests. I want you to tell me more about Pietro Agnoletti.'

Lena looked at Blake. 'He owned the painting,' she said. 'Why would he steal it from himself?' She had considered him herself, of course, and knew the answer before the word left Blake's elegant lips.

'Insurance.'

The door swung open and Gullins strolled in, eating an enormous bar of chocolate. 'There you are,' he said to Blake. 'It's so hot out there that this Mars Bar melted in my pocket. I can still break you off a piece, if you don't mind it being a bit soft.'

Blake grimaced. 'We're in the middle of an interview.'

'Tape running?' said Gullins. It wasn't. 'Then it's informal, is it? Good, I'd hate for you to leave me out.'

'This is my case, Constable,' replied Blake. 'I will seek your assistance when I need it. Currently there is no grunt work to be done.'

'Excellent,' said Gullins, taking a seat. 'Then you won't mind me joining in.' He grinned at Lena, displaying brown chocolate-coated teeth.

Blake shifted in her seat. 'Lena, you were going to tell me more about Pietro. I understand from PC Cartwright that he confided in you. Did he have money troubles, that you were aware of?'

Gullins almost choked on his chocolate, sending tiny sprays of sweet spittle on to Lena's face. 'That guy having money troubles? And my mum is the Queen!'

Lena hesitated for a moment. Pietro had plenty of troubles, without the police investigating him too. But then, they'd be bound to find out in any case. And was she sure that he was innocent? Sarika was family. She had to come first.

'Yes,' replied Lena. 'He is being threatened by a loan . . .' Lena paused, trying to remember the expression Pietro had used. 'Fish,' she said, feeling pleased with herself.

'You've cheered me up no end,' said Gullins, still laughing as he licked the remains of the chocolate from the wrapper. 'I'll put an armed guard on him, shall I? And maybe start a collection round the boys at the station so he can keep his Bentley running?'

'PC Gullins,' said Blake. 'If you continue to make a mockery of this investigation I will be forced to—'

'Don't worry, I'm off,' he said, hauling himself to his feet, still chuckling. 'I'll leave you two to your girl power.'

'Now,' said Blake, leaning in to Lena once Gullins had shut

the door. 'Tell me what you know about Pietro. Then I'll take you to see Sarika.'

Patrick was turning into her best client, thought Lena, as she made her way towards his house after leaving the police station. He had called her back a third time, eager that she should come and clean at his that afternoon. As long as he had remembered to leave the cash this time, she thought grimly. She wouldn't clean a third time without payment. At least it was a chance to have another look around his house, to see if she could figure out his plans.

The last time she had been in a bit of a daze. Hearing about the death of Mr Theopolis had quelled her enthusiasm for investigating, but it hadn't dampened her cleaning efforts. She'd mourned Mr Theopolis with each wipe of her cloth, mop of the floor, sweep of the duster. She'd thought about Mrs Theopolis, on her own in her clean house, polishing the cutlery with salty tears travelling down her cheek. Lena hoped she'd go back to Greece to enjoy her days with her children and grandchildren. Fish in her belly and the Aegean sun on her face.

Sarika had been in reasonable spirits. She'd heard that Kat had confessed that Sarika didn't ever use the laptop and seemed to think it was only a matter of time before she'd be released. Lena wasn't so sure. Even with what she'd told Blake about Pietro, the painting still eluded them all. And without the painting there was no proof that Sarika was innocent. Still, it was good that the girl felt positive. That would make her miserable situation more bearable. Temporarily, at least.

Lena reached to tip Patrick's window box to retrieve the key, then jerked her hand away. It was different. Full of red geraniums, their petals stretched out towards the sunshine. The pot still had the price tag. Fifty-five pounds for a tub of geraniums! She could plant something herself for much less than that. He must really want to sell this house. Perhaps she should start a flower business too, she mused. She could market herself to anyone moving house. A thorough clean, and plants, flowers and scented candles scattered around in key places. She'd mark them up, of course, to make a profit. She could even get Sarika, once this was solved, to make bread to bake in the oven. The scent of baking bread would definitely sell a house. She reckoned for that she could easily charge £10 per loaf and the ingredients would cost pennies. Well, maybe not Sarika; she seemed even less likely to be capable of baking bread than Lena. Lucia, perhaps?

The door swung open, breaking her recruitment reverie. 'Lena!' exclaimed Patrick, a smile spreading across his face. 'You're my saviour. Come in, please.'

Lena followed him, puzzled. This was the most enthusiastically he had ever spoken to her, and she didn't think she'd seen him smile before.

She followed him into the living room, which was a floral mortuary. 'I bought the cut flowers too early,' he said. 'But no matter, I can get some more before she comes. Here, come into the kitchen. I've got a few houseplants and I'm not sure where to put them. Or how to keep them alive.'

The kitchen was a jungle of luscious ferns, small orange trees laden with fruit, tall rubber trees, jasmines in full bloom and, to Lena's delight, orchids. All sat with their price tags still stuck to their pots. And all were slowly drying out.

'Where should they go?' he asked, his eyes looking worried. 'Will you put them where you think?'

'Okay,' said Lena, feeling a little overwhelmed. 'I will water them and find them a place to live.'

'Water. Of course. You are brilliant. Do you think she'll notice that they are not the same plants as the ones when she left? I tried to get the same but I never really looked at them before. No idea what we had. Some had flowers, I think. She loves flowers.'

Lena opened her mouth to ask who he was talking about just as his phone rang. He jumped up and ran to search for it.

Patrick was like a completely different person, she thought to herself as she poured water from a jug into the grateful plants. Like a schoolboy at the start of the summer holidays. Or a teenager, love-struck for the first time.

That sounded right. Not quite right, but better. Lena picked up an orchid and a fern and went to look for a shady spot in which they could live. The bathroom, perhaps, where they would appreciate the humidity.

Lena trudged up the stairs and found the perfect homes for them. She looked around the room, which had stone flooring and tiles the colour of a sunset: the last moment of muted purples before darkness took over.

She collected another plant from downstairs, a little orange tree clinging to its still tiny fruit. She took it into a small study and moved a pile of papers to find it a sunny spot. The address at the top of the first page was Mexico. She put the plant to one side and read the letter carefully.

Patrick was no money launderer for a gang, trading in art crime. He was not preparing to flee the country. He was a man, lost, unable to look after himself. But he had hope again. That was why he had wanted to buy the painting. For the woman who had so carefully decorated this house, who loved flowers and loved art. And loved purple.

The letter was from a cancer clinic in Mexico. It said that his wife was well enough to come home. Her tests were clear now.

So that was what the money had been for.

One fewer suspect. But a happy ending. She'd get this house spotless for him. And for his wife. Convalescence was easier in a clean house.

213

CHAPTER 22

Lena sat at home, fiddling with her suspect board. Gertrude was innocent and she was convinced Patrick was too. From these three clients who had been suspects at the gallery reception, Malcolm still stood out as a loose end. Lena hated loose ends. When you pulled on them everything unravelled.

She glanced at her watch. She still had two hours before she was meant to be at Cartwright's house for dinner. Plenty of time for a phone call and to get ready. She pulled out the list of names from the gallery and found Malcolm's plus one at the reception. Leonora Taylor. She closed her eyes and tried to remember what she looked like. A tall blonde woman came into her head. He'd said she was a potential client, but he'd also said the painting was for the reception in his clearly abandoned office. She needed to talk to this woman.

Lena thought for a moment of what she'd say if she called her. Could she offer her a cleaning service as well? Perhaps it wasn't necessary. She dialled the number on the paper. The words would come to her.

'Leonora speaking,' said the cultured voice at the end of the telephone.

'My name is Lena,' she said, an idea forming with the words. She found herself putting on her poshest voice. 'I hope you do not mind me contacting you, but I am a marketing director at . . . Lena's Elite

Evenings,' she said. She was right about that name. It did sound like an escort agency. Never mind. 'We are a Hungarian entertainment firm. I was given your details by Malcolm Paulter. You are his reference before I hire his agency to do my marketing.'

There was a pause and then a chuckle. 'He's got some front,' said Leonora. 'I suppose he thinks that no one ever checks references.'

'He has not been a good agency?'

'He has been no agency at all,' said Leonora. 'He used to be one of the hottest creative directors in town; his agency was famous. But then his OCD got the better of him. What started as attention to detail spiralled out of control. He tried to get every one of his clients to change their logo to purple. Insisted the world would end if everything was not a purple triangle.'

'I do not want a triangular purple logo,' said Lena, hoping she'd say more.

'No one does. His staff realised he was barmy and left one by one. Then his clients did the same. He had to close the agency.'

'But you were with him at the Agnoletti Archer Gallery reception?' said Lena.

'How do you know that?' said Leonora, a little sharply. 'Oh, I suppose he told you. Yes, he invited me and I felt sorry for him, but he spent the whole time straightening the picture frames. I left early, I couldn't face him any more. All those ridiculous brags about buying the painting. He's in more debt than Argentina. And that nonsense about Chinese clients. I think he is delusional.'

Lena thought a moment, wondering how desperately he needed cash. 'Did he try to get money out of you?'

'Only for work he thought he could still do. Sad, really, that's what he's become. I heard a rumour he can't walk past a road if he sees a traffic cone. Has to go and admire its shape. Cones are as lucky as triangles, in his book.'

'Thank you,' said Lena. She put the phone down. That was what he was doing in the alleyway, she thought, remembering the traffic cones she'd seen there. And that was why he had to get home. The dirt on his clothes would be killing him. It made sense. But still, he needed money. Badly. Could he be involved?

It felt as if she was getting closer to the truth. She found it hard to think of anything else. So when she got ready to go to Cartwright's flat for the first time for his dinner invitation, she didn't even think about what to wear. It wasn't until she was standing outside his door that she realised she was wearing old denim shorts, a faded green T-shirt and she hadn't brought any wine with her. Initially the invitation had seemed so casual, but here, with the petunias in his window box glaring their disapproval at her, Lena suddenly felt nervous. She carried on walking past the house.

She wanted to talk to Cartwright about her theories and see if he could help. So there could be no cancelling at the last minute. She didn't have time to go home and change. But she could try and find a bottle of wine. Lena looked up and down the residential street hopefully. She knew Stoke Newington well; she just had to get her bearings. Lena went left and stumbled upon a small café with organic sprouting mung beans and despaired of her chances to purchase alcohol. On closer inspection, though, she found a bottle of organic wine and a tub of fiercely priced olives. Purchasing both and wishing most of her work at the moment wasn't for free, she hurried back to Cartwright's house.

He lived on the lower ground floor of a three-storey Victorian house divided into flats. Lena took a deep breath and rang the doorbell. Cartwright opened the door. Lena felt a little flutter. He was wearing chinos and a loose blue cotton shirt that matched his eyes. They had an awkward cheek kiss and she came inside.

After the shock of Malcolm's immaculate flat, Lena was pleased to see that Cartwright's house was normal. Fairly clean and relatively tidy, with a multitude of well-watered houseplants and a sofa with arms so scratched it looked like it was growing stubble. 'Kaplan is around here somewhere,' said Cartwright. 'Perhaps try the garden?'

Lena went outside. Kaplan shot out of a tree laden with inchoate apples and wound his hairless body around Lena's legs. She hadn't felt his bare skin on her own bare legs before, and she had to stifle a shudder. Even though she could see his baldness, she still mentally expected the soft caress of fur from the cat. Cartwright was right, the animal had put on weight. But as Lena scratched his ears and listened to him purr, she was pleased. This was a happy cat.

Cartwright came out to join her, holding two glasses of prosecco. 'He is pleased to see you,' he said, handing Lena a glass. 'He is also pretty excited about the lamb in the oven.'

Lena smiled at him. 'I am excited about the lamb also,' she said. 'I cannot remember the last time anyone but my mama cooked for me.'

Cartwright smiled back. 'The way to a girl's heart is her stomach,' he replied. Lena looked at him and he began to redden under her gaze. 'Talking of which,' he continued, 'I need to check on my starter.'

While Cartwright disappeared into the kitchen, Lena looked around. She didn't enjoy gardening herself but she could tell this garden was loved. It was fairly small, with a table and chairs set up and lit by candles. The sun had not fully set and she could make out a pink rose bush in full bloom, a clematis with flowers like stars sprawling over the fence, luscious green foliage and a small pond covered in water lilies.

She sat on a chair and helped herself to some kind of cheesy pastry nibble as she sipped her drink. Lena's mother loved gardening and had tried to encourage Lena when she was growing up. But she'd never taken to it: it brought dirt into the house and things would never grow in neat lines. But she admired people who could. She wondered if this was all Cartwright's work.

Cartwright came out holding two plates, which he lowered ceremoniously to the table. 'Goat's cheese and beetroot salad with a pomegranate vinaigrette,' he said, his voice full of pride. 'I thought something light would be nice before the lamb. More prosecco?'

'Yes please,' replied Lena. She bit into a piece of salty goat's cheese. 'This is delicious,' she said. She scooped some salad on to her fork and took a gulp of prosecco. She knew that they were not meant to be talking about the investigation, but Lena found she could not chat any more about cheese until she'd shared her most recent discovery. 'I have found the frame *A Study in Purple* was in,' she blurted out. 'It is downstairs in the gallery. It looks the same as the others, but I recognise a mark on it.'

'That's amazing,' said Cartwright, picking up his fork. 'What did Detective Blake say?'

'I have not told her,' admitted Lena. 'I want to investigate first. But I do not know what to do next.' She looked at him expectantly.

'That explains why they couldn't see anyone on CCTV with the picture,' said Cartwright. 'It would be much easier to smuggle it away unnoticed without the frame. You wouldn't even need a getaway car. Just roll it up and at that time of night no one will even notice you carrying it.'

'They might notice,' said Lena, thoughtfully. 'You would need to hide it on yourself . . .'

'What?' said Cartwright, watching her face.

'I have got it!' said Lena. 'Of course.' She leapt up. 'Come on, we need to go now.'

'Go where?' said Cartwright. 'The lamb is almost ready. And you've hardly touched your starter.'

Lena looked regretfully at the white goat's cheese, still sitting on its bed of leaves.

'I cannot eat knowing that proof is out there,' she said.

'I understand,' muttered Cartwright.

'And we can have the lamb later?' said Lena. ' We need to see that CCTV. We need to see it now.'

'There,' said Lena. 'That man. Can we zoom in?'

'This isn't *24*,' grumbled Cartwright. 'What you see is what you get.'

Lena watched the man. He was in the shadows, he wore a hat and his face was turned away from the camera. She analysed how he walked. The limp was as she thought she remembered it from the CCTV footage she had watched for Mr Theopolis. He never bent his right leg, instead swinging it gingerly from his hip. He was coming from the direction of the gallery.

'He is the thief,' declared Lena. 'Look at how he walks. He must have the painting, rolled up and in his right trouser leg.'

Cartwright looked more closely. 'I think you could be right,' he said. 'But we can get a gait expert to analyse this, just to be sure,' he said. He looked at Lena's confused face. 'Gait, as in how you walk,' he explained. 'Not as in garden.'

'Where does he go next?' asked Lena. 'Is there more footage?'

Cartwright went to the cupboard and came back with a small pile. 'It is lucky we still have these from the council,' he said. 'They are part of the evidence in Mr Theopolis's case. There's no guarantee that we'll be able to track that man,' he said. 'But let's see what we can do.'

The two spent several hours glued to the screen, watching for the man with the limp. It would have been impossible to tell from his face, but his limp made him easy to spot. They traced him from Upper Street, right up to St Paul's Road, before they lost him at the New River Path. He never emerged from the other side of the park.

'I know that area,' said Cartwright. 'We can go there tomorrow and look around. See where he might have gone to.'

'We go now,' said Lena, grabbing her bag and Cartwright's arm. 'Let us see what we can find.'

It was almost eleven p.m. by the time they arrived at the entrance to the New River Path. It was a narrow park around the thin canal intersecting a council estate on one side and a row of expensive Georgian townhouses on the other. There was a pub near the entrance. Cartwright went in to enquire while Lena investigated the park gate, now locked.

If it was locked now it would have been locked then, she thought. She looked at the gate, taller than her and made of cast iron. Lena pushed against it, and then thought of trying to clamber up it. She thought better of it. It would be impossible for anyone but a gymnast. Even if she could make it up, she doubted their suspect could. Lena looked around. There was a road leading back around to the estates, but that had been thoroughly covered by CCTV and they hadn't seen their limper. Could he have hidden the painting somewhere, wondered Lena.

She looked around again for a hiding place, shivering now in her shorts. There was a row of tall, smart houses, a telephone box long since abandoned and a few parked cars. She didn't know what she expected to find. It had been over three weeks since the painting had been taken. It would have been sold by now. Possibly on its way to China, like Detective Blake had said.

Lena opened up the phone box anyway. Since she was here she might as well look thoroughly. She was rewarded by the smell of urine and an eyeful of postcards lining the wall, advertising chat lines and prostitutes. Everyone had a mobile phone now, even her, so the telephone sat there sadly, not enjoying its seedy retirement.

'No one can remember him in the pub,' said Cartwright, crossing the road to join her. 'Let's go back to mine. I'm sure I can do something nice with cold lamb chops while we work out what to do next. Turn it into curry, perhaps. Kaplan has probably devoured the goat's cheese though. I think I left it on the counter by mistake.'

'Just a minute,' said Lena. She'd noticed that, though most of the postcards were shoved haphazardly wherever they would fit, the ones that lined the top right corner of the box were much more symmetrical, running down in neat order for about a metre. Lena pulled them off, one by one.

'I didn't see you as a sex-line fan,' said Cartwright, with a nervous laugh. 'The police used to take those down, but we stopped a few years ago. No one else wants to use the phone boxes anyway.'

'Shush,' said Lena. Behind the cards she found a cardboard tube, wrapped in cellophane and affixed to the corner with Blu-Tack. She pulled the tube away and peered into it, as though it were a telescope.

Lena wiped her hands on her shorts and then reached inside, moving to stand directly under the streetlight. Very carefully she pulled out the rolled-up canvas inside. She held her breath and unravelled it. Red circles, a collection of tadpole-like creatures and a purple triangle greeted her. '*A Study in Purple*,' she said. 'We have found it.'

CHAPTER 23

'I am so glad to have you back,' said Lena, meaning it. Sarika sat on the floor in Penelope's house helping Casper to draw a dragon while Lena cleaned the living room. She'd been freed the day after the painting was found – whoever the person was on the CCTV, it was clearly a man and not Sarika. Now, six days later, things were getting back to normal. Penelope was having lunch with her friends from her NCT group of new mothers, and Crispin was dozing in the corner crib.

'The dragon has scales,' Sarika told Casper. 'You draw them by making lots and lots of U's with the purple crayon. See?'

'Can this go on the fridge when it is done?' asked Casper.

'Of course. If you draw it very well,' said Sarika. 'And don't colour in outside the lines.'

Lena balanced herself on the mantelpiece, finally reaching up to the coving she'd wanted to clean since she had first visited Penelope's house but had never had the chance.

'It is good to be back,' said Sarika in Hungarian, while Casper industriously focused on the scale creation. 'It was hell being in custody.'

'It was only for four days,' said Lena.

'Four days too long,' replied Sarika. 'Thanks to that boyfriend of yours.'

'It was not Cartwright's fault that you were caught,' said Lena. 'I didn't give him your address. And he is not my boyfriend.'

'Whatevs,' replied Sarika, dropping some English into their conversation.

'When are you getting rid of that awful blue hair?' said Lena. 'What will your mama say?'

'Dragg says it matches my eyes,' said Sarika. Lena rolled her own eyes at that. 'About Dragg,' Sarika continued. 'It is actually Kat's name on the lease . . . and now we're together, and both have work in London, and I'm living with you . . .'

Lena jumped down from the mantel. The parquet floor shuddered a little in response.

'You made me go outside the line!' reprimanded Casper. 'I need to start again.'

'No you don't,' said Sarika, looking at the picture. 'Look, if we just extend that line a bit we can cheat.'

Casper grinned and continued. 'We do fire next,' promised Sarika. 'I'll show you how to make it come right out of the dragon's nose.'

'Like bogeys,' shrieked Casper, delighted. 'Dragons are much cooler than dinosaurs.'

'Dragons are the coolest,' agreed Sarika.

Lena wiped away the dust that had fallen from the coving on to the mantelpiece. 'I still don't know who took the painting,' she said in Hungarian again, hoping to change the subject.

'As long as they know it wasn't me,' said Sarika, 'I am happy.'

'But I'm curious,' said Lena. 'The police still cannot tell who that man was. And he was wearing gloves so there are no fingerprints. And why leave an expensive painting in a phone box? It makes no sense.'

'If you don't let Dragg live with us, I will have to move out too. We will have to find somewhere else to stay,' said Sarika. 'Somewhere we can be together.'

'That might be best,' said Lena, thinking of the state of the flat they used to live in. She wasn't sure she could bear it. 'There is not much room at my flat and you would both need to be on the sofa bed. It will not be comfortable.'

'Okay,' replied Sarika. 'I will leave tomorrow. I think there is a squat in Stoke Newington with a bit of spare floor space. Dragg says Druggie Joe has been missing so long they are giving up on him. So we could take his spot.' She looked at Lena.

'I will get you both a key cut,' said Lena, fetching the vacuum cleaner before she could change her mind. 'He can move in tonight.'

'Thanks Lena,' said Sarika, enclosing Lena in a massive hug that knocked the wind out of her.

'Just temporary,' she said. 'Then you can get a place of your own.'

'Did you hear that?' said Sarika to Casper, bending down to talk to the child. 'Lena is letting me live with her. Until I am back on my feet.'

'My dragon has brilliant feet,' contributed Casper. 'Feet with claws. Better than both your feet put together.'

Lena ran her duster over *A Study in Purple*. It was back in its original position on the wall, but in a brand-new frame. Simon had chosen it. Apparently, brushed metal was more appropriate for the colour tones.

Lena stood back to admire the painting. It was hard to imagine that it had caused so much fuss. Still all she could see was a mess of triangles and tadpoles. She was surprised. Lena liked Trudy and thought she seemed like the real deal. Someone who could actually paint. A proper artist.

Lena put her own feelings aside and dusted the giant clay eye. It also gazed disinterestedly at the painting. She was no art expert. But something bothered her. Lena went up to the painting and inspected it closely. She had no doubt that this was the painting she knew. She recognised the brush strokes, the precise colours. But something about the theft didn't make sense to her.

Why was the painting abandoned in a phone box? It seemed a strange hiding place. And Blake had told her that thieves try to sell a piece as quickly as they can, preferably abroad. Had a deal fallen through and someone panicked? Surely there was a safer place to stash a painting worth that sum than a phone box, concealed only by flyers for prostitutes? It was as if whoever had taken it thought it had no value. But then why bother stealing it in the first place?

'There's my hero,' said Pietro, interrupting her reverie. 'How's my very favourite cleaner?'

Lena smiled at him. 'I am good. I am pleased that Sarika is free and safe. I am pleased to have my job here back also. And you? Have you found a buyer yet for *A Study in Purple*?'

'It's a bidding war!' said Pietro. 'Perhaps more of my exhibits should be stolen and then returned.'

'The thief has not been caught,' said Lena. 'So perhaps more will.'

'Don't say that,' said Pietro with a shudder. 'I don't actually think my heart could take it.'

'So who is in your bidding war?' asked Lena.

'The same people who were all trying to negotiate me down before. Suddenly much keener. I expect they realise the painting is so much more beautiful than they thought.'

'No,' said Lena. 'They all have different reasons.'

'We are lucky at how the canvas was rolled,' said Pietro. 'It was nice and loose, and the paint was on the outside. If they'd done it the other way it could have cracked. Or if they had wrapped it in something like bubble wrap it could have got little pockmarks. Ferrotyping is the bane of the oil painting's world. Now, you were going to tell me about the psyche of my clients. Perhaps I can use it to sell more.'

Simon came into the room. 'I dropped Trudy off at the airport,' he said.

'She has gone?' said Lena, looking at him in surprise. 'I thought that you two . . .'

'She's a free spirit,' replied Simon. 'When New York calls to you, it calls, apparently. She had a big gallery opening there.'

'I can't believe she just left like that,' said Pietro. 'No goodbyes, nothing.'

'She said goodbye to me,' said Simon.

'Lena was just about to tell us about our clients,' said Pietro. 'Simon, tea for me and some ridiculously strong coffee for our Hungarian saviour.'

'Gertrude is an investor,' said Lena, watching Simon clatter around the kitchen. 'She does not trust the stock market or banks, so she will keep the painting in her secret attic for safety.'

'We should sell it to her,' said Simon, from the other room. 'It is a brilliant investment. When does she want to pick it up?'

'Never!' declared Pietro. 'The painting must be seen.'

'Malcolm is who you should not sell it to,' said Lena. 'He cannot afford it.'

'But he owns an advertising agency,' said Pietro.

'It is not doing so well,' said Lena. 'And I think that the painting is not healthy for him. Purple triangles are an obsession.'

'You cannot possibly know that,' said Pietro.

'Patrick is who you should sell the painting to,' said Lena. 'He deserves it.'

'Really?' Simon interrupted. 'He does not seem like an art lover. Where would he keep it?'

'He is not,' said Lena. 'He wants it for his wife. She is about to arrive back from the clinic. In Mexico. She has been very ill but is getting better.'

'I don't know how you get people to tell you all this, Lena. No one breathed a word of any of it to me,' complained Pietro.

'Their houses speak,' replied Lena. 'If you learn how to listen.'

The gallery door swung open. 'Miss me?' said Trudy, giving Pietro a kiss on each cheek and another right on his mouth.

'Darling!' exclaimed Pietro. 'Delighted you've come to visit. But what about your flight?'

'There are plenty of planes,' dismissed Trudy, with a lofty wave of her hand. 'I had unfinished business.'

Simon stepped out of the kitchen. 'I am glad to see you,' he said, with a nervous smile. 'But I thought . . .'

'Changed my mind,' said Trudy, pivoting on her heels. 'How's that genius cleaner and that gorgeous painting of mine?'

Lena went to greet her, but Trudy, unusually rude, pushed past her. She stared at the painting, transfixed.

'Isn't it exquisite!' said Pietro. 'Even the artist is mesmerised by her own work. I should take a picture of your expression, Trudy. For Instagram. Perhaps I could even put the price up.'

'This is not *A Study in Purple*,' said Trudy, slowly.

'Nonsense,' said Pietro. 'There's purple all over it. What else could it be?'

'This is not my painting at all,' Trudy continued. 'The brush strokes are all wrong. The colours are too muted. The triangles,' she turned to look straight at Pietro, 'they have no soul.'

'Of course they do,' said Pietro, trying to laugh. 'It must be yours.'

'This painting is a fake,' said Trudy. 'I am absolutely certain.'

'That's crazy!' exclaimed Cartwright. 'Why would someone place a fake painting in a phone box?'

'Why would someone put a real one in a phone box?' countered Lena.

'Perhaps it was the drop point?' suggested Cartwright. 'Where the thief left it for the buyer to pick up and leave the money.' He warmed to his theme. 'But the thief double-crossed the buyer and left the fake instead. It's like a movie.'

Lena scooped the foam from her cappuccino with a spoon and popped it into her mouth. She'd called Cartwright straight after the revelation and they'd met in a smart-looking bakery. It was only once they were there that Lena realised it was one of the many gluten-free bakeries that littered Upper Street. Coeliac disease seemed an epidemic in Islington. 'Maybe,' she said. 'But I am sure it is the painting that was hanging in the gallery. I recognise it.'

'But can you be sure?' said Cartwright. 'You are not an art expert.'

'That is what Pietro said too,' said Lena. 'But I am sure. One hundred per cent. It had the same little water marks on it when Sarika wiped it.' She looked at Cartwright's face. 'No real damage was done,' she said, quickly. 'Just dried little water drops, in the shape of a circle. No one noticed so I do not try to fix it in case I made it worse.'

'Pietro had no idea it was a fake? He is not much of an art expert in that case.'

'No,' said Lena. 'He says he did not know. But that is the only thing he can say, even if it makes him look stupid. Or he could be in trouble for dealing in fakes.' Lena put the coffee down and took a bite of her gluten-free chocolate cake. It tasted surprisingly good. She offered a forkful to Cartwright, but he was busy extracting the Earl Grey teabag from its tiny glass pot.

'I will need to look into what the procedure will be now,' said Cartwright. 'Pietro clearly can't sell the painting. I wonder what attitude the insurance company will take. Presumably they won't pay? I'll ask DI Blake. It's her area of expertise.'

'Sarika is home safe,' said Lena, polishing off the cake. 'And my agency's name is clear. I am sorry for Pietro, but my case is solved.'

'But we need to find out who that man was in the CCTV. It could lead us to something bigger.'

'I am sure DI Blake will want your help,' said Lena. 'But after my experience with Yasemin Avci I am done with gangs.'

'I'm ruined!' declared Pietro. He was slumped on the floor in front of the door to the storage cupboard, blocking Lena's path to the mop.

'You will be okay,' said Lena, wondering if there was a spare mop in the basement.

'It would have been better if you'd left that damn fake in that seedy phone box,' said Pietro, his voice full of bitterness.

'Better for you perhaps,' said Lena. 'Not better for Sarika. She would still be in custody.'

'But what about me?' said Pietro. 'The insurance company will never pay out now. And that Turkish psychopath is coming back.'

'I can talk to the police and get you help? Protection?'

'And even if he doesn't murder me in my very own gallery,' continued Pietro, talking over her, 'I am still ruined. A laughing stock. Couldn't even tell a painting was a fake.'

'Plenty of people are fooled by fakes,' said Simon, walking into the gallery. 'And what's this about murder?'

'Nothing,' said Pietro, jumping to his feet. Lena took the opportunity to squeeze behind him and gain entry to the cupboard. She emerged triumphant with the mop and bucket, then grabbed the cleaning spray and a cloth duster as well, in case her path was blocked again later.

'People will understand,' said Simon. 'Even some of the world's most famous art dealers have been fooled by fakes in the past. It happens. No one will blame us.'

Pietro walked up to Simon and hugged him. 'You've been a true friend,' he said.

'I wouldn't let any harm come to you,' said Simon. 'Now, I need to get going. I'm late for an appointment.'

He left.

'You should tell him about the money you owe,' said Lena, as soon as the gallery door was closed. 'Perhaps he could help?'

'There's nothing he can do,' said Pietro miserably. 'He doesn't have any goddamn money. I'm the one with the money, and I can't get hold of a single penny when I need it!'

Lena allowed herself a moment, standing outside her front door. She took a deep breath, remembering how it used to feel to come home. To enter the calm oasis of a space that was hers. That was ordered. That was clean. Then she put the key in the lock and pushed open the door.

Dragg's skinny frame was draped over the sofa bed, his skin only just distinguishable from Lena's once white sheets. 'Lena, is that you?' called a voice from the bathroom. 'Could you give me a hand?'

Lena picked her way through the melange of mess. A large rucksack sat on the floor, its contents erupting into the living room. Twisted trousers spilled out like entrails. Trainers were dotted around the room, kicked off to form a haphazard assault course. A dirty sock stared up at her, a hole in its sole. I know how you feel, she thought.

'Lena?'

She went into the bathroom and gasped. Sarika had filled the sink with blood and was leaning over it, more pouring from her head.

'*Istenem!* What has happened? Here, sit down. I call ambulance. And police.' She looked for a weapon in the bathroom to protect them both from the newly violent Dragg.

Sarika laughed. 'It's just red hair dye,' she said, with a giggle. 'You are such a drama queen, Lena.'

Lena sank down on the toilet seat. '*Hála Istennek*,' she said. 'You must not do that to me.'

'In fairness, the packet does say the colour is called "Bulls' Blood",' said Sarika, flicking her hair backwards. Splatters of the colour hit Lena's white wall behind her. 'Here, help me wash it out.' She rotated herself over the small bath. Lena picked up the shower head and sprayed Sarika's head, watching the colour drain from her hair into the white expanse beneath, dancing and spinning before finally escaping into the plug hole. Sarika had something pink and damp wrapped around her neck. Lena's once white hand towel. Lena could hardly bear to look at the rest of the room. Red splatters on the bathmat and walls. Pink towels. Red sink.

'It looks like there has been a massacre here,' she said. She fiddled with the tap to increase the water pressure.

'It does look a bit more sinister than the blue,' admitted Sarika. 'But red is Dragg's favourite colour. The colour of fire. Ouch, that's hot!'

'Oops,' said Lena, pausing a malicious millisecond before turning off the tap. 'All done.' Sarika reached for a fresh towel and wrapped it around her head before Lena could stop her. 'You should not change yourself for a man,' advised Lena, watching her cousin admiring herself in the mirror. 'He should love you for who you are.'

'Do you think I've lost weight while I was away? I expect it was all the stress. Being a fugitive.'

Lena took another look around the bathroom. 'No,' she replied. 'And clean up.'

When she emerged back into the living room, Dragg was standing with his back to her in his boxers, leaning out of the window.

'No smoking in the flat!' said Lena. 'I told you that.'

'I'm not smoking in the flat,' reasoned Dragg, pulling his head back in to look at her. 'The cigarette is out the window.'

'That is not the point,' said Lena. 'Downstairs on the street, if you must. And put some clothes on.' She watched as Dragg stubbed out the cigarette on her white windowsill, expressing his disdain for her orders with a shrug of his shoulders. He left the apartment, climbing into some trousers he'd peeled from the floor as he did so.

Lena sank on to the sofa bed, still unmade. She took another deep breath, but the smell of smoke made her cough. She noticed a large blank canvas, leaning against her kitchen stove. Spray cans of paint littered the windowsill, shading her small orchid garden.

Lena couldn't stand being in the flat any longer. What had once been her sanctuary was now a hellish bed of chaos. She decided to leave Sarika and Dragg to it and seek the cleanliness of the gallery. Pietro might still be there, bemoaning his fate. And misery loves company.

It was raining; the special hot rain of the tropics that seemed to have taken a wrong turn and got lost in Islington. It fell in angry drops on to the pavement, the force of each landing causing a splashy rebound. At least it would clean the summer grime away. The upturned ice-cream cones with ants feasting on the remains; the syrupy juices from melted lollies; even the vomit from too many Pimms. Rain was what summer in the city needed. Lena shook the water from her umbrella and let herself into the gallery with the key Pietro had ceremoniously presented to her when he'd given her her job back. She'd already popped Ophelia's key discreetly back in her drawer. She placed her umbrella neatly in the stand at the entrance. She could hear the rain assaulting the conservatory roof at the back of the gallery like a percussion band. Then she heard something else. Something much less pleasant.

A thud. A grunt of pain. A whimper.

The noises came from the basement. Lena ran down the stairs.

Pietro was curled up in the foetal position on the floor. Erjan, the loan shark's bailiff, stood over him, a broken picture frame in his hand that he was brandishing as a weapon. He turned to face Lena.

'Hello,' he said. 'Perhaps you would like to join your boyfriend on the floor. We're just having a little chat.'

'No, thank you,' said Lena, looking around for a weapon of her own. She wished she'd brought that hedgehog sculpture down from upstairs. It would finally have come in useful.

'Tough,' said Erjan. He walked over to Lena. 'Are you going to give me that bag of yours and sit down nicely, or am I going to have to hit you with this?' He lifted the piece of wood threateningly.

'Sit down, Lena,' said Pietro. 'That frame is ebony. It's one of the hardest types of wood. That's why I picked it. It gives the pictures a necessary sense of permanence.'

Lena would have rolled her eyes if they weren't fixated on that wood. She could see a nail protruding, its point glinting even in the dim light of the basement.

'Okay. I sit,' she said.

'Sorry about this,' muttered Pietro to Lena. He struggled to sit up, clutching at his ribcage.

'We just need more time,' Lena told Erjan. She was rewarded with a sharp poke to the stomach from the ebony picture frame.

'You've had your two weeks. Plus an extra day. Because I'm a nice guy. But no more messing. We want the money. Now,' said Erjan. 'With interest.'

'Just a couple more days,' said Pietro. 'That's all we need.' He looked at Lena. 'Actually, there is no "we". Lena is just my cleaner. She has no part in all of this so you can let her go.'

'Sniffs around here an awful lot for someone who has nothing to do with this,' said Erjan. 'Wouldn't want her getting left out of the fun.' He raised his weapon again. 'Now, am I getting my money or are you both getting a beating?'

'That won't help you get your money any quicker,' said Pietro. 'In fact, it will be quite a hindrance, if I'm in hospital.'

'It will make me feel better,' said Erjan, with a laugh. 'And the boss won't think I'm doing my job otherwise. Some of us need to work for a living. Now, here's the plan. You get a nice gentle beating today, like a deposit. Because I'm a fair man and working for a fair boss, that buys you one more week to get the money together.'

'Then what happens?' asked Pietro, immediately looking like he wished he hadn't.

'I'm glad you asked that,' replied Erjan. 'Because, in seven days, if we don't get our money, this gallery is ours. Remember that deed you signed over as collateral?'

Pietro smiled wanly. 'So be it,' he said. 'Maybe you should just take the gallery now and spare me the beating. I think my days as a gallery owner are numbered. Perhaps it isn't my *raison d'être* after all.'

Erjan smiled back. 'Your days as a man at all are numbered,' he said. 'Can't have the other businesses think we're going soft now, can we? Not punishing people if they don't pay up on time.'

Pietro looked at Lena, panic in his eyes. 'He's bluffing,' whispered Lena. She looked up. Erjan held the picture frame up as if it were a baseball bat. 'I do not bluff,' he said. 'You are first.'

Then he swung.

The last thing Lena remembered was the sound of ebony, the hardest of the woods, whizzing through the air.

CHAPTER 24

Lena blinked. She had a hangover. There was something sticky on her temple and an almighty banging in her head. She rolled over. The banging wasn't in her head. It was the sound of Erjan's foot kicking Pietro in the stomach.

'Stop,' she croaked. She realised no sound had come out. She cleared her throat, wishing she could do the same with her head. 'Leave him.'

'Want some more, do you?' said Erjan, leaving a whimpering Pietro and coming over to Lena. 'I didn't give it much welly last time. And I used the side without the nail. 'Cos you're a girl. You won't be so lucky next time.' She saw his face, flushed with excitement. He was enjoying this. Lena felt a flood of fear. He didn't want to stop.

'Yasemin Avci,' she said, remembering the gang leader she'd come up against in the past and hoping the name alone was enough to buy her some time. She saw excitement turn to confusion on Erjan's face. 'Also known as Fatima Moustafa, or Emine Adnan. Whatever you call her, she's a friend of mine.' Lena paused and watched his reaction.

'She's long gone from London,' said Erjan. 'Everyone knows that.'

'She is coming back,' said Lena, hoping that wasn't true. Yasemin was the only person she knew in the Turkish mafia, and after their last experience together she was no friend of Lena's. But he didn't know that. And he had to be stopped. Now.

Erjan looked at her for a long moment. She saw the excitement drain from his face.

'Tell her I send my respects,' he said, with a little nod of his head. He turned on his heels and left, taking the piece of ebony with him.

Lena handed Pietro a glass of brandy. They had almost run out. 'Let me see where you are hurt,' she said. 'You need help.'

'He just kicked me a couple of times,' said Pietro. 'You were only out cold for a minute or so. Seemed much longer. I thought you were dead.'

'I am not,' said Lena. 'Let me see where you are hurt.'

Pietro raised his shirt, displaying a hairy and sore-looking stomach.

Lena felt around his ribcage. 'I cannot feel anything broken,' she said. 'But I am not a doctor. You should go to hospital.'

'I'll go tomorrow,' said Pietro. 'I don't think I could face hours in A&E tonight. In fact, I'm not sure I can even face Ophelia.' He took a deep glug of his brandy.

Lena drank from her glass, feeling the brandy calm the pounding in her head, even as it burned her throat. 'You need to tell your wife,' she said. 'She might be able to help.'

'I'm such a failure. I can't even tell a fake when I see it. Even you could see something wasn't right. I don't deserve to run a gallery. Which is as well, because there's no way out of this mess.'

'We'll think of something,' said Lena. 'Every mess can be cleaned up.'

'It can when you are here.'

Lena looked at him in surprise. He put his glass down and continued. 'You can do amazing things,' he told her. 'You saved my life just moments ago. And you tracked down the stolen paint-ing before. Why not again – the real one this time?'

'What do you mean?' said Lena.

'That would solve all my problems, I know it. I've got buyers queuing up. Trudy is on hand to verify the painting. It would be a quick sale, I'm sure of it. All we need to do is find the real paint-ing.' He smiled at her, his face full of new hope.

Lena looked at him. Her head was sore and she could feel a scab beginning to form where the frame had hit her temple. 'I do not even know where to start,' she said. 'We do not know whether the painting you had was ever *A Study in Purple*. Even if it was, we do not know when it could have been switched. That means we have no timeline.'

'Perfect,' said Pietro. 'So you will establish the timeline first. I knew you'd know what to do.'

'We do not know who painted the forgery, or if it was the same person that took the painting . . .'

'A suspect!' declared Pietro. 'Lena, you are halfway there already.' He looked at her expectantly.

'I have my business to run,' said Lena, feeling frustrated that he wouldn't listen. 'Now Sarika is back and can work again, I need to find new clients for us.'

'Tell you what,' said Pietro. 'I'll hire you to investigate. Whatever you get cleaning, I'll double it. No, treble it. With a bonus when you find the painting.'

'The last thing you need is more people to owe money to,' said Lena, feeling herself relenting a little. Perhaps she could do this.

'Brilliant,' said Pietro. 'So you can do it. Excellent. You have full access to everything you need here. All our expertise, all our client files, every transaction we've ever made.'

'I do not promise anything,' said Lena, feeling excitement brew-ing despite herself at the prospect of continuing her investigations.

Professionally this time. 'And if I have nothing in one week, we go to the police and get you protection.'

Suddenly Pietro's mouth was kissing her cheek and she was encased in an enormous hug. 'Thank you, Lena,' he said. 'Thank you, thank you, thank you.'

Lena stood in the Summer Exhibition amongst the crowds, looking at Trudy's latest canvas. It was an enormous painting, three times the size of *A Study in Purple*. It mainly consisted of blue and green splodges, with a small brown animal, drawn with only a few brush strokes, staring out mournfully from the right-hand corner. The painting was entitled *Otter* so Lena guessed that must be what it was.

But the longer Lena looked at this painting, the more she liked it. The splodges seemed to travel around the canvas, as if dancing in the sunlight. Although she couldn't see the details of the animal, she could tell that it was terrified. A long red line intersected the painting and it made Lena feel uneasy. Something terrible was about to happen on the canvas and the otter knew it.

She was here to interview Trudy again, to find out more of the history of *A Study in Purple*. She felt flushed with excitement at the confidence that Pietro had shown in her. She decided not to worry that it was the act of a desperate man. It was her first paid detective assignment and there was no way she would let him down.

Lena drew her eyes away from the painting to look for Trudy, but found them drawn back. She had to physically turn away so the painting was outside her field of vision before she could concentrate on anything else.

'Lena!' Lena found herself on the receiving end of a jubilant kiss on each cheek. 'Glad you could come. What do you think of my painting?'

'It is not something that would fit in my flat,' said Lena, honestly. 'But I like it very much. Especially the worried otter.'

Trudy laughed. 'That's my favourite bit too. Come on, let's go to the members' room. We can chat there before someone tries to talk to me about symbolism. I can't face a symbolism conversation on a hangover.'

Trudy gestured to the man serving coffee in the members' room as they walked past the queue of pensioners waiting for tea and cake. He nodded understanding. She led Lena through another door to an area that felt like a tiny jungle. Luscious plants grew from all directions under a curved glass roof. They both took seats on plush rectangular stools. The man Trudy had waved to placed a tray on the table, containing two cups of steaming coffee and a plate of assorted cakes. Lena smiled. She could get used to the life of a professional investigator.

'So,' said Trudy, taking a sip of her coffee. 'What do you think happened to the real painting?'

'That is what I am trying to find out,' said Lena. 'First I want to understand the timeline.'

'The police are talking to me too, you know,' said Trudy. 'Asking questions.'

Lena flushed. They would know much better than her what to look for. For a moment, she considered abandoning the case and not wasting everyone's time.

'But I like you,' said Trudy. 'Have a piece of cake and I'll tell you what I know. The brownies here are excellent.'

Lena helped herself to a brownie, feeling better. 'When did you last see *A Study in Purple*?' she said. 'When were you sure it was the real thing?'

'I sold it years ago, when I was getting critical acclaim but not many sales. To some minor league art dealer. He got it for a song, but I was so grateful for any money back then. It meant I could eat.'

'When was that?'

Trudy looked up to the glass ceiling, as if her memories would be floating there. 'Maybe fifteen years ago, maybe more?' Lena put down the half-eaten brownie in dismay. 'It must have been sold many times over that period, before it eventually reached Pietro's hands.'

'So it could have been switched years ago,' said Lena. 'By any number of people.'

'No,' said Trudy. 'I saw it hanging in Pietro's gallery. It was the last time I came to London, for the Summer Exhibition, so it would have been in June, one year ago. I'd heard he'd bought it, and it had been so long since I'd seen it that I was curious. I wanted to see if it was as good as I remembered it. Plus I wanted to see Pietro too.'

'Was it?' said Lena.

'Yes,' said Trudy. 'That's why I was so surprised at the reception that I'd misremembered it. I thought it was just the drink. But no. That painting was full of emotion, full of joy, full of love.' She took a sip of coffee. 'I hate it when artists big up their own work, but I love that little canvas. Takes me right back to how I felt then. Before life pushed me down. When things were simple and I didn't know every relationship would end in someone's heart getting broken. Usually mine.'

'I am sorry,' said Lena.

'It's okay,' said Trudy, picking up a piece of cake adorned with a walnut. 'Things are looking up again now.'

Lena took a sip of coffee. She wanted to ask more about Trudy's love life, but forced herself back to the case. 'So you are sure then that it was your painting? Hanging in the Agnoletti Archer Gallery in June last year?'

'Absolutely,' said Trudy.

'That is excellent,' said Lena, putting down her coffee to write herself a note. 'I started cleaning the gallery three and a half months ago. I am sure the painting that was there then was the painting in the phone box. So that gives us a period from last June to this March when it could have been switched.'

'That sounds right,' said Trudy. 'I don't think you'll find anyone else who could say with any certainty that it was the real deal in that time. I would have thought Simon would have noticed, though. He's got an artistic soul. But he has his own struggles.'

Two ladies descended on their table as Lena went to ask her next question.

'Trudy Weincamp!' exclaimed one. 'Now my membership fee has paid off! Imagine having a cup of tea with the great artist herself. I recognise you from the RA magazine.'

'Really?' said Trudy. 'I thought I told them not to use my picture.'

'It's definitely you,' said the lady. 'Isn't it, Mabel?'

'Oh yes, it's her all right,' said Mabel. 'I keep that magazine in our downstairs loo. And with my troubles, I read that article many times.'

'Are you all right now?' asked her friend, distracted from Trudy for a moment.

'Oh yes. I took an Imodium before we came out. Better safe than sorry. That's what I always say.'

'Very wise,' agreed her friend.

'Did you want an autograph?' asked Trudy, interrupting their dialogue.

'Oh yes,' exclaimed Mabel. 'I wish I had the magazine with me now. That would be quite the thing.'

'Here,' said Trudy, hurriedly signing a napkin and handing it to Mabel.

'And one for me too,' said the other woman firmly. 'Dolores. That's spelt D O L . . .'

'I've got it,' replied Trudy. 'I had an Aunt Dolores.'

'Would you believe it?' said Dolores. 'It's not a common name these days, you know.'

'Sorry, Lena,' said Trudy, looking uncharacteristically flustered. 'I need to get going.'

'Of course,' replied Lena. 'I have what I need now.'

'Don't let us drive you away,' said Dolores, sliding into Trudy's chair as she rose.

'Not at all,' said Trudy. 'I have to give a lecture soon anyway.' She reached to take the plate with the leftover cakes.

'If you're done with those . . .' said Mabel, grabbing the plate. 'You might as well leave them. Waste not want not.'

Dolores murmured her agreement and reached to grab one. Trudy let go of the plate. 'The brownies here are first rate,' said Dolores, her mouth full already.

CHAPTER 25

'You've changed your tune,' said Cartwright. 'I thought you had decided to end your investigations.'

Lena took a sip of the homemade lemonade Cartwright had given her, feeling its sourness cool her throat, even as a curled-up Kaplan on her lap warmed her belly. She stroked him and looked around Cartwright's living room. In general she thought Victorian houses had too much coving and unnecessary ornament, but she had to admit this one, with its high ceilings and open sash windows, was a pleasant place to spend a hot Sunday morning.

'Pietro needs my help. And I would like yours.'

Cartwright smiled at her. 'Of course,' he said. 'I've been thinking about it since we last spoke. I had a feeling you wouldn't give up.'

Lena smiled back at him. 'I am stubborn,' she said.

'Perseverance is a virtue.' Lena didn't like it when Cartwright used words she didn't understand, but she took it as a compliment nonetheless. 'So how can I help?' he added.

Lena took another sip of the lemonade. Kaplan briefly woke and stretched out, needling his claws into Lena's knee. She stroked his ear, ignoring the fleeting pain.

'I know that the painting was definitely real in June one year ago. But by March, when I started cleaning for Pietro, it was a fake.'

Cartwright jumped up. 'This calls for a spreadsheet,' he said, grabbing his laptop from where it sat idly charging in a corner. 'Let's get all of this captured and see what we can do with it.'

Lena waited while the computer booted up and Cartwright entered the date information. 'That's a great start,' he said. 'What do you think is next? Shall I talk to Blake and see how she is proceeding?'

'No,' said Lena. 'I have my own ideas. We know there was a painting there, and that it was fake. We need to find out who painted that fake.'

'It is possible that whoever painted that copy did so in good faith,' said Cartwright. 'He or she might tell us who commissioned them.'

'We need to find out who it was,' said Lena. 'But I do not know how we do that.'

'Blake said it is a skilled job, forging a painting so well that only the artist can tell the difference,' said Cartwright. 'And the person who can forge a Rembrandt is not always the same person who can forge a Tracey Emin. There would be a limited number of people with the requisite talents.'

'So we can limit the suspects?' said Lena.

'We'd need access to the database.'

'Let me guess,' said Lena. 'Blake would be able to do that?'

'Of course,' replied Cartwright. 'She'll be way ahead of us.'

Kaplan bit Lena's finger and jumped down. Without realising it she'd been gripping his ear. 'Sorry,' she said to the cat. He looked back at her reproachfully then settled on the floor and proceeded to clean himself.

'Okay,' said Lena. 'Can you get the list from her?'

'I'll pop into the station this afternoon,' said Cartwright. 'I will talk to her then. We are quite friendly now. I think she would rather I was assisting her than Gullins. Not that that is much of an endorsement. Hopefully she will let me see the list.'

'Call me when you have it,' said Lena, getting up to leave.

'There could be quite a few names on that list,' said Cartwright, thinking. 'But I expect there is a way to cross-reference them against the timings and whether they have any connection to the gallery.' He began typing into his laptop. Kaplan meowed.

'There's fish in the fridge, Lena, if Kaplan's hungry,' he said, without looking up. 'Now, there must be a formula I can use for this. I'll get it figured out and then I can show Blake. I bet she'll be impressed. She seems like just the type of woman to appreciate one of my matrices.'

Lena went to the fridge and pulled out a piece of smoked salmon for Kaplan. The cat leapt up and snatched it from her hand. 'I will see you soon,' she said to the cat, scratching his ear again as he purred up at her.

'Yes, see you soon Lena,' called Cartwright. 'I'm going to focus on this until I go to work.'

Lena walked through the hallway and out of the door.

Lena was hot and cross by the time she reached her flat. For some reason the bus she caught home had its heating on, even though it was thirty degrees outside. She'd spent the journey with hot air being blasted on to her ankles. They were swollen with the heat so her legs resembled tree trunks. And by now Cartwright would be impressing the attractive DI Blake with his spreadsheets. The ones he used to share only with Lena.

She put the key in the lock and prepared to shout at Dragg if he were still in bed. That would cool her down. She opened the door to an empty flat. She smiled. They'd gone out, and had even made a half-hearted attempt to clean up. The sofa bed was folded away, albeit with bits of bedding sticking out of the sides like an overfilled sandwich.

Lena grabbed a glass of water from the reasonably clean kitchen and sat on her sofa, drinking the contents of the glass in a single gulp. She'd have a little rest, enjoy the quiet, and then take the opportunity to have a thorough clean. That would calm her nerves and distract her thoughts. Perhaps it would even help her figure out a way to track down the painting.

Lena opened her eyes again. She blinked a few times. She was still on the sofa and she had not cleaned the flat. She heard a knock and stumbled up to open the door.

Cartwright was standing in the doorway, still in his uniform, clutching his laptop. 'I have it,' he said. 'The list we need. Blake is much more open-minded than most detectives on the police force and she loved the work I've done. I think she might allow me to assist on this case, maybe even apply for her department..Let's go through this and then maybe I can take you out for a spot of dinner?'

Lena looked at her watch, thinking it must be the middle of the night and wondering where would be open for dinner still. It was seven p.m.

'Come in,' she said, rubbing her eyes. 'I make coffee.'

Lena tried to wake herself up while Cartwright took a seat and opened his computer.

'I've got it down to sixteen people already, using my spreadsheet,' said Cartwright. 'Blake was very impressed. She had forty-seven people on the list before that. Your date range was most helpful too. It would be great to limit it further. Are there any other times we might be able to find out if the real painting was there or not?'

'I do not think so but I will check with Pietro,' said Lena, bringing out a cup of coffee and one of tea.

'But how would he know?'

'I will ask if any experts visited the gallery,' she said, trying to work out a way to ask that tactfully.

Lena thought for a moment. She didn't have a lot of time before Erjan did more than just threaten Pietro.

'I have another idea,' she said. 'What information do you have on these people?'

Cartwright looked at the screen. 'Date of birth, nationality, criminal record if any.'

'I want to see if there is a connection with any of our suspects,' said Lena.

'That is hard to tell from this,' said Cartwright. 'What type of thing did you have in mind?'

'Can you see art schools?' asked Lena, on a hunch. 'Sandover College of Art? That is where Pietro, Ophelia and Simon all went.'

'Yes, should be able to. Oh, a few of them. It appears Sandover College of Art is a hotbed of fraudsters.'

'The bed is hot?' questioned Lena, then decided to let it go as Cartwright looked set to launch into a long explanation. 'Were any of them at the college between 1994 and 1999?'

'Yes,' said Cartwright. He looked up at her. 'Just one. And he is not going anywhere.'

'This whole notion of copying a painting by someone else being a crime is very modern, you know,' said Humphrey Bouverie. 'In the golden age of the Renaissance it was considered to be absolutely fine. To be expected, in fact.'

Lena looked at the man in front of her. It had been easier than she'd thought it would be to visit Pentonville Prison. Forty-eight hours, once Cartwright had put in a call to one of his contacts. And Humphrey had accepted their visit without question. Lena supposed he was lonely. She felt a flood of relief that it was him, and not Sarika, that she was here to see.

'We are not in the golden ages,' said Lena, trying to focus on what he was saying.

'Very true, young lady,' replied Humphrey. 'And extremely sad. In the golden ages, an artist could make an honest living without ending up in prison.'

'It wasn't an honest living you were making, though, was it?' said Cartwright. 'You're in here for burglary.'

'A simple misunderstanding,' said Humphrey. 'Most unfortunate.'

'I am sure it was,' said Lena. 'But paintings were found at your house? They were copies of valuable originals.'

'For my personal pleasure,' replied Humphrey. 'A hobby. Even the great Michelangelo created a statue of Cupid and added acidic earth to make it seem ancient. He is not vilified. The Romans produced reproductions of the most beautiful Greek statues by the hundreds. Then they conquered Europe.'

'So you follow in good footsteps?' said Lena.

'Exactly. You'd think in this digital world the lines between original and fake would become blurred again. Are people who inhabit a digital space suddenly not real? No. Is something that is sold online any less sold?'

Lena thought for a moment. What he said triggered something in her mind.

'And if people happen to like my copies,' continued Humphrey, 'I sell them in good faith. Later, if it is of such quality that it can be sold as a great artist's masterpiece, am I to be criticised?'

'So it is just coincidence that your paintings have ended up in the hands of so many shady people?' Cartwright said.

'Shady people, as you so ungenerously describe them, can be art lovers too,' replied Humphrey, with dignity. 'A love of art is not always consistent with conventional morality. In fact, history has shown that it is often quite the opposite.' Humphrey leaned back and crossed his arms.

Lena gave Cartwright an angry look. Putting Humphrey on the defensive was not helping.

'We are not here to get you in more trouble,' said Lena, leaning forwards a little. 'We are here to consult your expertise.'

'Perhaps you should tell that to your boyfriend,' said Humphrey, glaring at Cartwright. Lena felt herself flush at the mistake, but decided not to correct him.

'Sorry about him,' she said. 'He does not understand artists.'

'And you do?'

Lena thought about what Trudy had told her. 'A great painting can take you to emotions you thought you had forgotten,' she said. 'Like falling in love for the first time, before you understand the pain that it can bring.'

Humphrey smiled at her. 'I do not want to copy other artists, you know,' he said, more softly. 'It is never quite the same, no matter how careful you are. Because what you are doing is not from your authentic soul. The colours can be just as vibrant, but it will always be a shadow of the original.'

A few weeks ago, Lena would have rolled her eyes at this. But now she was starting to think it could be true. 'What are your own paintings like?' she asked him.

'Abstract representations of suffering, death and decay,' replied Humphrey. 'But beautiful through it all. Doesn't sell, though.' He laughed. 'When I get out I'm going to paint kittens in wine glasses. Maybe the odd dog begging for a bone. That's what people want to buy. I've even started here. They've decent art supplies in prison, you know, if you get into the right one.'

'I will bear that in mind,' said Lena, with a smile.

'We know that you went to Sandover art school,' said Cartwright. 'Did you know Pietro Agnoletti?'

'He was the year below me. Of course I knew him. No secrets there. Dreadful artist. Talked too much, painted too little.'

'And Simon Archer?'

'Same year as Pietro. They were firm friends but he was incredibly talented. His portraits were so full of truth they made me want to cry. It was as though he could see into your soul.' He paused. 'And of course I knew Ophelia too. Beautiful girl, started at the college a few years after me. We dated, you know, after Pietro messed things up with her. I'm not surprised she fell thrall to his trust fund in the end. They are married after all, now.'

'She is with him for his money?' said Cartwright.

'We're all with everyone for something,' said Humphrey. 'Maybe she loves him. Who can explain the ways of love?'

'And you say you dated her?' Cartwright pressed.

'For a brief while. Then I got bored. A pity such a heavenly face has been installed on an empty brain. Like painting the Sistine Chapel with crayons.'

Lena leaned forwards. 'We know that you painted the fake of A Study in Purple,' she said. 'You are the only one who could have.'

'You flatter me,' replied Humphrey.

'It has been exposed as a fake now. But I am sure you did not intend for it to be used to conceal a crime.'

'If I did paint it, that would be the case, of course. Everything I do is in good faith. But it wasn't necessarily me.'

'If it was you,' continued Lena, carefully, 'who commissioned you?'

Humphrey laughed. 'But we are speaking hypothetically, are we not? I couldn't possibly encroach from the abstract into the world of the concrete.'

'We can get you taken off the art programme,' threatened Cartwright. 'Transferred to a much less pleasant prison.'

'No, you can't,' replied Humphrey. 'Never bluff a bluffer. I think it's time for you two to leave.'

The guard approached. Lena and Cartwright got up. 'Well, that was a waste of time,' said Cartwright as they left.

'Not necessarily,' said Lena. 'It gave me an idea.'

★ ★ ★

'I've been through the computer records like you said,' said Cartwright, when he called Lena later that evening. 'It's a god-send, finally being able to have access to Pietro's files, disaster zone that they are. But I have found something odd. *A Study in Purple* was marked sold on the website for three hours back in August last year. But then it went back online as available.'

'Someone thought about buying it and changed their mind?' said Lena.

'Possibly. But there is no record of who. And there should be. No payment was received into the accounts. You said Ophelia runs the online side of the business?'

'Yes. But I don't think she knows very much about it.'

'Perhaps,' said Cartwright. 'But she was also in a relationship with our fraudster. There must be a connection.'

Lena thought for a moment. She closed her eyes. Ophelia's pretty face flashed in front of her, covered in the suspicion Lena had seen when she'd discovered Pietro and Lena in the gallery basement together. Could she be capable of more than they'd all thought? 'Can you find the name of the person who bought the painting?' asked Lena.

'I will try,' said Cartwright. 'It certainly smells like fish, as you'd say.'

CHAPTER 26

Lena sat outside the coffee shop opposite the gallery, sipping on her iced latte. She saw Ophelia dart out of the shop, her peach silky kaftan trailing behind her. Lena jumped up and followed her. Ophelia wandered like an autumn leaf floating in the breeze, pausing to look in shop windows and occasionally greeting people she knew with a series of sounds as dainty as a dove cooing.

Lena watched as she walked, noticing the admiring looks Ophelia attracted. She had an ethereal quality that, coupled with her interesting wardrobe choices, made her extremely striking.

Ophelia turned left into Camden Passage. Lena was not surprised. With its series of antique jewellery stalls, vintage shops and quirky boutiques, it was just the type of place Ophelia seemed made for. Lena quickened her pace and carried on along Upper Street so she could head Ophelia off at the other end of the market. She wanted this meeting to seem accidental so Ophelia would feel at ease.

There was a flaw to her plan, realised Lena, pushing through the people meandering along the narrow streets. She'd lost her. Lena scanned the people admiring the second-hand jewellery and peered into the window of a shop selling oriental prints. Nothing. Lena had almost given up when she fell over Ophelia coming out of the most expensive jewellery shop in the market, specialising in elegant art deco pieces. Ophelia was carrying a small paper bag.

Lena felt a wave of antagonism towards this woman, shopping while her husband owed so much money he was fearful for his life. But he had chosen not to share his troubles with Ophelia, Lena reminded herself. His wife was in blissful ignorance.

Ophelia was smiling and looked right through Lena with her angelic eyes. 'Hello, Ophelia,' said Lena firmly, determined to bring Ophelia's lofty focus to herself. 'Have you found something nice?'

'Lena, lovely to see you,' replied Ophelia, with her distracted air. She made to carry on.

'I bet that it is beautiful,' said Lena, gesturing to the paper bag, determined to initiate an impromptu chat. 'What is it?'

'A brooch by Lalique,' said Ophelia. 'Eighteen nineties, I think. It's an enamel dragonfly set with opals. Absolutely exquisite.'

Lena fell into step with Ophelia.

'This street is my favourite,' said Ophelia, obviously accepting that she was in Lena's company now. 'Oh, look at that stunning hat. I'll try it on and you can tell me if it suits.'

Lena made the appropriate noises of admiration as Ophelia placed various feathery, furry and sparkling objects on her shiny hair or around her milky-white neck. Lena couldn't understand the appeal of vintage to the wealthy. If she had enough money she would buy everything brand new and sparkly clean. Who knew what other people had done with these objects? She especially objected to the feathers. They had not only belonged to another person, but a bird as well. Lena knew how filthy the chickens in her village could be and wouldn't dream of putting something plucked from one of them on to her own head.

'It is much better, trying things on, than shopping online,' said Lena.

'Oh, I do agree,' said Ophelia. 'I never buy anything online if I can help it. You need to feel the material in your hands. See the colours in the sunlight.'

'Is the gallery the same?' said Lena, trying to make her voice sound casual. 'Do people buy the art online?'

'Never,' said Ophelia, with a charming laugh. 'It sounds dreadful, with me running the website for the gallery, but we haven't sold a single thing online. People need to see paintings in the flesh, so to speak, before they'll buy. So the website is just like a shop window, enticing people to visit and come inside. I do keep it looking beautiful.'

'So nothing has been sold that way?' said Lena.

'Not a thing,' said Ophelia, cheerfully.

'Never?'

'Never.'

'Has anyone ever bought anything and then cancelled the order?'

'We haven't even got that far, I'm afraid,' said Ophelia.

'Never?'

'I'd remember something that unusual. Now, what do you think of this peacock feather fascinator? Isn't it divine?'

Lena sat in her room with the door closed. She could hear Sarika giggling loudly at something Dragg had said. Although Lena had found herself warming to Dragg a little, she doubted anything he said could really be all that funny. She wanted to go to the kitchen and make herself a cheese and paprika sandwich, but she didn't feel like being sociable. And she wasn't sure if she could cope with the constantly messy state of the kitchen. Lena took a deep breath and tried to think about how nice it should feel to hear Sarika giggle. Sarika safe. Sarika not in prison.

Feeling more in control of her own thoughts, Lena turned her attention back to the suspect board, propped up on her dressing table. The crime had changed. The suspects were no longer the ones who'd been at the gallery reception. She got up and started to take down the names. She paused when she got to Pietro. He had hired her to find out what had happened, but did he really want to know? She left his name there, along with Ophelia, Simon and Trudy. Picking up a new Post-it note and trying to ignore the rumbling in her stomach, Lena wrote down Humphrey Bouverie, the forger's name. She drew a line from his name to Pietro and Simon, and a double line to Ophelia. Then she drew a crude depiction of a computer screen and stuck it next to Ophelia. Did the woman know more than she was letting on?

The doorbell rang. Lena listened. Eventually she heard Dragg's distinctly unimpressed voice as he opened the door.

There was only one person she knew that Dragg disliked that much. Lena picked herself off the bed, smoothed her hair and hurried into the living room. 'Cartwright,' she said, before she'd even seen him. 'It is good that you are here.'

'I have brilliant news,' said Cartwright. He stopped and looked at his feet, stepping back carefully. 'What on earth?' His shoe had become entwined in a pile of Dragg's discarded underwear.

'Sorry about that,' said Lena. 'Dragg, Sarika, I go out now with PC Cartwright. Clean up.' She looked at Sarika. The girl had turned a fuchsia pink with sunburn and was peeling off bits of dry skin from her shoulders, flicking them on to Lena's fleecy blanket. Lena shuddered.

'Dragg has to catch the train to Brighton in an hour,' objected Sarika. 'For three whole days.'

'An hour is plenty of time,' said Lena. 'If you focus. I do not want to find dirty underwear on the floor when I am back.'

'They are clean,' said Dragg, moving forwards to disentangle them from Cartwright's shoe. 'They were clean,' he said, giving Cartwright a menacing stare.

'Just do it,' said Lena, grabbing her bag and Cartwright's arm to pull him out of the flat before more misfortunes befell him.

'And Sarika, rub aloe vera on your sunburn. There is some in the bathroom cupboard. And put my blanket in the washing machine.'

'Do you have time for a sandwich?' said Cartwright, once they were in the hallway.

'All the time,' said Lena, picturing exactly the sandwich she wanted in her head. There was a clean little deli around the corner that stocked paprika. That would be perfect.

'Excellent,' said Cartwright. 'You're going to be pleased with what I've found out.'

Lena bit into her sandwich and felt the soft white bread sink into her palate, before the spice of the paprika tickled her tongue. She took a sip of coffee and watched Cartwright bite into his ham and cheese roll. 'I am very impressed that you found out who bought the painting online,' she said. 'What is the name?'

'Most people don't realise that nothing is ever really deleted from the internet,' replied Cartwright. 'Just temporarily hidden.'

Lena grinned at him. 'You are so clever,' she said. 'We will solve this together. I know we will. What is the name?'

Cartwright looked up from his sandwich. 'There is one issue,' he said. 'I can't tell you the name. Amy, DI Blake that is, has let me officially assist on the case now, so as soon as we have a warrant I will be able to go as well to see what's what.'

'And me?' asked Lena, her enthusiasm dampening like *hideg meggyleves*, chilled sour-cherry soup.

'We'll do it for you,' said Cartwright, looking intently into his sandwich. 'But do not worry, Amy and I will find the painting. She was already very impressed that I found Humphrey Bouverie and the connection to Ophelia.'

'You told her about our investigations?' said Lena.

'Don't worry,' said Cartwright. 'I've kept your name out of it.'

Lena put her sandwich down and looked at him. So he was taking credit for the work that they had done together. Most of which she had done.

'So now you work with DI Blake?' said Lena, feeling the sandwich stick in her throat. 'Not with me?'

'Now we can pool resources,' said Cartwright. 'Work together on this. It will be much better.'

'She will work with me as well?' said Lena.

'Well, of course we'll not be able to work with you officially . . .' said Cartwright. 'But behind the scenes you and I can carry on with, you know, what we are doing.'

'Right,' said Lena, feeling the urge to wash her hands. Why did this arrangement make her feel grubby? 'But Pietro has hired me to find his painting,' said Lena, putting down the coffee she'd been holding to her lips with so much force that the hot drink spilled over the edge of the cup. 'I am investigating too.' She grabbed a napkin automatically and wiped up the spillage, keeping her eyes on Cartwright.

'I'll find the painting quicker with Amy's expertise,' said Cartwright. 'And that means we'll be able to get the proof we need against Ophelia.'

'I am not sure it was Ophelia,' said Lena. 'Not yet.'

'Amy is very experienced,' said Cartwright. 'And she thinks Ophelia is our prime suspect. The evidence all stacks up. The connection with the forger, the website, this dodgy transaction.'

'But why?'

'Amy has a theory,' said Cartwright. 'And I think her theories are likely to be a bit more accurate than ours!'

'Fine,' said Lena. She stood up to go just as Cartwright took another bite. Let them arrest Ophelia, if they were so certain. Perhaps it would even help her own investigations.

'Hold on a minute,' he said, his mouth full. 'I'll walk you back.'

'No need,' said Lena, already halfway out of the door. 'I have things to do.'

Lena was too upset even to stroke Jasper's ear. The rabbit gazed up at her for a moment, then gave up and found satisfaction by nibbling a stick of celery instead.

'I think it's disgusting,' said Mrs Kingston, presenting Lena with a strong cup of coffee and a plate of Hobnobs. 'Dropping you after all the work you've done.'

'Pietro trusted me to find out what happened,' said Lena, grabbing a biscuit and dunking it in her coffee. 'I feel like I am so close to getting that painting,' she added, popping the biscuit in her mouth before it got too soggy. 'And I have been cut up.'

'Cut out,' said Mrs Kingston. 'But you have come to the right place. If that PC Cartwright can find out who bought the painting, I don't see why we can't.'

'I am not good with computers,' said Lena. 'We had to go to the library in the next village to use one. I could barely turn them on until I started to work in Debrecen. Even then I shared mine with a colleague.'

'You think they had computers in my day?' said Mrs Kingston, also grabbing a biscuit and feeding half to Jasper. 'I still miss the noise of my typewriter, the soundtrack to every great news story I wrote when I first got into journalism. And don't get me started on the intoxicating smell of correction fluid . . .'

Lena sipped her coffee. 'It is hopeless,' she said. 'I will tell Pietro to keep his money. He cannot afford to pay me anyway.'

'Not so fast,' said Mrs Kingston. 'I may have been brought up in a land before mobile phones, but I do have some contacts. Now, where's my Rolodex? I've got just the girl in mind to help us with this. Broke some pretty big stories with her, before I retired.'

Lena jumped up to help Mrs Kingston as she strained to get to her feet. Jasper chewed his Hobnob, nonplussed. 'Thank you, dear,' said Mrs Kingston, shuffling into the next room. 'Have another biscuit. This shouldn't take a minute once I've got through. Name and address do you, or do you want email too?'

CHAPTER 27

After a train ride down to East Sussex later that afternoon, with a still-peeling Sarika in tow, Lena found herself tramping along an immense gravelled driveway. She could barely see the country house, enormous as it was, as the drive seemed to go on for ever. Like most things in the countryside, it was designed for someone with a car, not someone on foot. But she had taken Sarika here by train, determined to find out for herself what this man had in his house before the police stuck their noses in.

Bartholomew Worthington. It had taken Mrs Kingston's contact only ten minutes to find his name, and another five to get his address. Lena had no idea how she managed it, but she felt decidedly less impressed by Cartwright now. She didn't need him at all – or his precious DI Amy Blake.

'This place would be a nightmare to clean,' said Lena, breaking into Hungarian at the strain of the long walk. 'By the time you'd finished, it would be dirty again, and you would have to start all over. Good for business, I suppose.'

Something rustled in the bushes next to them and Sarika let out a screech. 'What the hell was that?' the girl said.

'A bird?' said Lena, doubtfully. 'Nothing to worry about.'

Sarika continued, her steps more tentative now. 'I don't like it in the countryside,' she said. 'Not now that I'm a Londoner.'

Lena took a deep breath. The healthy but unpleasant aroma of cowpats filled her lungs, taking her back to the village of her youth. 'No,' she said, 'I don't like it much either. It smells like the worst bits of home. Let's see what we can find out and then get the train back to London.'

'So what do we say when we get to the house?'

Lena thought. She'd been debating that point with herself the whole journey. 'The free cleaning session has worked well so far,' she said. 'But I haven't been able to call him to arrange that. So we will have to take our chances.'

'Do you think he will just let us in?' asked Sarika.

'We'll find a way,' said Lena.

Finally they reached the front door. Lena rang the doorbell and stood back to look for signs of life inside.

They waited.

'It will take a long time,' said Lena. 'If he is in a different part of the house.'

Sarika began to fiddle with her hair, searching it for split ends. Lena felt her back aching. She considered taking a seat on the gravel, but decided that would not look professional when the door was finally opened.

'No one is here,' said Sarika, plucking out an offending strand and releasing it into the air.

'I agree.' Lena looked at her. 'But we have come a long way,' she began. 'And I'm sure he wouldn't mind . . .'

Sarika looked at her blankly. 'Let's go around the back,' said Lena, starting on her way. 'So many doors and windows. There's bound to be one open.'

She ignored Sarika's objections and made the long journey around to the back of the house. Before they'd even reached it she'd found a side door. With a forceful shove and a squeak of complaint, it yielded them entry.

'Come on,' said Lena. 'Let's investigate.'

Sarika hung back. 'What's wrong?' said Lena.

'Breaking in. I don't want to go to prison,' said Sarika. 'I can't face it.'

'It will be fine,' said Lena. Then she saw the fear in the girl's eyes. 'But it is best if you stay here and keep guard,' she said. 'That is an important job.'

'Yes, I can do that,' replied Sarika, instantly more cheerful. 'I will sound the alarm if needed.' She settled down on an upturned flowerpot and proceeded to pout into the camera lens of her phone.

Lena entered the house. The door led into a kitchen, large but cluttered, with loose lino on the floor and a selection of dead wasps on the windowsill. It smelt musty, of old fruit and closed windows. Lena suppressed the urge she always felt when confronted by mess and left it as it was. There were no dirty plates, just a bowl of apples slowly turning to cider on the counter. She left the kitchen, feeling increasingly confident that the occupant of this house was away.

She found herself in a narrow corridor and followed it round. Pushing through a door, she gasped.

She was in the most beautiful hallway she'd ever seen. A huge chandelier glistened over her head. The stairway was expansive and elegant, with a rich burgundy carpet. Paintings adorned the high walls.

Lena realised the kitchen must have been the servants' quarters. Now she was in the part of the house that welcomed honoured guests. She stepped on to the staircase, feeling the carpet sink beneath her feet as if it wanted to hug them. Lena looked at the paintings as she went up the stairs. There were all styles of art here. Old-fashioned dark oil paintings, fresh pastel watercolours, charcoal line drawings. Then she saw it.

A Study in Purple.

Only it was not the *A Study in Purple* that she knew. It was brighter, deeper, more intense. And full of joy.

Lena found herself unable to look at it without smiling. The triangles were no longer just triangles, they were temples to happiness. The tadpoles were life-giving and beautiful. The red circles lit up the canvas like the sun. She stood, entranced.

Then she heard a bang. Gunfire.

Lena froze. She felt a stab of pain through her shoulder.

Instinctively she reached her hand up to the pain, expecting to feel the warm stickiness of blood oozing through her fingers.

There was none.

Confused, Lena looked at her shoulder. She breathed deeply and sat down on the soft, carpeted step. It took her a moment to process the information.

It was her scar that hurt, revisiting its memory of pain past.

This shot was outside, far away from her own shoulder.

Sarika was outside.

Lena jumped to her feet and charged back down the stairs, ignoring the dizzy sensation in her ears. She ran through the kitchen and pushed open the door. Straight into the barrel of a gun.

'What the hell do you think you're doing?' The man did not so much speak the words as growl them. He was in his late fifties with dark, greying hair and overgrown eyebrows.

'Where is my friend?' Lena hissed back, ignoring the gun in her face. 'Did you shoot her?' Lena looked around for Sarika. 'Where is she?'

'Calm down,' he said. 'I didn't shoot anyone. I simply fired a shot in the air to scare her.'

'If she is hurt . . .' said Lena, her voice riddled with threat.

'I told you. I didn't shoot her. Look, there she goes, scarpering off without a second thought for you.'

Lena looked. She could see Sarika in the distance, running across the field. She was giving the cows a wide berth. Lena breathed a sigh of relief. 'Lucky for you she is okay,' she said.

The man laughed and lowered his gun. 'Big talk for someone standing there with diddlysquat while I've got a hunting rifle in my arms.'

'Like I said, you are lucky,' said Lena, braving it out.

'That brings me back to my first question,' he replied. 'What are you doing in my house?'

Lena racked her brain for an explanation. It quickly found her most common response. 'I clean,' she said, trying to regain her composure. 'I am the cleaner.'

The man looked at her doubtfully. 'Then why did your little friend run away?'

'Because you pointed a gun at her,' reasoned Lena.

'I didn't order a cleaner.'

'You live here?'

'I own the place. And I didn't hire you.'

'Your wife called me,' bluffed Lena. 'She said that she wanted to surprise you.'

A dog barked across the field, presumably delighted to have Sarika as a running companion. They both paused to look in that direction.

'She's surprised me all right,' said the man. 'She's been dead a year and a half.'

'Oh,' said Lena, feeling dreadful. 'I am sorry.'

'Not your fault,' said the man briskly. 'But it doesn't explain what you are doing here. You don't look like a burglar.'

'I am not,' said Lena. 'I have come about the painting. *A Study in Purple*.'

The man looked her up and down. 'I don't get many visitors,' he said. 'And you don't look too dangerous. You had better come in. We'll talk about this properly.' He allowed her inside. 'Then I'll decide whether to call the police. We might as well have a drink in the meantime. Tea?'

'Coffee,' replied Lena, sitting down in one of the small wooden chairs scattered around the kitchen table.

'I suppose now you're in my house and I'm making you a drink instead of shooting you I should introduce myself. I'm Bartholomew.'

'Lena.'

'Pretty name,' said Bartholomew. 'German?'

'Hungarian,' said Lena.

'And what do you want with my painting?'

'I think you know.' Lena looked at him.

'I really don't,' said Bartholomew.

'It is stolen,' replied Lena.

'No, it's right up the stairs.' He left the kitchen. Lena followed. He climbed the stairs. 'There.'

'No,' said Lena, starting to feel confused. 'It is stolen from the Agnoletti Archer Gallery. On Upper Street, Islington.'

'No,' echoed Bartholomew, giving her a funny look. 'It is bought, with good money, from the website of the Agnoletti Archer Gallery. On Upper Street, Islington.'

'I will call the police,' said Lena. She would enjoy telling Cartwright that she had found the painting. No thanks to him.

'By all means,' said Bartholomew. 'Do you want to turn yourself in for breaking and entering? You really aren't much of a burglar, are you?'

Their baffled looks were interrupted by a clattering from outside. The gun went off again. Lena raced down the stairs for the second time that day, Bartholomew close behind her.

'Sarika!' she said. 'Dragg! What are you doing here? Who is shot?'

Sarika threw herself at Lena in a fervent embrace. 'I thought you were dead.'

'Well I am not. What is Dragg doing here?'

Dragg looked shaken. 'I could have been killed,' he said, ashen-faced. He sank to the floor.

'What happened?'

'I sent Dragg a text from the train and said we were coming here and he said it wasn't that far from Brighton and he would meet me,' said Sarika. 'But then I saw him on the path and told him you were in danger so we came to rescue you. He picked up the gun and it went off.'

'You shouldn't just pick up strangers' guns,' said Bartholomew. 'It's very dangerous if you don't know what you're doing.'

'It's him,' said Sarika, pointing at Bartholomew. 'The man who tried to shoot me.'

'This joker is more likely to have shot you than I was,' said Bartholomew. 'He's had a bit of a fright. Come in and I'll get him a stiff drink. Actually,' he said, looking at the women, 'I think we could all use one.'

Sarika and Dragg looked doubtfully at Lena. 'Come on, it is fine,' she said to them. 'And when you have calmed down I have something to show you.'

By the time Cartwright and Blake arrived, they'd been having stiff drinks for a good three hours and were thoroughly calmed down. Dragg was telling Bartholomew about the amazing dragon he could paint if he had a wall the size of this house. Sarika gazed at him adoringly and Bartholomew seemed ready to fetch the paints he kept in his basement.

'There you are,' said Lena, pulling herself up from the incredibly comfortable sofa. The exertion sent the whisky up to her brain and she wobbled for a moment before stumbling over to Cartwright. 'We found it,' she said, feeling her earlier anger replaced by a surge of affection. She embraced him in an enormous hug. Her arms still wrapped around his body, she looked up.

He was only a couple of inches taller than her, and she could reach his lips with her own. Suddenly that was all she wanted to do, and she leaned in closer.

Cartwright pulled away. Lena noticed DI Blake frowning at them.

'Come on,' she said, grabbing Cartwright by the hand and gesturing for Blake to follow. 'Come see it. We have found *A Study in Purple*.'

She ran up the stairs and pointed to the picture.

Lena felt Cartwright's hot breath in her ear and smiled. 'How could you do this, Lena?' he said. 'Just come here, no warning? It could have been dangerous.'

'Who is responsible for this?' said Blake, her eyes on the painting.

'It is my painting, if that's what you mean,' said Bartholomew, who had followed them up the stairs. 'But I bought it legitimately, from the gallery website,' he added, slurring his words a little. 'I have all the paperwork to prove it. Somewhere.'

'Then you had better find it, sir,' said Blake. 'And accompany us to the station back in London to give a statement.' She looked at Lena, swaying a little on the step. 'I don't know how you found this man,' she said, casting a glance at Cartwright, who had found something interesting on the carpet to stare at. 'But please leave this to the professionals now.'

CHAPTER 28

Lena fell asleep on the train ride back, waking to find herself still miles from London and already with a stinking hangover. She struggled out of her seat, climbed over an assortment of other drunk, sleepy or similarly afflicted individuals and narrowly avoided stepping in a generous pool of vomit. She vowed never to take the last train back to London again. Locating the buffet car, she purchased a bottle of water and a stewed cup of coffee. Pausing a moment, she added a forlorn egg sandwich to her miscellaneous haul and trudged back to her seat.

Sipping on her coffee and struggling to figure out the mysteries of how to open the sandwich packet, Lena reflected on what had happened. She'd found the painting. The painting that had caused so much drama. Bartholomew was being driven back to London to be questioned by the police. But she believed him. He'd bought that painting, online, in good faith. Whoever had sold it to him was behind the theft. Much as she hated to admit that DI Blake was right, it had to be Ophelia.

Lena picked up her phone and looked at Pietro's number. She could see her reflection on the screen staring back at her, bleary-eyed and ghostly. She'd been told not to interfere with the investigations. But she'd also promised Pietro that she would find the painting for him. Did it still count as a success if it resulted in his wife being arrested? Surely he deserved a warning, at the least. Her finger hovered over the dial button.

She put the phone back down and stared out of the window. She looked past her reflection and into the dark night. The blackness of the countryside reminded her of her village back home, without the constant orange haze of London streetlights. She thought about Timea, her friend who had been murdered. And Timea's son Laszlo, back in the village with no mother. All because of jealousy.

Could this be the same motive? Why else would Ophelia steal the painting? According to Pietro, she had no idea of the money struggles that they suffered. She didn't need the money from the painting. Unless she had secret money troubles of her own?

Ophelia knew about the affair between Pietro and Trudy, but it was so long ago, before they were married. Was seeing the painting her husband's ex-lover had painted hanging in the gallery, their gallery, too much? Surely she couldn't still be holding a grudge?

Unless the romance had been rekindled. Lena remembered the look in Ophelia's eye when she had discovered Lena and Pietro in the basement of the gallery. Suspicion. And anger. Were Trudy and Pietro seeing each other once more? The unlikely romance with Simon could be a convenient front for such activity.

Lena determined that she would find out.

'Ophelia Agnoletti, we would like to ask you some questions at the station,' said Blake. Ophelia looked startled; Pietro outraged.

'What the hell does my wife have to do with this?' asked Pietro. He turned to Lena, who was relieved that she had decided to come straight to the gallery the next morning. 'You've been investigating. Surely you can tell them this is nonsense.'

'It is nothing to do with Lena Szarka,' said Blake. 'I am in charge here.'

'They just need to ask some questions,' said Lena. 'Do not worry.'

'This is ridiculous,' said Pietro. 'An outrage.'

'Calm down, sir,' said Blake, clearly unimpressed. 'Now, Mrs Agnoletti. Will you come with me?'

'I haven't done anything,' said Ophelia. 'I don't know why you'd think I had?'

'Then you've nothing to worry about,' said Blake, shepherding her out and into her car. She drove off as Simon arrived.

'What's going on?' he asked. Pietro had sunk down to the floor with his head in his hands.

'I've found *A Study in Purple,*' Lena told him, watching his face carefully. 'And the police want to question Ophelia.'

'Ophelia?' said Simon, his face whitening. 'Why on earth . . . ?'

'The real painting was sold on the website over a year ago,' she told him. 'A fake was put in its place, painted by an ex-boyfriend of Ophelia's. They think that she is responsible.'

'It is too ridiculous,' said Pietro. 'Why would she do such a thing? She's my wife, for goodness' sake.'

'She wouldn't,' said Simon. 'I'm sure she wouldn't.'

'Do not worry,' said Lena. 'I will find out what is true. And what is false.'

The good thing about arty people, Lena decided, was that they were easy to follow. Trudy's short but fiercely bright pink hair bobbed along in front of her like a buoy floating in the grey waters of Lake Balaton. From time to time Trudy would pause to gaze at the sky, a tree or a piece of graffiti, as if imprinting the experience on her memory. Perhaps to use for a later painting. In any case, it allowed Lena a chance to catch up.

Pietro had said he was going to the police station, but Lena was not sure she believed him. Trudy was meant to be back in New York by now, but here she was, walking along Kingsland Road. She couldn't bear to leave. Had she stayed to be with Pietro, now his wife was likely to be behind bars?

Lena thought. Something didn't feel right about that story. Lots didn't feel right. Trudy had turned down a small alleyway and was standing outside a block of flats. It had the square lines and grey colours of an ex-council property. Lena stood behind a surprisingly verdant tree and watched. Trudy pressed the bell. Lena leaned round. Trudy pressed again. Lena strained her eyes to see which button she pressed. Flat D, the top floor. Impatient, Trudy looked at her watch, then turned around and walked back in the direction she had come from. Right past Lena, who stood still, doing her best impression of a tree. Trudy disappeared. Lena breathed a sigh of relief and went up to the building.

Was this where Trudy and Pietro had their trysts? The paint on the doorway was starting to flake off like Sarika's sunburnt skin. She looked down and saw large splodges of bird poo on the steps. She looked up. The doorway was sheltered and not an ideal spot for a bird, a large bird, by the look of those splodges, to perch. She bent down to take a closer look.

It wasn't bird poo. It was white paint.

Lena was rising to her feet just as a skinny girl charged out of the building and jumped over her like a gymnast. Lena leapt up quickly and caught the door. Just in time.

She avoided the lift, smelling the customary elevator urine aroma from the hallway, and made her way up the cold stone staircase to flat D. The paint splodges led to the same place. Lena tried the door. It was the other good thing about following artists. They were terrible at locking doors. She pushed it open and stepped inside.

Sun poured in from the skylight, warming the paint-splattered concrete floors. The walls were white and covered in artwork. The paint splatter intensified under a blank canvas set up on an easel. She ran her finger over the top of the canvas. It was covered in dust.

Lena turned to look at the paintings. They were all abstract, all different but with the same colour scheme. A flash of auburn running through milky-white curves. Beautiful. Lena leaned in to admire the paintings. She could see emotion running through every brush stroke.

Love.

She stepped back. There was something familiar about the figure. And even she could tell that these paintings were done by someone filled with talent. She didn't think it was the work of Pietro. It was too single-minded and too intense.

She heard a sound at the door and looked for a hiding place, but in this large expanse of room there was none. The door swung open. A man stared at her, a paper coffee cup in one hand and a newspaper in the other.

'Simon,' exclaimed Lena.

'Lena,' said Simon, looking at her in confusion. 'What are you doing here?'

Lena took a deep breath, allowing oxygen to flow from her lungs to nourish her brain. What did this mean? She looked to the paintings on the wall for inspiration.

They provided it.

All at once it hit her. The fragments that had been building up in her mind suddenly came together. There were gaps, sure, but gaps could be filled. Coloured in. The outline of the image was there.

'I am looking for you,' said Lena.

'But how did you find my studio?'

'I followed Trudy,' she replied.

'I knew I should never have brought her here,' said Simon. 'Even once. It is meant to be my sanctuary. A room of my own.'

Lena took another breath. The fragments she had were circumstantial. She needed a confession. 'The police told me that Ophelia will be charged with the theft of *A Study in Purple*,' she lied.

'But she is innocent.'

'I know that,' said Lena. 'And you know it too.' She stared at him. He stared back, then broke her gaze. 'But the police do not.'

'I never imagined she would be blamed,' said Simon. 'I won't let her suffer,' he said.

'Not for something you did,' said Lena.

'Of course not.'

They stood in silence for a moment.

'Trudy was not meant to come here today,' said Simon.

'That does not matter,' said Lena. 'Why did you steal the painting?'

'That doesn't matter either,' said Simon.

'Yes it does,' insisted Lena. 'Tell me.'

'I've always loved her,' he said, gesturing around the room. 'Ophelia was my muse.' Lena looked at the paintings. The white curves. The flashes of brilliant auburn. 'For a while she was all I could paint; I had to keep my work hidden. When she broke up with Pietro I could paint anything. I felt so free, like anything was possible. I started the gallery with him. Then they reconciled; hope was gone. After that, I couldn't paint anything any more. Not even Ophelia. But I wanted to stay near her.'

'I am sorry,' said Lena, meaning it. 'But I still do not understand. Why take the painting? Revenge?'

'Never,' replied Simon. 'Pietro is my best friend. I knew Ophelia was lost to me, but I thought that, just maybe, I could get my other passion back. My art. I needed a space to paint. A studio of my own, away from the miserable flat I inhabit. But without painting, I could never afford one. Not with what I make at the gallery.'

'Why did you not sell one of these?' said Lena, gesturing to the paintings on the walls. 'They are beautiful,' she added.

'Can you see the love in them?' he asked. 'The passion?' Lena nodded. 'Of course you can. Everyone can. Even Pietro. And he will know it is his wife. These paintings can never be in the world. He can never find out how I feel. That's if I could even bring myself to part with them.'

Lena frowned at him. 'So you stole someone else's painting instead?'

'It seemed perfect. No one would know, and I desperately needed a place to paint. But I couldn't get a deposit together. Not even afford to rent a place, let alone buy it. So it would properly be mine.'

'So when *A Study in Purple* came into the gallery . . .'

'I took it. I knew Pietro would never notice. He pretends to know so much about art, but he is no artist. I had an old friend from art school do a copy for the gallery and I sold *In Purple* online. That was the brilliant thing – I could sell it legitimately at full price. It was enough for a deposit on my studio and to supplement a mortgage. I thought it was perfect. No one would suffer. And I could paint again.'

'But what about the gallery?'

'I thought we'd sell the fake too. Pietro would still get his money and some punter who didn't know any better would get the fake *In Purple* and be happy with it. But then we couldn't shift the damn thing. It's like people could tell it was no good. Could sense it didn't have the magic of the original. And it didn't even help me.' Simon gave a bitter laugh. 'I can't paint any better in this studio than I could anywhere else. I put up my paintings and splattered paint at a canvas, but nothing ever worked. I couldn't do it.'

'Perhaps it was your guilt?' suggested Lena.

'And then Pietro announced Trudy was coming,' continued Simon. 'He didn't tell me till the very day she was meant to show up. You were there. I couldn't get the original back, so I had to make the fake disappear. I didn't have much time to plan. That's why I took Pietro's keys, as well as trying to make it look like a break-in. I wanted there to be as many suspects as possible so they couldn't blame anyone. I'm so sorry about your friend, but I couldn't know she'd run away and make herself look so guilty.'

Lena thought. 'But Trudy saw the painting at the reception.'

'I plied her with vodka tonics before we got to the studio, and slipped a little something in there too to make her drowsy. I just had to hope that it would work well enough for her not to notice that the painting was a fake until I had the chance to get rid of it.'

'But why put it in a phone box?'

'Phone boxes are a victim of the modern world,' said Simon. 'It seemed fitting. No one uses them any more. And I couldn't bring it here. What if someone discovered my studio? I had to think quickly.'

'You could have destroyed it.'

Simon smiled. 'It wasn't as brilliant as the original, but I cannot destroy art. I was going to move it to a storage unit once things settled. And I thought I might be able to bring it back one day, or sell it, if things got really bad. Only Trudy would be able to tell it was not the real thing.'

'Trudy really likes you.'

'I know,' Simon smiled. 'I like her too. A lot. I let her see these paintings because I knew I could trust her to keep my secret. We're both artists who paint about love: we understand each other. Being with her is like being free. I almost feel like I could start to paint again.'

'You must go the police,' said Lena. 'And confess.'

'If I do that, Trudy will hate me. They all will,' said Simon.

'Maybe,' said Lena. 'But it is the right thing to do.'

Simon grabbed her arm and looked into her eyes. For a moment, Lena could see what Trudy saw in him. His intensity. His focus.

'You are right,' he said finally. 'I will tell the police what I have done. Perhaps it will be a relief.'

'We go together,' said Lena. 'Now.'

CHAPTER 29

Lena drew her brand-new portfolio out of the bag, moved a book about butterflies out of the way, and spread it out on the coffee table with a flourish. Ophelia and Pietro both made the 'ooh' sound that she'd been hoping for as she opened it to the first spread.

'This is option A for the canapés,' she said. 'Rhapsody in red.' Sarika's flatmate Lucia had used her night off from cooking at the Black Zenith to create a complete tasting platter of exquisite canapés for herself, Dragg and old Mrs Kingston. Mrs Kingston had used her journalistic skills to help her come up with themes, names and descriptions, and Dragg had faithfully drawn illustrations of each dish before it was devoured. Lena flicked over the page. 'But I think for your next exhibition you might prefer the luxury option. Rainbow dreams. Of course, as well as the canapés I can provide matching cocktails plus cleaning and the room-dressing before, full service throughout, and then I will get it spotless afterwards so that you can open again the next morning and all traces of the evening before will be only a pleasant memory. If you like I can bring tasting samples on my next visit.'

'Exquisite,' said Pietro. 'Is there no end to your talents?'

'I have had some help,' said Lena. 'And now that Sarika is back I have even more.' She could hear Sarika downstairs now, the

277

swish of the brush over the floor. The girl was getting better, decided Lena, but she'd still give it a quick going-over herself before she left. Lena's Cleaners stood for perfection, after all. Cleaning would remain the main focus of her business, but she liked the idea of having another service to offer alongside. It was a competitive market.

'Those drawings are simply marvellous,' said Ophelia. 'You could almost display them in the gallery.'

'I will give you the artist's details,' said Lena, with a smile. 'He can also do much . . . larger pieces too.' She closed the portfolio and picked up her coffee. 'But tell me. What is the news with Simon?'

'Being in a cell did wonders for him,' said Ophelia. 'He has been painting non-stop. That nice detective Amy Blake made sure he could have his paints in custody.'

'We've already sold two of his paintings,' said Pietro. 'A third one is downstairs. Have a look as you go out. It's of the Atlantic Ocean.'

'I could do prison food canapés for the next event,' said Lena with a laugh. 'Porridge cocktails.'

'I love it!' said Pietro.

'I was joking,' said Lena.

'And your . . . troubles?' Lena cast a glance at Pietro.

'I've told Ophelia all about it,' said Pietro, taking his wife's hand. 'But it's okay. The money from Simon's paintings have already paid off our most, um, pressing debts, and Mr Worthington has kept the original *A Study in Purple*.' He smiled. 'Simon being incarcerated really helps our sales, you know. The press love it. It almost seems a shame that I have told the police to withdraw the charges.'

'Withdraw them? So he will not face trial?' Lena thought about all the stress that man had put her and Sarika through. And Pietro.

'My husband is very forgiving,' said Ophelia, taking his hand. 'I have learnt from him.'

'Doesn't seem much point in holding a grudge,' said Pietro. 'That's no way to live your life. And being in love with Ophelia. One can hardly blame him for that. She's the most beautiful creature that has ever walked this earth.' He leaned in and kissed his wife.

'The new exhibition will be all about the sea,' said Ophelia. 'Blues and greens and boats and fishes. Simon likes to paint the ocean. Trudy has been back and forth over it a few times now. To visit.'

'We could do a seafood-themed canapé menu,' said Lena, feeling inspired. 'You should try Lucia's *polpo fritto.*'

'Perfect,' exclaimed Ophelia.

'We can do dinner parties as well,' said Lena. 'Here in the gallery. If you wanted something more intimate for your best clients. I will clean too, of course. Before and after.'

'Patrick would come,' said Pietro. 'And his wife. They bought most of the butterflies in the chrysalis collection. Excellent eye, that lady. Still can't shift that damn hedgehog though.'

Lena got to her feet. 'I should help Sarika now. I will be in touch to arrange the tasting.'

'No need,' said Pietro. 'We trust you.'

Lena smiled. She'd earned that.

Sarika hadn't done a bad job downstairs, thought Lena, as she cast an approving eye around the gallery. She wiped her finger along the top of a picture frame and found it came away clean. 'Well done,' she said to the girl. 'You do good work.'

Sarika broke into a smile. 'Thank you,' she said. She glanced at her watch, a timekeeping present from Lena. 'But I should go to Penelope's house now. I teach the boys Hungarian. Then Dragg has his art class with Casper. They will make dragons out of plastic bottles, loo roll and tubes of glitter.'

'Dragg is good with the children,' admitted Lena, dreading to think of the mess that activity would create. 'Perhaps he is not a bad boyfriend after all.'

'What about your love life?' asked Sarika. 'Have you seen Cartwright?'

'He is very busy with DI Blake,' replied Lena. 'She has selected him for a special assignment. Quite an honour, apparently, for someone just out of their training programme. He is most pleased.'

'I think he will find time for you,' said Sarika, with a smile. She pushed open the gallery door. 'Are you coming?'

'One moment,' said Lena. 'I want to see Simon's painting. Then I will come with you.'

It was hung where *A Study in Purple* used to be. The clay eyeball gazed at it appreciatively.

As did Lena. The canvas was huge, spanning the wall. It was made up of myriad dots of paint, each a subtly different hue of blue, green and the white of ocean spray. A dart of grey penetrated the blue sky: a seagull's wings caught in flight. The tiny bird was traversing the vast ocean. Brave and free.

ACKNOWLEDGEMENTS

Thanks to my agent Euan Thorneycroft at AM Heath for making the mysteries harder to solve, as well as Jo Thompson for all her help. Special thanks to the talented editorial team at Constable: Krystyna Green, Amanda Keats and Eleanor Russell, for all their valuable feedback, enthusiasm and hard work. Thanks also to Penny Isaac for her meticulous and insightful copy-editing.

Jo Wickham has done an excellent job generating press for the books. I'd like to thank her and Amy Donegan, who had to field my enthusiastic ideas about marketing with mini bottles of washing-up liquid. The designer Hannah Wood and illustrator Sara Mulvanny deserve a special mention for the splendidly gorgeous covers.

A million thank yous to Philippa Pride, AKA The Book Doctor, for her wonderful teachings, editorial expertise and constant support. All aspiring writers should attend one of her courses. I'd like to thank the talented members of her Next Chapter writing group for their help too: Tanya, Kelly, Jenny, Debbie and Elvie.

Thanks to the officers of the Metropolitan Police who helped me with my research and impressed me with their integrity. Thanks also to Dante Zacherl for showing me the beauty of graffiti art.

My mother Susan gets a special thank you for her creative feedback and my father Roger for his impeccable logic. My Hungarian grandmother is no longer with us, but her culture, recipes and a few choice swear words live on through Lena.

And of course, thanks to my husband Sui. If he hadn't left piles of worn underwear to gather dust on the bathroom floor, I never would have had the idea for the series in the first place. He is my muse.

The biggest thank you goes to the littlest person, my baby son Teddy. He waited patiently to be born until a few days after I delivered this manuscript to my publisher. I've dedicated *A Clean Canvas* to him.